"Oh, rea
she supposed
"I told Sa_____ ___ ____ ___ ____ ____ ____ ___,
but she insisted she could spare you." His hand rubbed over his chin. "If you'd rather not, I'll hire someone."

She unfolded her arms and pushed out her hands in protest. "No, no, I'll drive you. After all, your accident was my fault—"

With a shake of his head, he held up his forefinger. "Don't go there, Molly. My accident wasn't your fault. Or Karli's. I keep telling you that."

"But—"

"No 'but's.' I'll be fine. My work will be fine. Okay?"

"Okay."

Steve's brown eyes gleamed.

He was much too close. She wanted to step back, but before she could, he slid his finger under her chin and tipped up her head.

"Molly?"

When she looked up and met his heated gaze, corresponding warmth spun through her. Her heart thudded, her breath faltered.

He stepped closer, while she stood rooted to the spot. The air sizzled. His lips parted and his warm breath slid over her cheek.

Run, Molly!

Too late. His lips closed over hers, softly, yet firmly. She leaned into him and felt his heart beating underneath his shirt, felt the heat of his body, breathed in his masculine scent. Their lips engaged in a familiar dance, yet as new and exciting as though she'd never experienced it before.

Praise for Linda Hope Lee and...

FINDING SARA:
"A modern western, packed with secrets, intrigue and old-fashioned romance. *FINDING SARA* is a romance that won't be forgotten."
~*Joanne Hall, Writers and Readers of Distinctive Fiction*

~*~

"Lee takes a cowboy and an heiress and combines them into a refreshingly sweet tale. Readers can easily relate to the main characters as Sara searches for herself while Jackson overcomes a devastating loss."
~*Karen Sweeny-Justice, Romantic Times, (4 Stars)*

LOVING ROSE:
"*LOVING ROSE* is a sweet, heartwarming read that will tug at your heartstrings."
~*Melissa, Sizzinghotbookreviews.net (4 Hearts)*

~*~

"What a beautiful story! *LOVING ROSE* is full of characters who face real-life situations."
~*Nikki, sirenbookreviews.blogspot.com (4.5 Siren Stones)*

Marrying Molly

by

Linda Hope Lee

The Red Rock, Colorado Series, Book Three

This is a work of fiction. Names, characters, places, and incidents are either the product of the author's imagination or are used fictitiously, and any resemblance to actual persons living or dead, business establishments, events, or locales, is entirely coincidental.

Marrying Molly

COPYRIGHT © 2013 by Linda Hope Lee

All rights reserved. No part of this book may be used or reproduced in any manner whatsoever without written permission of the author or The Wild Rose Press, Inc. except in the case of brief quotations embodied in critical articles or reviews.
Contact Information: info@thewildrosepress.com

Cover Art by *Tina Lynn Stout*

The Wild Rose Press, Inc.
PO Box 708
Adams Basin, NY 14410-0708
Visit us at www.thewildrosepress.com

Publishing History
First Sweetheart Rose Edition, 2013
Print ISBN 978-1-61217-852-3
Digital ISBN 978-1-61217-853-0

The Red Rock, Colorado Series, Book Three
Published in the United States of America

Dedication

To Max

Acknowledgements

Special thanks to TWRP editor Leanne Morgena
for her expert editing and guidance
during the writing of this series.

Chapter One

Molly Henson leaned forward to gaze out the TransAmerica coach car's window. Any minute now, the Rocky Mountains would appear. The train chugged around a corner, and, yes, there they stood, still off in the distance, but unmistakably her beloved Rockies. Her heartbeat quickened. The sight of the jagged ridges of purple granite, veined with snow even on this June day, and silhouetted against the deep blue sky, never failed to thrill her. The mountains remained faithful guardians of the country she called home.

Doubt eroded some of her excitement. After a two-year absence, would she still call Red Rock, Colorado home?

"Mommy?"

Molly pushed away her troubling thoughts and turned to her five-year-old daughter, Karli, sitting beside her. She brushed a ringlet of blond hair from the child's forehead. "Yes, darlin'?"

"Are we there yet?"

At the frequent question posed by her impatient daughter, Molly smiled. "Almost. Why don't you take a little nap? Then we'll be there before you know it."

"'kay." Karli snuggled down in the seat and closed her eyes.

Molly regarded her child for a long moment, conscious of the love overflowing her heart. Her daughter was her most precious possession, more dear than anything else in the world. She hoped returning to Red Rock was the right move.

She drew in a deep breath and leaned back against the seat. Maybe she should take a nap, too. The journey from Chicago had been long. They could have flown, of course; but, thinking Karli might enjoy seeing the country, Molly chose the train.

After a last look at the mountains, growing ever closer, she closed her eyes. The clack-clack of the train's wheels faded as she drifted off to sleep...

Something was wrong. Molly's eyelids popped open. She clutched the armrests and jerked upright. An innate sense of trouble had pierced her sleeping mind like a silent alarm. She turned to make sure Karli was all right.

Karli's seat was empty.

Molly's stomach clenched. Karli had the habit of going off without telling her. What was she up to this time?

Heart pounding, she scooted into Karli's seat, leaned into the aisle, and peered ahead. No sign of her daughter. She swiveled and scanned the back of the car. Karli stood in the aisle talking to a male passenger. Molly's relief lasted only a moment then anger heated her cheeks. Hadn't she warned her daughter many times about talking to strangers?

She bounded from her seat and marched down the aisle. "Karli? What are you doing back here?"

Karli gazed up at Molly with innocent eyes. "I was looking for Mr. Muggins. I lost him, and he found him." She pointed to the man seated on the aisle.

The man in question appeared to be a few years

older than Molly, probably in his early thirties. He was dressed in navy blue slacks, a light blue sports shirt, and a tan nylon windbreaker. Dark brown hair was neatly combed over a high forehead, and he had deep-set brown eyes.

She'd noticed him earlier in the dining car. He sat alone, reading a newspaper. He glanced up as she and Karli passed by. His gaze lingered longer than a stranger's should.

Molly had to admit he appeared harmless, although appearance alone was not proof that someone was good or bad. Where her child was concerned, she couldn't be too careful.

"I found Mr. Muggins on the floor next to my seat," the man explained, nodding at the small doll Karli clutched to her chest. "Figured he belonged to someone not far away, so I set him right here." He pointed to the armrest.

"And when I got up to look for Mr. Muggins, I saw him," Karli said. "Mr. Mug-gins, Mr. Mug-gins..." She sang the theme song to the doll's animated TV show.

"That was very nice of you." Molly spoke in a crisp, polite tone then turned to Karli. "Say 'thank you,' honey, so we can go back to our seats."

Karli waved the doll. "Thank you."

The man smiled. "My pleasure." He switched his attention to Molly, and their gazes collided.

Her heart started to pound. Why? The danger had passed. Karli was safe.

The new danger had nothing to do with Karli. Like an arrow shot from a bow, the warning was aimed directly at Molly.

With a quick intake of breath, she grabbed Karli's

hand and marched them down the aisle. When they reached their seats, Molly put Karli next to the window and herself on the aisle. She leaned over and, in as calm a voice as she could muster, said, "Karli, honey, I'm glad you found Mr. Muggins, but I've asked you not to talk to strangers. Even if I'm nearby."

"But he had Mr. Muggins." Karli's brows knit. "Mr. Muggins is mine."

"I know. But here's what I wish you would have done." She smoothed the collar of Karli's pink cotton blouse. "When you spotted Mr. Muggins, you would've told me first. Then we would have gone together to talk to the man. Please remember for next time. Okay?"

"'kay." Karli shrugged. She turned away and held the doll up to the window. "See, Mr. Muggins, that's the desert out there."

Her tension melting away, Molly leaned back and listened to her daughter talk to her doll as though he were real. Perhaps to Karli, he was. On his TV show, Mr. Muggins was nanny to a brood of six children whose busy parents had little time for them. Dressed in a black suit, white shirt, red string tie, and black felt hat, Mr. Muggins always thought up fun things to do and fun places to go. Karli loved the show, so Molly had given her the doll at Christmastime. She never thought Karli would become so attached to Mr. Muggins, but she took him with her everywhere.

Molly wondered if the doll might be a father-substitute. Helping her daughter adjust to a one-parent family was one of the many challenges she'd faced after Buck's death two years ago.

The image of her late husband popped into her mind—tall, handsome, broad-shouldered, with blond hair and eyes bluer than any Colorado sky. And, as always when she thought of him, a mixture of anger and love filled her. Anger because he'd left her and Karli all too soon, and love because she loved him today as much as she ever had while he was alive.

Buck's image faded, replaced by that of the stranger she and Karli had spoken to, sitting only a few rows behind them. When their gazes met, her heart had thundered so fast she had to break eye contact. What was that all about? Molly straightened and set her jaw. Never mind. The stranger didn't matter, nor did her troubling reaction. After she and Karli left the train at Red Rock, they'd never see him again.

****

Steve Roper leaned into the aisle, his gaze fastened on the woman and her daughter as they made their way back to their seats. The child—Karli, her mother had called her—looked back over her shoulder. She smiled and waved the Mr. Muggins doll. Steve smiled back and gave a little salute.

She was a cute kid, and they'd been having a perfectly innocent conversation about Mr. Muggins. Steve was familiar with the doll because his niece and nephew back in New York watched the TV program.

Karli's mother interrupted them and swept her daughter back to their seats. He really couldn't blame the woman for her protective attitude. The world sometimes was a dangerous place, and children shouldn't be talking to strangers.

Earlier, he'd noticed the mother and daughter in the dining car when they passed by his table. But he hadn't seen whether or not the child carried a doll, or anything else. He'd been too busy looking at the mother.

A redhead, she had a sprinkling of freckles across her pert, up-turned nose. While he'd never been particularly attracted to redheads, he couldn't take his eyes off this one.

Their gazes met for one brief, yet highly charged moment, and he had a wild urge to leap up and invite her and her child to share his table. Fortunately, before he could make such an impulsive and probably stupid move, the hostess appeared and led the pair to another table.

"You goin' to Denver?" Steve's seatmate interrupted his thoughts.

Steve glanced at the man, who'd boarded the train a couple stops ago. In his sixties, he had watery eyes and leathery skin. His receding chin sprouted a white goatee.

"Not my final destination," Steve said. "But I'll be doing business there."

"That's where I'm headed," the man continued. "Goin' to live with my son. He don't think I should be alone now my wife's gone. She passed on a couple months ago."

Steve murmured his sympathy. He knew about losing a wife, although his loss was different from this man's. His wife, Angie, had disappeared. Even though he'd divorced her in absentia, he'd not been given the closure he needed to eventually move on. Instead, he'd been left in a nightmarish limbo.

A chance existed, although a slim one, that this trip to Colorado would answer the question of what had happened to her. Then he would truly be free.

He hoped.

"Don't think I'll like the big city," his seatmate

said, stroking his goatee. "I'm used to my place in Clancy. Know where that is?"

Glad for a diversion from his depressing thoughts, Steve turned his attention to the conversation. "I've heard of Clancy," he said, "but I don't know anything about it..."

****

As the train slowed on its approach to Red Rock, Molly's nerves tingled with anticipation. Eager to see some familiar sights, she leaned across Karli to peer out the window. Yes, there sat the red brick station house, and next to it the warehouse with a blue slate roof. In the parking lot, aspen trees planted in circular oases of greenery waved in the breeze.

Bringing her gaze back to the small crowd gathered on the station's platform, she searched for her friends, Jackson and Sara Phillips.

Ah, there they were. Sara had her arm linked through Jackson's, and he held their three-year-old son, Ryan. Molly's heart swelled with love. Although she was not blood-related to either Sara or Jackson, they were more like family than the sister and brother-in-law she'd left back in Chicago.

"Are we there now, Mommy?" Karli asked, her nose pressed against the window.

Molly took her gaze off the trio outside long enough to bestow a smile on her daughter. "Yes, darlin', we're finally there."

With a loud squeal of brakes, the train eased to a stop, and soon she and Karli joined Sara, Jackson, and Ryan on the platform. The air, as fresh and dry as she remembered, washed over Molly, and the bright sun and blue sky welcomed her.

"You're here at last!" Sara enveloped Molly in a hug then stood back and regarded her at arm's length. She slowly shook her head. "You haven't changed a bit in two years."

Molly swallowed over the lump in her throat. "You haven't either, Sara."

Tall and slim, Sara always managed to look regal, even in the jeans and blue-checkered, western-style shirt she wore today. Her long, blond hair was tied back in a jaunty ponytail.

Jackson slipped an arm around Molly's shoulders. "Good to see you again, Molly."

"You, too, Jackson." She leaned close to plant a kiss on Ryan's cheek. The toddler had his daddy's dark hair and his mother's vivid blue eyes. "Hey, big boy, you've grown."

"So has Karli." Sara stooped to eye-level with Karli and clasped the child's hand. "Do you remember me?"

"Nuh uh." Karli shook her head.

"This is your Aunt Sara, darlin'." Molly laid a hand on Karli's shoulder. "And your Uncle Jackson, and your cousin, Ryan."

Wide-eyed, Karli gazed up at Jackson. "Mommy says you have horses. Can I ride them?"

Jackson grinned and ruffled Karli's hair. "Why, sure. I've got one in mind especially for you."

"Oh, goody." Karli jumped up and down.

Molly clenched her jaw. Considering what happened to Buck, she wasn't sure she wanted Karli riding horses yet. But now was not the time to discuss the matter. She'd wait until later. She caught Karli's hand and started toward the station house.

"Hold it, Molly," Jackson called out.

Molly stopped and turned.

"We're meeting someone else from the train." Sara gestured to the passenger car.

Who could the person be? Molly looked around. As far as she could tell, only a couple with two children and an elderly man had left the train.

And then her gaze lighted on the man who'd found Mr. Muggins. He stood at the other end of the platform, a black briefcase slung over one shoulder, looking around as though he waited for someone. Her throat tightened. Surely, he couldn't be the one Jackson and Sara were meeting. She didn't want him to be. He was...dangerous, somehow, although she didn't know why.

Her hope vanished when Jackson said, "There he is," and started toward the same man.

The other man grinned and stepped forward. His gaze slid from Jackson to Sara and then to Molly and Karli. His eyes widened.

Sudden heat, which had nothing to do with the bright sun overhead, rushed to Molly's face.

Karli jumped up and down. "That's the man who..."

"Hush, darlin'." Molly held up a warning hand.

Thankfully, Karli quieted.

Gripping Karli's hand, Molly hung back while Jackson and the newcomer shook hands and clapped each other on the shoulder. Apparently, they were old friends.

Sara joined them, and Jackson introduced her.

Jackson turned and gestured to Molly. "Molly, Karli, come meet Steve Roper."

Molly allowed herself and Karli a few steps forward, but not enough to be a part of the group. "We, ah, met on the train."

"Sort of." Steve raised his eyebrows and grinned at Molly.

"You're the man who found Mr. Muggins." Karli finally got to say her piece.

At Jackson's and Sara's puzzled looks, Molly offered a brief explanation of the incident with Karli's doll.

Steve gazed down at Karli. "I see you're taking good care of him."

"Yes, I am." Karli clasped the doll to her chest in a tight hug.

"Steve and I knew each other when I lived in New York," Jackson explained, referring to the time when he was a Wall Street stock broker. "He designs computer software for businesses, and he has a couple of accounting programs for us. You're going to install them, right, Steve?"

"You bet." Steve patted his briefcase. "One for your ranching business and another for Sara's bakery. Customized for each."

"My business has really grown," Sara said to Molly with a wide smile. "And I'm so glad you're here to take over the office work."

"I'm looking forward to working there." Molly still struggled to accept the reappearance of the man she thought she'd never see again.

"Let's go collect your luggage." Jackson led the way to the station house.

Sara fell into step beside Steve, leaving Molly and Karli to trail behind.

"Where are you staying, Steve?" Sara asked.

"The Bingham Hotel."

"Are you sure you want to stay there? Oh, it's a nice place, but we have plenty of room at the Rolling R."

"No, thanks, Sara." Steve stood aside to allow Sara, Molly, and Karli to pass through the station's automatic door. "I'll be fine at the hotel. I'll be in and out, driving to Denver and other places to see potential clients."

Hearing Steve's refusal, Molly blew out a relieved breath. She and Karli would be living at the ranch, and, although it really wasn't her business or her choice to make, she didn't want Steve to stay there, even for a short time. Even though she barely knew him, his presence unsettled her in ways she didn't want to think about.

They collected their luggage and trooped out to the parking lot to Jackson's SUV. Worried about who would sit where, Molly silently thanked Jackson when he said, "You ladies sit together. I know you have a lot to catch up on."

Molly and Sara secured the children in their third row car seats, and then climbed into the middle row, while Steve joined Jackson up front. Once they were underway, Molly managed to answer Sara's questions about their train trip, but her gaze kept straying to Steve sitting just a foot or so away. When he turned to talk to Jackson, she caught a glimpse of his profile. She had to admit he was an intriguing man. In addition to those deep-set brown eyes, he had a high forehead that spoke of intelligence, and a firm jaw that indicated strength and determination.

When Sara turned to retrieve a toy car Ryan had dropped, Molly forced herself to look out the window and focus on the scenery. She'd been eager to renew her acquaintance with the town. They were passing Jasper's Drugstore on the corner of Fifth and Mountain View. Then came the Roundup Restaurant, with its neon sign in the shape of a lasso, and then Bolson's Hardware, all places she had frequented when she and Buck had lived here before.

As they passed Timber Ridge Road, Molly spotted the brick medical clinic belonging to Dr. Mike Mahoney.

"How're Mike and Rose?" Molly asked Sara. Rose was Jackson's sister, who married Mike two years earlier, before Molly and Karli left Red Rock.

"They're doing fine." Sara gave Ryan his toy and settled back in her seat. "They moved into their new home not too long ago. Rose is still working for TransAmerica, although now that she's pregnant, she's not traveling."

"She's about seven months along, right?"

"Yes, and they're both so excited." She looked across the seat with a laugh. "They're coming to dinner tonight."

"I look forward to seeing them." Like Sara and Jackson, Mike and Rose were as close as family.

Sara leaned forward and tapped Steve on the shoulder. "You're invited to dinner, too, Steve."

He turned to look over his shoulder, a frown on his face. "Sounds like you have a family reunion planned. I don't want to intrude."

"You won't be." Sara shook her head.

Jackson added, "Come on, you can't turn down a

home-cooked meal."

"Steve, please come," Karli said.

Steve twisted farther around to fix his brown-eyed gaze on Molly. "What about you? Are you in on this?"

Was she? Something about this man surely spelled danger. Not in the physical sense, but danger to her emotions, fragile and vulnerable in the wake of Buck's death. Sara and Jackson were the hosts, though, and if they wanted Steve to come, their word was final. Molly lifted her shoulders in a slight shrug and said, "Fine with me."

Steve's frown faded into a grin. "Well, okay, then."

The vehicle pulled up in front of the Bingham Hotel. Molly had always liked the stately look of the three-story building and the way pyramid-shaped bushes in terra cotta pots stood like guardians on either side of the door.

Jackson and Steve got out and walked to the back of the SUV where Jackson retrieved Steve's suitcase. While he and Steve stood on the sidewalk talking, Sara turned to Molly. "He seems like a nice man, doesn't he?"

Molly brushed a bit of lint from her jacket. "I suppose."

"You two timed your arrivals perfectly."

Molly jerked up her head. "What do you mean?"

"He's installing the new accounting program you'll be using at the bakery."

"Yes, I remember accounting was included in the job description."

"Right. And having Steve here to help you learn the program will be good, won't it?"

"I guess." Molly lowered her eyelids.

Sara touched Molly's arm. "Is anything wrong?"

Trust Sara to be perceptive. Molly forced a smile. "No, not really. I'm just tired from the long train ride."

"Of course, you are. Well, you'll have time to rest when we get to the ranch."

Apparently satisfied with Molly's reply, Sara sat back.

Molly turned her gaze toward Steve Roper just as he leaned over to pick up his suitcase. His back was to her, emphasizing his broad shoulders. Her chest expanded with a soft sigh. Okay, he was attractive. So what? She wasn't looking for a man. One of the reasons she'd fled Chicago was to get away from her sister Paige's constant matchmaking. Molly hoped that on the ranch, she and Karli could live in peace and quiet with their memories.

She hadn't counted on Steve Roper.

Good thing his presence was only temporary. She'd make sure any association they had would be strictly business, nothing more.

Chapter Two

After leaving Steve at the hotel, Sara joined Jackson in the front seat. Left more or less to herself, Molly put aside her worries about the troublesome newcomer and gazed out the window at the passing landscape. The dry, dusty land, broken up by occasional pastures and fields, and the ever-present blue bowl of sky, were so different from the narrow streets and high-rises she'd left behind in Chicago.

Twenty minutes later, Jackson turned off the freeway onto an asphalt side road. When they passed under the wooden arch emblazoned with *Rolling R Ranch*, waves of emotion swept through Molly. Her first visit to the ranch had been as a newlywed. Buck had hired on as Jackson's ranch foreman and she as cook for the ranch hands. They drove down this road deeply in love and full of dreams for the future.

"Working for Jackson is a great opportunity for us," Buck told her. "We'll save our money and buy our own spread someday."

Then his buddies introduced him to rodeo, and that had been the beginning of the end...

Don't think about that. You can't change the past. Concentrate on the future. Your and Karli's future.

She glanced over her shoulder at her daughter, absorbed in looking out the window. Yes, making a good life for Karli was Molly's goal now.

A herd of grazing cattle came into view, and then the grove of aspen trees by the main house. In the front yard stood the familiar weeping willow tree with the old, bleached white wagon wheel propped against the trunk. The tree's long, thin branches waved lazily in the breeze.

As waves of nostalgia rolled through her, Molly shifted her gaze to the house, built of wood and faced with fieldstone, with a porch across the front. She had fond memories of the dinners and parties she and Buck had attended there. Buck and Jackson grew to be best friends as well as employer and employee, and he and Molly were included in many gatherings.

Sara turned to face Molly. "The house we have for you and Karli is down the road a ways. I hope you'll like it."

"I'm sure I will." Molly gave her friend a reassuring pat on the shoulder.

They drove past the main house, the barn, and the stable and on down the road that wound through the property. When they came to the cutoff leading to the house she and Buck had occupied, Molly's stomach jolted and she tore away her gaze. The new foreman and his wife lived there now, Sara had told her in one of their phone calls. Life went on.

At last, they reached the house that was to be hers and Karli's. The wood-framed, one-story home had a fresh coat of white paint and pots of red and orange geraniums sitting on the front porch.

"I hope you didn't go to too much trouble," Molly said as Jackson swung the SUV onto the gravel driveway.

"Not at all," Sara said. "I've always wanted to fix

up the place, and your coming gave us a good excuse."

Jackson braked to a stop and cut the engine. "I'm pleased to find a use for this house. It was on the ranch when I bought the place, but no one's ever lived here."

They all climbed from the SUV and headed up the walk to the porch. Jackson unlocked the door and made a sweeping gesture for Molly to enter ahead of him. "You first, Molly."

Holding Karli's hand and trembling a little inside, Molly stepped over the threshold. The small house had no formal entry, and they were immediately in the living room. The smell of fresh paint filled Molly's nostrils.

Entering behind her, Sara pointed to the beige walls. "We chose a neutral color, so that you can accent with whatever colors you like."

"What a good idea." Molly's gaze swept the room's furnishings, which included a comfortable-looking sofa, a couple of easy chairs, and a stand with a TV.

They continued on to the kitchen, where a round table and several chairs occupied a sunlit corner. Two bedrooms with a bath between them, plus a small alcove containing a washer and dryer, completed the floor plan.

"This will do just fine," Molly said, when they had seen all the rooms and were back in the living room. "More than fine—it's wonderful." In a sudden rush of emotion, her eyes filled with tears. She reached out and hugged Sara.

"We're so glad you're here," Sara said, returning Molly's hug. As she stepped away, she swiped a tear from her cheek.

"Okay, you two." Jackson grinned. "This is supposed to be a happy occasion."

"It is." Sara met her husband's gaze and smiled. "Sometimes we women cry when we're happy. You should know that."

Jackson tossed back his head and laughed. "I guess I should. Thanks for reminding me."

Suddenly remembering her daughter, whose hand she had dropped somewhere along the way, Molly looked around. Karli was nowhere in sight. Tension rippled along Molly's shoulders. She turned to the others. "Where's Karli?"

"She was here a minute ago." Jackson turned to Ryan standing beside him. "Did you see where Karli went?"

"In there, Daddy." Ryan pointed toward the kitchen.

Molly hurried into the kitchen. Karli wasn't there, but the door leading to the back porch stood open.

Heart pounding, Molly ran out the door, calling, "Karli! Karli!"

"She can't have gone far," Sara said, as she and the others followed close on Molly's heels.

"Oh, yes, she could. You don't know her. Karli!" Molly ran down the porch steps, her gaze sweeping the back yard. The yard had a wooden fence, but with slats a child Karli's age could easily crawl through. Bushes filled one corner, and a small storage shed stood in another. Had Karli escaped the yard, or was she hiding somewhere near? Molly bit her lip. Where should she look first?

She was about to investigate the shed when her roving gaze spotted her missing daughter. She sat on the wooden seat of a rope swing hanging from the branch of a huge maple tree. She swayed back and forth, crooning to Mr. Muggins, tucked in her lap.

Molly pressed her palm to her chest and whooshed out a breath. But her relief lasted only a moment. Then, setting her jaw, she ran to Karli.

Her daughter looked up. Her blue eyes, so like her father's, shone. "Look, Mommy, a swing."

"Yes, I see. But you must tell me when you want to go somewhere."

"I'm sorry." Karli lowered her eyelids and turned down her mouth.

Molly regretted spoiling her fun. But, given Karli's habit of going off on her own, Molly considered her reaction justified. The ranch was huge, much of it untamed and wild. Here, above all places, Karli needed to stay close.

Aware Sara and Jackson stood nearby, Molly turned and mustered a smile. "Sorry for the scare. Karli tends to wander."

Sara nodded, her brow furrowed. "We'll keep that in mind."

"And is this swing safe?" Molly fingered the swing's coarse rope. "It looks old."

"The swing was on the property when I bought the place," Jackson said as he walked closer. "I replaced the rope and secured the seat. I thought Karli would enjoy it."

"That was thoughtful of you, Jackson." Molly spoke more calmly, now that Karli's safety had been assured. "I'm sure she will. Won't you, honey?" She smoothed Karli's hair from her forehead.

"I like to swing. So does Mr. Muggins." She held

up the doll.

"Swing, swing." Ryan waved his arms. "Me, too."

Jackson leaned over and touched his son's shoulder. "Sure, buddy, you can have a turn sometime. But right now, we'd better let these folks settle in."

With a smile, Sara hooked her arm through Jackson's and said to Molly, "Yes, you and Karli can rest awhile before dinner."

"That would be nice," Molly said, aware of the fatigue coursing through her body. "The trip has been a long couple of days."

****

In his third floor room at the Bingham Hotel, Steve unpacked his clothes into a walk-in closet and an antique oak dresser with an oval mirror. He carried the leather bag containing his shaving supplies into the bathroom and set it on the counter. That was about it, except for his briefcase, which held his laptop and software programs. Those he placed on the round table near the window, which would serve as his desk.

He stepped to the window and let his gaze skim the buildings across the street, past the outskirts of town, and on to the mountains in the distance, where sunlight glinted on the jagged peaks. Was Angie out there somewhere? The detective he'd hired to find her had traced her to a small town not far from Red Rock. But then the trail had gone cold, and Steve eventually gave up the search.

Now that he was here, though, he planned to investigate on his own. With any luck, he'd find her yet. His gut feeling told him she was still alive. Divorced or not, he wanted to know what had happened to her.

He checked his wristwatch. Three-thirty already. Soon it would be time to head out to the Rolling R. He needed to rent a car and pick up a hostess gift for Sara. A bottle of wine? Flowers? As he locked the door to his room and caught the elevator, he considered his choices.

After looking around the lobby's gift shop, he settled on a bouquet of flowers. A display of boot-shaped plastic containers of candy reminded him of the kids, Ryan and Karli. The image of Karli's mother, Molly, with her red hair, pert little nose, and soft mouth, sprang to mind. She was pretty and appealing, but he had the feeling that for some reason, she'd taken a dislike to him. Was it because they'd gotten off to a bad start over Karli's lost doll? Or something else?

She probably wouldn't like him giving Karli a gift. Well, too bad. He wasn't going to give something to one child and not the other. Fairness upheld, he added two of the candy-filled boots to his purchase. He left the store and headed down the street to the car rental agency.

****

"They're here," Jackson said from his post in the armchair near the living room window.

Molly ran to look over his shoulder at the silver SUV coming down the road.

The car pulled into the driveway and stopped. Mike Mahoney stepped from the driver's side. He rounded the car and helped his wife, Rose, from the passenger's seat. One hand cradling her stomach, she slid from the seat to the ground.

Molly smiled to herself. Yep, Rose was pregnant, all right. No doubt about that.

The couple linked arms and headed up the path to the house. They looked so good together and Molly's heart warmed. She'd missed them almost as much as she'd missed Sara and Jackson.

They reached the top of the porch steps just as Jackson opened the front door. "Hey, you two." He stood aside for them to enter the house.

Once inside, Rose hugged her brother then stepped back and said, "Mike got a call from the hospital as we were leaving, but he didn't have to go in."

"One of my patients is about to deliver." Mike came in behind Rose, and he and Jackson clapped each other on the shoulder. "But we should be okay for the evening."

"Ah, the life of a doctor," Jackson said. "But look who's here." With a swing of an arm, he stood aside and motioned to Molly.

"Molly." Rose rushed to Molly's side and gave her a hug. "So good to see you."

"You, too." Molly returned Rose's hug. "You haven't changed a bit," she added as they drew apart, and then grinned. "Well, except for your pregnancy. Otherwise, you and Jackson still look enough alike to be twins." Like her brother, Rose was a dark-eyed brunette with a warm and friendly smile.

Mike put his arm around Molly's shoulders. "Molly, you're looking good."

"Thanks, Mike." Molly's gaze took in Mike's hazel eyes framed with dark lashes, and his thick, reddish-brown hair. "And you're still the handsomest doctor I know."

"Here's Karli." Rose bent to greet the child, who'd left her coloring book to come over and see the newcomers. "You've grown. What a big girl you are."

"Can you give Rose a hug?" Molly said to her daughter. "She's Uncle Jackson's sister."

Clutching Mr. Muggins in one hand, Karli hugged Rose.

With a beaming smile, Rose put her arms around Karli. "I'm your Auntie Rose, and I'm so glad to see you again."

"Who's that with you?" Mike asked as he too bent and took Karli's free hand.

"Mr. Muggins." Karli waved the doll.

"Well, he must be a very good friend of yours."

Molly rolled her eyes. "You don't know the half of it. She won't let him out of her sight."

"I lost him on the train." Karli twirled around on one foot. "But Steve found him."

"Right," Jackson said as he closed the door. "Steve Roper, and you're going to meet him tonight."

Mike stood, and then circled a hand around his wife's elbow and helped Rose to her feet. "Oh, yeah, your friend from New York with the new accounting system. I might be interested in that."

"Yes, I remember your telling us about him." Rose smoothed her white T-top over her stomach.

Sara came in from the kitchen. "Hello, you two. Let me have your jackets, and Jackson can get you something to drink." She gestured to the portable bar at one end of the room, where bottles of wine and sparkling water chilled in ice buckets.

"Anna has everything in the kitchen under control," she added, referring to the Phillips' cook and housekeeper, Anna Gabraldi. "So I can be hostess now."

Mike and Rose had barely been served their drinks and sat, and Karli returned to coloring with Ryan when Steve Roper arrived.

From her chair near the children, Molly caught her breath as Jackson led Steve into the living room. He looked every bit as handsome as when she'd first met him. So much for hoping her initial reaction was a fluke.

"These are for the hostess." Steve presented Sara with a bouquet of flowers. While Sara left to search for a vase, Jackson introduced Steve to Rose and Mike.

Spotting Steve, Karli dropped her crayons, jumped up, and ran to him. "Steve's here. Steve's here."

"Hey, Karli. I've got something for you." Reaching into his jacket pocket, he pulled out a small plastic boot filled with candy and handed it to Karli.

"For me?" Karli squealed with delight.

"Yup. And one for Ryan, too." Steve took out another boot and held it out to Ryan, who had toddled up to stand beside Karli.

"Say 'thank you,' son," Jackson prompted with a hand on his son's back.

"Tank you." Ryan reached out for the boot.

Molly was about to remind her daughter when Karli echoed by saying, "Thank you."

"Wait until after dinner to open it, Karli," Molly said, as Karli tore the paper wrapper from her gift.

Her warning captured Steve's attention, and he met her gaze. "Oh, hi. Didn't see you over there."

"Hi." Rather than rising and stepping forward to greet him, Molly remained seated.

Sara returned with a vase containing the flowers, which she placed on the coffee table. "Yes, let's keep the candy for dessert." She managed to get the gifts from the children without too much resistance and set them on the fireplace mantel. She took Steve's jacket while Jackson poured him a glass of wine.

Glass in hand, Steve joined Mike and Jackson, and the three men stood in the center of the room talking. Molly pursed her lips. This was supposed to be her and Karli's homecoming, and she'd looked forward to spending the evening with her "family." Steve was an outsider. He didn't belong here. Not tonight, anyway.

When they trooped into the dining room for dinner, Sara placed Steve on the other side of Karli, where Buck would've sat. Molly's stomach clenched, and she looked around to see the others' reactions. No one else seemed to notice, though, and Karli bubbled with delight to have Steve nearby. She chattered to him about Mr. Muggins, who sat on the table near her plate, and Steve helped her to unfold her napkin when it tangled with the silverware.

Conversation flew back and forth, the men talking about sports, and Rose and Sara about furniture for the new baby's room. Molly concentrated on eating her chicken baked in marinara sauce. Ordinarily, she would have enjoyed the meal, but tonight every bite stuck in her throat.

"You're awfully quiet, Molly," Sara observed during a lull in the conversation. Her brows were drawn together in a question.

Molly shifted in her seat and forced a smile. "Guess I'm a bit trip weary. But I am glad to be here."

"It's good to have you here," Rose said, and the others chimed in their agreement.

As conversation resumed, Molly tried to keep up,

but her eyes suddenly filled with tears. She ducked her head and dabbed her lips with her napkin. She thought her display of emotion had gone unobserved until she looked up again and met Steve Roper's gaze. Was that concern radiating from his eyes? Stiffening her spine, she turned her head away. She didn't want his sympathy.

When everyone finished eating, Anna Gabraldi, gray hair in its usual neat bun and round cheeks rosy from the kitchen's warmth, bustled in with a plate of cookies and a carafe of coffee.

"Sara's latest cookie creation," Anna announced. "Hot out of the oven."

The plate was passed from hand to hand around the table, each person taking a serving.

With a twinkle in her eye, Sara put a finger to her lips. "Don't ask what's in them. The recipe's a secret."

Rose tilted her chin and sniffed the air. "I'd bet cinnamon is one of the ingredients."

"A bakery on a ranch is something I haven't heard of before," Steve commented, and then bit into his cookie.

"I love working here at home." Sara picked up the cream pitcher and added some to her coffee. "And we've been expanding the operation."

Mike helped himself to another cookie from the plate that now sat in the center of the table. "Pretty soon, your baking business will take over the entire ranch."

Sara laughed and shook her head. "Not likely. My husband still has a thriving business of his own with his quarter horses."

The group moved the party into the living room,

settling the children with a set of plastic alphabet blocks and the candy boots. The talk centered on Rose and Mike's new addition to their family.

Molly joined in the conversation, careful to add a lightness she didn't feel to her tone. She genuinely was happy for Mike and Rose. They'd had a difficult time getting together again after a two-year separation, and no one deserved happiness more.

Still, she couldn't help feeling a touch of envy. Didn't she deserve some happiness, too? Here she was, a widow at the young age of twenty-five. All her hopes and dreams of family life had shattered that fateful day two years ago...

After a while, even though the subject changed to other topics, the voices grated on her nerves, and the room closed in. Casting a glance at Karli to make sure she and Ryan were absorbed with the blocks, she rose, crossed to the front door, and slipped outside.

Perhaps the explanation she'd offered earlier for her behavior was true—she was tired from the trip, riding the train, making connections, and the emotional parting with her sister, Paige, and brother-in-law, Harlan.

Whatever the reason for her strange mood, she needed a moment or two alone. Hugging her arms, she walked to the top of the steps. As she looked out, her gaze caught the long branches of the willow tree as they brushed the weathered wagon wheel propped against its trunk. Beyond the yard, a rosy dusk had settled over the meadows and the asphalt road leading to the highway. In the distance sat the ever-present mountains, their formidable peaks reaching into the sky.

Molly sighed. Such a peaceful scene. If only she

could feel as peaceful inside. Instead, she was a prisoner on a roller coaster of emotions, one minute happy to have returned, the next, fighting the impulse to flee.

Her thoughts turned to Buck, and her throat tightened. Many a night, after dinner with Jackson and Sara, the four of them would sit out here on the porch, the men discussing ranch business, while she and Sara talked about their children.

Buck. How she wished he were here by her side tonight. Then her world would be complete. Tears rolled down her cheeks and a sob caught in her throat.

"Molly?" a deep voice said.

Molly jumped. Buck? She turned, half expecting to see him.

Of course, the speaker wasn't Buck. He was Steve Roper. Her stomach churned. The one person she especially did not want to see. "Oh...hi," she managed to say.

He lingered near the door. "Nice evening, isn't it?"

"It is." Not wanting him to see her tears, she turned away to swipe at her wet cheeks.

He took a couple steps closer. "Seems like an interesting town, Red Rock. What I saw of it today."

Molly turned back around and offered a smile. "I like it."

Silence fell. From nearby bushes came the evening's first cricket chirp. Overhead, an airplane droned.

Finally, Steve shuffled his feet and spoke. "Guess I'll go back inside." He grasped the screen door's handle.

On impulse, Molly said, "Steve, wait."

He stopped. "Okay..."

Molly bit her lip. "I want to apologize. For today. On the train."

With a subtle shake of his head, he held up a hand. "No need..."

"Yes, it's something I need to do. If I came across as rude and abrupt, I'm sorry."

"You were worried about your daughter—"

"Yes. But, where she's concerned, I can't seem to help overreacting." She could have dropped the subject, but, for some reason, she wanted him to know more. "I'm a single parent. Her father, my husband Buck, died two years ago. She's all I have now, and she means the world to me."

His brow wrinkled. "I'm sorry about your husband, and I can imagine how tough losing her dad has been on Karli." His voice dropped to a low tone. "And I know where you're coming from. I lost my wife."

Molly pressed her fingers against her lips. How self-centered she'd been. Her thoughts about Steve Roper hadn't gone beyond attempts to fight her disturbing attraction. She'd never considered what his situation might be.

Hoping he'd elaborate, she waited.

Instead, he stared out at the yard, hands jammed into his slacks' pockets.

Finally, she asked, "Do you have children?"

"Nope. Never had any."

The regret in Steve's voice prompted her to offer more sympathy. Before she could, he turned and gave a smile that looked forced. "Anyway, apology accepted. Friends?" He held out his right hand.

"Sure, friends." She put her hand in his, intending

only a light contact, but his grip was strong and tight. He stepped closer, and she caught the pleasant, woodsy scent of his aftershave.

Her personal space invaded, she stepped backward. Her shoe's heel slipped over the edge of the steps, and she lost her balance.

"Watch out!" Letting go of her hand, he grasped her shoulders and pulled her to safety.

His warm breath brushed her cheek, sending shivers down her spine. Heartbeat pounding in her ears, Molly struggled to catch her breath. In a few seconds, they'd gone from a simple handshake to a near-embrace.

"You okay?" Concern shadowed his eyes.

Although still shaken, she nodded. "You can, ah, let go of me now."

"Oh, sure." He dropped his arms and stepped back.

"Think I'll go in now," Molly said with a nod toward the door.

"Yeah, me, too." Steve opened the screen door and stood aside for Molly to lead the way.

Once inside, Molly hurried across the room to sit by Karli and Ryan, as far away from Steve Roper as she could get.

Chapter Three

"Dinner was great, Sara." Steve slipped into his jacket and prepared to leave the Rolling R. "Thanks for inviting me tonight."

"We're glad you could join us." Sara opened the front door and held it. "Aren't we, Ryan?" She looked at her son, balanced on her hip. "Can you say 'bye to Steve?"

Ryan raised his hand and flexed his fingers. "'Bye."

"See you later, Ryan." Steve gave him a high-five.

Jackson joined them, stepping close to his wife. "When do you want to get started with our programs?"

"How about Tuesday? That will give me Monday to make some phone calls and line up some appointments." *And time to check around town to see if anyone remembers seeing Angie here.*

"Works for me," Sara said after a glance at her husband. "Then Molly can get acquainted with her job duties before she learns your new system."

So, instead of working with Sara, he'd be dealing with Molly. For just a moment, his body stilled. That was cause for concern, but he'd worry about it later.

"How long will you be here?" Jackson asked, looping an arm around his wife's shoulder.

Steve dug in a jacket pocket and pulled out his car keys. "I haven't decided on a return date yet. This is a combination vacation and business trip."

"Great. We'll plan some fun things to do," Sara said with a bob of her head.

"I'll look forward to that."

Steve glanced over their shoulders to where Mike and Rose sat close together on the couch looking at a photo album. "'Bye, you two. Nice meeting you."

They looked up and smiled. "See you later." Mike lifted a hand in a wave.

Steve swung his gaze to the easy chair where Molly had been sitting, but she was gone. So was Karli. Well, so much for saying good-bye to them.

On the drive back to Red Rock, with a faint glow from the setting sun lingering in the sky, Steve thought how glad he was to reconnect with Jackson. They'd been good friends when they both lived in New York. Sara was a jewel, and Mike and Rose were friendly and welcoming.

The only rough spot in the evening was Molly. He honestly hadn't known she was on the porch when he stepped out for a breath of fresh air. When he first met her on the train, he sensed she was sad and troubled, and now he knew why. Yes, he could relate to the loss of a spouse.

Maybe he should have explained that his wife had not passed away, as her husband had, but instead had disappeared. But they barely knew each other and, besides, he was never comfortable telling the story. He hoped Molly hadn't thought he was making a pass when he rescued her from falling off the porch. She was an attractive woman. But, even if he were ready to move on, he wasn't about to push himself on a woman who clearly wasn't interested.

In his hotel room, Steve flopped on the king-size bed and folded his arms behind his head. He was mulling over whether to watch TV or go to sleep when his cell phone rang. He recognized the special ring of his business partner, Jerry Templeton. Steve glanced at his wristwatch. Nine o'clock. That meant eleven back in New York. On Saturdays, Jerry usually hit the clubs.

"Hey, buddy, what's goin' on?" he said into the phone.

"Big news, man."

"You got Sotheby's. Yes!" Steve fisted his hand and pumped the air. They'd been trying for months to land the big auction house as a client.

"Nah, this is personal. We wanted you to be the first to know."

He ran a hand through his hair. "We?"

"Candace and me. We're engaged."

"What?" Steve bolted upright. "Where are you?"

"In a limo, driving through midtown. We had dinner at The Manchester, and then I popped the question. She said 'yes.' I put the ring on her finger. Done deal. You don't believe me? Here, talk to my bride-to-be."

As Jerry passed the phone to Candace, horns honked in the background. Steve pictured the coziness of the limo, the lights of Manhattan a blur of neon as the car sped along the streets. A wave of homesickness rolled over him. What was he doing out here in Red Rock, Colorado when he could be at home enjoying an evening out on the town?

A high, lilting voice said, "Hello, Steve."

"Candace, is it true? Did you let my big lug of a partner talk you into hooking up with him permanently?"

She laughed. "He made me an offer I couldn't refuse."

She sounded like she'd had one glass of champagne too many. But then, they were celebrating.

"You think you can settle him down, huh?" Steve said with a teasing laugh.

"Oh, yeah." Her voice took on a sultry tone.

"Well, that's great. I'm happy for both of you."

Jerry's voice sounded in the background.

"Jer wants to talk to you again, so I'll say 'bye now."

"'Bye, Candace. And congrats to you both."

"You old son-of-a-gun," Steve said when Jerry came back on the line. "When's the wedding?"

"Around Christmas. And it's gonna be big, man. Candace must have a million relatives, not to mention all of her father's business connections."

A wide grin broke out. "I'll be there."

"You better be. You're the best man."

"I'll be honored."

"Good. And, you're next."

Steve shook his head, even though the gesture was lost on Jerry. "No way. I don't want to get married again, not after screwing up the first time."

"Come on, you did the best you could for Angie."

"Oh, yeah? Then why did she run away?"

"Who knows? Whatever, you're divorced now and free to get on with your own life."

Steve tensed, as he always did when Jerry challenged him about moving on. "It's not that easy. What about my promise to her folks to take care of her after they died?"

"Like I said, you did the best you could. Quit beatin' yourself up. But, hey, gotta go now. We're almost to Candace's. I'll call you tomorrow and we'll catch up on business."

After disconnecting the call, Steve laid the phone on the nightstand. He sank back onto the pillows, his brain whirling with Jerry's engagement news. He was genuinely happy for them both.

He wished Jerry hadn't used his happy occasion to nag him about moving on with his own life, though. Yeah, he was free now, legally. He'd waited the five years New York State law required to divorce a missing spouse in absentia. But guilt and worry that Angie might be alive somewhere and need his help kept him an emotional prisoner.

Move on, Jerry said. Yeah, right.

****

Molly gazed around the bakery's kitchen, noting all the improvements. "Wow, Sara, you've really done a lot since I've been gone."

Sara nodded. "Last year, we put in the wall ovens and then those new counters and sinks. And no more mixing by hand." She gestured to several huge revolving metal vats. "I have lots of help, too. Come and say hello to my crew."

She led Molly to two women in their twenties, one tending a vat, the other arranging cellophane-wrapped cookies in a cardboard box. White aprons covered their clothing and hairnets corralled their hair.

A flash of recognition hit, and Molly approached the woman at the vat. "Aren't you Anna Gabraldi's daughter, Doreen?"

Doreen's round face broke into a grin. "I am. I

heard you were coming, Molly. Good to have you back at the Rolling R."

"Thanks." Molly raised her voice to be heard over the machine's rumble. "I'm glad to be back."

Sara introduced the second woman as Lupe Gonzalez. "Lupe's husband, Hector, is one of Jackson's ranch hands."

"How do you like living at the Rolling R?" Molly asked Lupe.

Lupe's smile was shy but her black eyes sparkled. "*Muy bien*. Very well," she said in her accented voice.

After Sara finished showing Molly the kitchen, she led them to a separate room at one end of the building. "Here's your office."

"This is bigger than the one I had at the real estate company in Chicago." Molly's gaze took in a metal desk, a file cabinet, a worktable, and several straight chairs. Next to the door hung a corkboard for notices. Sunshine beamed in a window facing the road, and several potted plants and a colorful wall calendar gave the place a homey touch.

Sara crossed to the desk and picked up a three-ring binder. "Everything you need to know is in here. All the procedures, from ordering supplies to taking phone orders, to supervising the crew are included."

Worry crossed her mind as Molly stared at the thick notebook. "Sounds like a big job."

Sara put down the binder and patted Molly's shoulder. "You'll do great. I wouldn't have hired you if I didn't think so. But before you get started, I want you to meet Teresa Halston."

"Another of your crew?"

"No, she's Isaac's wife. He's one of Jackson's

men. She has a childcare service for the children here and from a couple of neighboring ranches. She takes care of Ryan, like you used to do."

"Okay..." Molly narrowed her eyes. What was Sara leading up to?

"And she'll be taking care of Karli, too."

So that was it. She should have guessed. Molly lifted her chin. "That won't be necessary. She can stay here in the office with me. I'll get her a little table and chair, and she can sit in the corner."

Sara shook her head. "No, Molly, that's not a good idea. She needs to be active and to be with other kids. Teresa's yard is fenced, so you don't need to worry about Karli wandering. Besides, Teresa won't let that happen. She's very responsible. And this fall, when Karli goes into town to kindergarten, Teresa will see that she gets down to the main road for the bus."

Her body went stiff at the mention of kindergarten. "I'm home-schooling Karli. I've planned that from the very beginning."

Sara raised an eyebrow, her hand gesturing back at the kitchen. "And how will you do that when you're working full time?"

Molly had given the matter a lot of thought, and the answer rolled off her tongue. "I can teach her in the evenings and she can practice her lessons during the day."

Sara was quiet for a long moment then she said, "I understand how you want to be with Karli. But Teresa's a wonderful caretaker. She's well trained, licensed, and bonded. Do you think I'd trust her with Ryan if she weren't qualified?"

Heat crept up her neck. Sara didn't understand that

her situation was different. "I'm sure she is all you say, but that's not the point."

"No, the point is, Molly, that you have to let go of Karli, at least a little. She has to learn to make her way in the world."

A knot formed in Molly's stomach. She didn't want to quarrel with Sara. Still, she had the right to raise her child as she saw fit. "No, I don't have to let go of her. Maybe someday. But not now. Think about it. What if Jackson were gone and you were raising Ryan alone? Wouldn't you want to keep him close?" Her hand fisted at her side. "Why can't you understand?"

"I do understand, Molly, but that doesn't mean I agree."

Molly swallowed against the rising lump in her throat. "So I can't keep Karli here while I work?"

Sara's eyes clouded with apology, but she shook her head. "No, you can't. There are safety and insurance issues to consider, too. I'm sorry. We should have discussed this at the time I hired you, but we didn't. And now you'll have to make a choice. I'll give you some time by yourself while I check on Doreen and Lupe." Sara turned and stepped into the other room.

Molly pursed her lips. Who was Sara to tell her how she should raise her daughter? She said she understood, but she didn't. If Molly wanted to home school Karli, that was her business, wasn't it? If she didn't want her daughter thrown into the mix of someone's daycare, that also was her decision.

Returning to Red Rock and the Rolling R had been a big mistake. She and Karli didn't belong here. Too many memories. Too many problems.

If she returned to Chicago, she probably could get

her old job back at the real estate office. Her boss, Mr. Cass, had allowed Karli to come to work with Molly. Karli had been a bit of a problem, though, because sitting still for very long was difficult. Mr. Cass had hinted once or twice that Molly should make other arrangements.

Molly chewed her lip and sank into the office chair. What would Buck want her to do?

The answer to that was easy—stay here on the Rolling R. He always said he wanted to raise his children in the wide, open spaces, not in the big city.

Sara and Jackson had gone to a lot of trouble to bring her and Karli to Red Rock. Molly glanced out at the other employees and knew Sara could have hired someone locally to help with her business.

Molly and Karli had been back only a few days. Of course, adjusting would take awhile. Didn't she owe Sara and Jackson and everyone else concerned at least a try?

Decision made, Molly stood and crossed to the door leading to the kitchen and called to Sara. When Sara joined her, she said, "Okay, Karli and I will meet Teresa. But I won't make my final decision until after that meeting."

"Fair enough," Sara said, and squeezed her hand. "I'm betting you're both going to love her."

****

Molly had expected Teresa to be someone close to Anna Gabraldi's age. Instead, she was in her twenties, tall and thin, with chocolate brown hair pulled into a single, thick braid. Over her jeans and T-shirt, she wore a huge apron with many bulging pockets. A teddy bear's head stuck out of one, a doll from one, and a packet of tissues from yet another.

Teresa flashed a wide smile and led them into her house. She leaned down to eye-level with Karli. "So you're Karli. I've heard a lot about you."

"And this is Mr. Muggins." Karli held up her doll.

"Hey! We watch his program every day."

"You do?" Karli's eyes shone and a smile graced her mouth.

"Yup." She rose and turned to Sara and Molly. "The kids are outside with my high school helper, Jasmine, so this is a good time for a tour." She showed them a large playroom full of toys and games, a kitchen that included child-size tables and chairs, and several bedrooms furnished with twin beds for naptime.

"How many children do you have here?" Molly asked.

"Seven, including my two. David will be in first grade this fall, and Lani in second. Plenty of room for one more." She patted Karli's shoulder. "Now, let me show you what's outside." Teresa led them through the kitchen and out the back door.

Molly's eyes widened. In one corner stood a huge, multicolored playset with swings and a slide. Teresa's helper, Jasmine, pushed a girl on the swings, while two more used the slide. Nearby, Ryan and another boy played with toy cars in a sandbox, while an older boy and a girl sat at a table working a jigsaw puzzle.

"Wow!" Karli exclaimed and then ran toward the playset.

"Karli!" Molly's voice caught in her throat. "You haven't been invited yet."

"It's okay, Karli," Teresa called. "Go ahead and try out the equipment."

Karli raced up the steps to the slide.

"Be careful, darlin'!" Molly's throat dried. Would Karli be able to land on her feet without Molly to catch her at the bottom?

"I will." Karli sat at the slide's top. "Here I go!" she called and swooped down.

Expecting her to tumble onto the ground, Molly held her breath.

But Karli landed on her feet, laughing and waving Mr. Muggins. Then she ran to join Ryan and his friend in the sandbox.

Molly gazed around. "The yard certainly looks secure." She nodded at the cyclone fencing.

"It is," Teresa said. "And so is the house. When we're inside, the screen doors are always closed and locked. The children don't go out without either me or Jasmine."

"Karli tends to run," Molly said, her gaze following her daughter's movements.

Teresa smiled and stuck her hands into her apron pockets. "She sounds like a typical five-year-old."

"No, I mean it." Molly's tone was firm. "She runs away."

"She won't run away from here." Teresa smiled and slowly shook her head.

The three women stood awhile longer watching the children play. How carefree and innocent they were, Molly thought. No sadness about the past. No worries about the future. And for a moment, she yearned for someone to take care of her, so she too might be worry-free.

She straightened her shoulders. Silly thought. She was an adult now. She could take care of herself. And of Karli, too.

"So, what do you think?" Sara's voice broke into Molly's thoughts.

"I'm impressed." Molly turned to Teresa. "You've thought of everything. Still, could Karli start out on a trial basis? To make sure she adjusts?"

"Of course." Teresa nodded. "Why don't you let her stay for the rest of the day?"

Today? Molly wasn't prepared for Karli to begin so soon. Still, they were here and, other than her own anxiety, Molly couldn't come up with a reason to refuse Teresa's invitation.

"Well...all right. Let's exchange cell phone numbers, though. In case anything comes up."

Teresa nodded. "Good idea. And I'll give you a brochure to look over."

Molly stepped to the back door and called to Karli, "I'm going now, darlin'."

Karli stopped pushing a toy car through the sand long enough to wave. "'Bye, Mommy."

On the way back to the bakery, once Teresa's house was out of sight, a sinking feeling hit the pit of Molly's stomach. Was she doing the right thing to let someone else take care of her daughter?

Chapter Four

"Sorry to leave you alone so soon," Sara told Molly on Tuesday morning. "But I need to leave now if I want to reach Denver in time for my appointment." She crossed the bakery's office to the filing cabinet, opened a drawer, and removed a file folder.

Molly looked up from making an entry in the computer. "No problem." Sara had explained earlier that an appointment she'd had next week had been changed to this week.

"I know, but I've thrown a lot at you all at once." Sara glanced at the contents of the folder, and then stuck it into her brown leather briefcase sitting on the worktable. "Okay, any questions before I take off?"

"No, but I'll probably have plenty by the time you return."

"Don't forget to fax a reply to Donovan's letter."

"Right." Her gaze landed on the letter in the inbox.

"And check our supplies to see if we can cover those orders that came in last week."

"That's on my list." She pointed to the clipboard at her elbow. "Everything will be fine." Molly hid a smile. Sara was as nervous about leaving her business with Molly as Molly had been about leaving Karli at Teresa's.

"You think this suit is too dressy?" Sara smoothed the wide lapel of her navy blue cotton jacket then fingered the matching slacks.

"Not at all. It's perfect. And your hair in a bun instead of a ponytail looks professional." She made a shooing motion with one hand. "Go already, or you'll be late."

"Yeah. Okay." Sara started for the door then stopped and turned. "Don't forget Steve Roper's coming this morning to install the new software."

The reminder tightened Molly's brow into a frown. "I know." She couldn't help the sigh of resignation that escaped her lips.

"Anna will make lunch for the two of you."

Molly jolted at this news. "What? I planned to have lunch at Teresa's."

"Have Karli join you and Steve instead. I'll tell Anna on my way out to make enough for three. Gotta run." She darted out the door, but in the next instant she ran back in. "Almost forgot my briefcase." She snatched up the case and slung the strap over her shoulder. "Okay, now I'm really off."

Sara's "good-bye" to Lupe and Doreen drifted into the office, followed by the kitchen's screen door opening and closing. Molly sat back in her chair and folded her arms. Gazing out the window, she glimpsed Sara climbing into her car. If only Steve Roper weren't coming today. She needed more time to get used to the routine. She wanted to eat lunch with Karli and the other children, not with him.

Yesterday, she'd picked up Karli after work. Her daughter had been full of chatter about her afternoon at Teresa's. They'd both been too tired to do much in the evening, although Molly made sure she read Karli a bedtime story. She and Buck had read to Karli from the time she'd been born.

Molly sighed. He'd been such a good father.

She shook her head to clear away the memories. She'd better get back to work.

While she was lost in her thoughts, the computer switched to screen saver, a montage of ranch scenes. She punched a key to return to the order form. Studying Sara's notes, she added two dozen gingerbread cookies to the order. But when she punched the Tab key to go to the next line, the screen froze. Irritation tensed her muscles, and she scowled at the monitor. She hated glitches, had little patience with them. Hitting the Tab key repeatedly brought no results. Now, she'd have to force quit the machine and restart. Sara had warned her this might happen.

Before she could perform the task, someone knocked on the screen door that led outside. Scooting her chair toward the door, she looked up and met Steve Roper's gaze.

"Hey." His lips broke into a broad smile.

Molly's heart beat faster. "Hello. Come on in."

Steve opened the door and stepped inside. "Looks like you're hard at it." He crossed the room to stand in front of her desk.

He wore jeans and a brown cotton shirt that matched the color of his eyes. The shirt's short sleeves showed off his muscular arms. His black briefcase was slung over one broad shoulder.

Hoping to calm her over-active heartbeat, she took a deep breath. "Trying to be, but the program froze." She pointed to the computer.

He leaned around to glimpse the screen. "Good thing I came, isn't it? Once I install our program, that will never happen again."

She raised an eyebrow and, with undisguised skepticism, said, "Oh, really?"

He nodded, his eyes solemn. "Guaranteed satisfaction or your money back."

"You sound awfully sure of yourself."

"Where our programs are concerned, I am. You'll see." He set his briefcase on the worktable next to the desk and shrugged off the strap.

She wanted to look away, but couldn't keep her gaze off him. Judging by the precise cut at the nape, his hair had been professionally styled, probably at a fancy New York salon.

With a snap, he opened the briefcase and took out a box. His long fingers had neatly clipped nails with not a speck of dirt underneath.

Molly had to smile. He was such a dude and so out of his element here on the Rolling R.

He glanced up and caught her before she could erase the smile.

"What?" His brows knit into a frown.

Heat flooded her face. "Nothing. I was, ah, nothing." She made a dismissive wave.

"Oh. I thought maybe I was wearing my breakfast on my shirt, or something." He glanced down at the front of his shirt.

"I'd better get out of your way." Gripping the arms of her chair-on-wheels, she prepared to scoot to the side.

He raised a hand. "No, stay put. I want you to see what I'm doing. You need to learn the program from the bottom up. Then if you get into trouble, you'll know what to do."

"Okay." Like a dutiful student, Molly clasped her hands in her lap and leaned forward.

"Of course, we have good technical support, and our programs don't have glitches. But we always make a point of putting the customer in the driver's seat."

Steve's confidence impressed Molly. "Good to know."

Opening the box, he took out a couple of booklets and CDs then pulled up a chair and sat beside Molly. As he adjusted the monitor so they both could view it, his elbow brushed hers.

A little shiver spiraled up her arm. She should move away. Again, he'd encroached on her personal space. Instead, she sat there as though frozen.

Steve slipped the CD into its slot. "So, what other accounting programs are you familiar with, if any?"

She turned and, caught in the warmth of his brown-eyed gaze, couldn't form a single answer.

"Accounting programs?" he prompted, eyebrows raised.

"Oh, right. On my last job, I used Martin's Bookkeeper."

He nodded. "What exactly was your job?"

"I worked in a real estate office, in Chicago. Mostly, I prepared contracts."

"Residential? Commercial?"

"A little of both."

Encouraged by his interest, Molly told him more about her job while he finished installing the program.

At last, he picked up the manual and opened it to the first page. "Okay, we're ready to begin."

As Steve explained the program, Molly struggled to ignore the fluttering sensation in her stomach and the sudden palpitating of her heart whenever his arm brushed hers and instead to concentrate on what he was saying.

Enough of her brain must have been functioning, though, because after he'd guided her through the program, he sat back and grinned. "Hey, I think you've got it."

His praise warmed her cheeks. "Thanks for your patience. The program does seem like a good one."

With his forefinger, he tapped the manual's cover. "Here is everything you'll need for ordering, inventory, bookkeeping, all sorts of graphs and charts for analysis and projections, and then some."

"And you developed all this?" she asked, truly impressed.

Steve nodded, his eyes shining with pride. "Yep. I could have gone to work for Microsoft or one of the other software giants, but decided to strike out on my own. Hooked up with my partner, Jerry, and we've done well."

A beat of silence went by while he checked his wristwatch. "Almost noon. I'd better get going."

Apparently, he hadn't heard that he was invited for lunch. Molly studied her hands while she considered what to do. If she kept quiet and let him go on his way, she could have lunch at Teresa's, as planned. Afterward, she and Karli might be able to spend some one-on-one time.

But what about the lunch Anna was preparing for the three of them? And later, when Sara returned, she surely would question Molly about lunch. Molly wouldn't lie to either of them. She prided herself on being a truthful person.

She cleared her throat. "Sara wanted me to invite you for lunch at the ranch house. But you probably have other plans..." She held her breath, waiting for his answer. Part of her wanted him to refuse, while another, traitorous part, wanted him to accept.

One eyebrow peaked. "Sara wants me to stay for lunch? What about you?"

"Of course, you're welcome," she said, carefully avoiding his question. "I planned to have lunch with Karli at Teresa's, where she's in daycare. But if you stay, she can eat with us. I'm sure she'd like to see you again."

"Sounds like you had your plans all set. I wouldn't want to intrude..."

"You wouldn't be," she said, hoping her bright tone sounded sincere rather than forced. "But it's up to you."

Steve rubbed his hands together. "Well, then I'll stay. Anna's cooking is the best. And I won't mind the company, either," he added with a teasing grin.

"How's Karli doing in daycare?" Steve asked later as they walked down the asphalt road to Teresa's.

Better than I am, Molly wanted to say. "She enjoyed yesterday's play, but it's too soon to tell."

"I have to admit I'm surprised you're letting her stay there. I mean, considering how protective you are—by your own admission," he added, as though afraid of offending her.

Molly tugged on the brim of her straw hat. The noonday sun, as usual, was hot and unrelenting. "I didn't have much choice. Sara was firm. But I'll spend as much time with Karli as I can."

They made small talk for the rest of the short walk

past the hay fields and meadows where cows and horses grazed. At last, they turned down the side road that led to Teresa's. As they neared the house, the sounds of children playing in the yard drifted along the airwaves. Happy, carefree sounds. But Molly was anything but carefree. Her stomach had knotted up.

It's only lunch. Why are you making the meal such a big deal?

Because she wanted time alone with Karli? Because Steve was an intruder?

Or because his nearness kept her senses on high alert?

Pushing away her concerns, she scanned the yard looking for Karli, finally spotting her at the top of the slide.

"Mommy, look at me!" Karli whooshed down the slide, landed on her feet, and ran over to the fence.

"Hi, darlin'." Molly gestured to Steve. "Look, we have a visitor."

"Steve! Steve!" Karli jumped up and down.

"Hey, Karli. How'ya doing?" He stooped to Karli's eye level. "I see you have your friend with you." He nodded to Mr. Muggins sticking out of Karli's pants pocket.

"Uh huh." Karli pulled the doll free and held him up. "He likes the slide. He likes everything here, same as me."

"Same as I do," Molly corrected.

Teresa appeared, wearing her usual apron with the bulging pockets, and Molly introduced her to Steve. They chatted for a few minutes then Teresa opened the gate for Karli to leave.

Before Molly could take Karli's hand, Karli turned

to Steve and grabbed his hand. Something akin to jealousy shot through Molly. She'd looked forward to spending time with her daughter, and now she had to share her with Steve.

Steve smiled down at Karli. "Your mom asked me to stay for lunch. That okay with you?"

"Goody! Goody!" She skipped along beside him, tugging his hand.

"Slow down, Karli," Molly cautioned in an attempt to make clear her position of authority. "We'll get there soon enough."

At the ranch house, Anna had their places set at the dining room table, two on one side, and one on the other. Karli ran to the side with two settings. "Sit by me, Steve. Sit by me."

"You and I need to sit together." Molly stepped to Karli's side and caught her hand. "You might need help with your food."

"Steve can help me. Huh, Steve." Karli smiled up at him.

"I'd be honored, but we need to do what your mom says." His gaze met Molly's.

"Please, Mommy?"

Molly released an exasperated breath. "Oh, all right." She dropped Karli's hand and went to the other side of the table.

Steve pulled out Karli's chair then headed around to help Molly.

Molly slid into her chair before he reached her. "I'm fine," she said over her shoulder. She picked up the lemonade pitcher from the table and filled their glasses.

Anna bustled in with a plate of ham sandwiches, a

bowl of potato salad, and a tray of fresh vegetables.

While they ate, Karli chattered to Steve about her favorite subject—horses. "Can you ride a horse?" she asked him.

He sipped his lemonade. "I have, but it was a long time ago."

"When you were five?"

As she picked up the plate of sandwiches and held it out to Steve, Molly heard the hopeful note in Karli's voice.

Steve laughed and took the plate. "A little older than that."

"Uncle Jackson says he can teach me. He could teach you, too."

Steve nodded. "That's an idea."

Karli scowled at Molly. "'Cept my mom says 'we'll see.' I think that means 'no.'"

After helping himself to another half sandwich, Steve put down the plate and shot Molly a questioning look.

"I think she's a little young yet." Molly scooped a bite of potato salad onto her fork.

"But you'll let me, huh?" Karli said to Steve.

What? Molly's mouth dropped open. "Karli! Steve has no say in what you do. He's not—" She almost said, "Your father," but stopped herself in time.

"Your mom's right, Karli. She's the one who'll decide."

Steve's support helped to settle Molly. She took a deep breath and leaned back in her chair.

Karli's lips pushed into a pout, but when Steve asked how she liked staying at Teresa's, she brightened and launched into a tale about playing in the sandbox.

When they finished eating, Molly suggested Karli help Anna clear the table, while she and Steve took their lemonade out to the front porch.

Karli agreed and ran off to the kitchen to find Anna.

When she and Steve were on the porch, Molly sank into one of the log chairs, placing her glass on the matching table. She turned her face to the soft breeze, which smelled of hay and the wildflowers growing along the side of the road.

Steve pulled up a chair and sat beside her. He set his glass on the table, and then leaned forward and clasped his hands between his knees. "Good lunch. I'm glad I stayed."

Molly brushed back a lock of hair caught by the breeze. "I apologize for my daughter. She's a little much, sometimes."

"No apology necessary." Steve straightened and gave a dismissive wave. "She's fine."

"She likes you." Molly cast him a covert glance to gauge his reaction.

Steve tossed back his head and laughed. "I do seem to hit it off with kids. I have a niece and a nephew, a few years older than Karli. I spend time with them when I can." He was silent a moment then continued in a more sober tone, "I know it's none of my business, and I don't want to bring up a troublesome subject, but I was wondering about Karli's father...how he..."

Molly's stomach twisted. Talking about Buck's death was always painful, but she wanted to answer his question. She took a deep breath. "Buck was killed in a rodeo accident while riding a mean bull, almost two years ago."

Steve slowly shook his head. "Wow. What a tragedy. You have my sympathy."

"Thanks. But, how about your wife? When did she pass away?"

His mouth tightened. "She didn't pass away. She disappeared."

Molly gasped. How awful. "Disappeared!" She hadn't expected that.

"Yep. One day, she left our house to go shopping—or so she said—and that was the last I saw of her."

"She didn't leave a note or anything?" Molly couldn't imagine a spouse just walking off without a word.

He shook his head. "And she didn't take anything, except her purse and the clothes she was wearing."

Molly bit her lip. "I had no idea..."

"I did everything I could to find her. I put her description in every missing person's database, hired private investigators, even consulted a psychic. There were a few leads, but none that amounted to anything."

Molly picked up her glass and sipped the lemonade. "Maybe she got amnesia. Sara had amnesia after she was mugged in the train station here in Red Rock. That's how she and Jackson first met."

He nodded. "I've heard the story. And I thought of amnesia regarding Angie."

"So there's a possibility you'll find her yet."

"Maybe." He shrugged. "I waited five years and then divorced her in absentia."

"Were you together long?"

"A year. She was only eighteen when we married. Her parents had passed away, and she was an only child. Our relationship was...different."

She wanted to ask what he meant by "different," but that was too personal a question. "I was eighteen when Buck and I married, too. And my parents were both gone. Dad had died of pancreatic cancer. Mom overdosed on prescription drugs. We never knew whether her death was intentional or accidental. She and Dad were devoted to each other and were inseparable."

"That must have been hard."

The sympathy in his voice sounded heartfelt, and she warmed toward him. "It was. My older sister, Paige, was already married, and I went to live with her and Harlan."

Steve shifted in his chair. "How'd you meet your husband and end up out here?"

"Paige and Harlan and I came to Colorado for a vacation on a dude ranch where Buck worked. We experienced love at first sight." She propped her chin in her hand and smiled at the memory, remembering those special days. "When Paige and Harlan went home, I stayed. They didn't want me to, but I was eighteen, and they couldn't stop me. Buck and I were married, and soon after that Jackson hired him, and we came to the Rolling R."

"Any regrets?"

"None. We were very happy. Until he got hooked on rodeo," she added in a low voice, pushing the words out through a tight throat.

"You didn't approve."

His words were a statement rather than a question. "Only because the sport was so dangerous." She angled her chin.

He looked off into the distance and then back. "Life is dangerous. You could get hit by a car crossing the street."

Molly gripped her glass. "You can save your breath with that kind of talk. I've heard all those arguments, and they're no comfort at all."

"I'm sorry." Steve leaned forward and spread his hands. "I didn't mean to tell you how to feel."

Molly put down her glass and folded her arms against the ache in her chest. At the same time, she gritted her teeth. The reminder of Buck's tragic death always brought this combination of sadness and anger. If only he had listened, he might still be with them today. Then she wouldn't be sitting here on the porch with Steve Roper. Which she shouldn't be, anyway. She scooted to the edge of her chair. "I'd better get back to work."

"Right." Steve pushed to his feet. "And I need to head back to town."

The screen door squealed open, and Karli burst onto the porch. She skipped forward, skidding to a stop in front of Steve. "Let's ride horses now," she said, looking up with bright and shining eyes.

Steve laughed and ruffled her curls. "You are determined, aren't you? But even if your mom says okay, now's not a good time. She and I have to go back to work, and you need to go back to Teresa's."

"So when can we?" Karli bounced up and down on the balls of her feet.

"That's up to your mom."

"And not something we're going to discuss right now. Steve is right. You need to go back to Teresa's." Molly stood and took Karli's hand then cut her glance to Steve. "Thanks for coming out to install the program."

He gave a slight nod. "Thanks for lunch. And, give a holler if you have any trouble with the program."

"I will." She and Karli stood on the porch holding hands while Steve headed down the steps and along the stone walkway to his car. Before climbing behind the wheel, he turned and gave a little salute.

"'Bye, Steve!" Karli called, cupping her free hand around her mouth.

"'Bye," Molly echoed.

"I like Steve," Karli said as he drove away. "Do you like him, Mommy?"

"He seems like a nice man," Molly hedged. "Come on now, we'd better get you back to Teresa's." She turned their steps toward the screen door. "And on the way, you can tell me all about your morning..."

Back in her office, Molly sat at her desk, paging through the new program's manual and reviewing what Steve had taught her. Although she tried to concentrate, her thoughts kept returning to the lunch they'd shared.

As much as she'd wanted to spend time with Karli, she couldn't deny she'd enjoyed Steve's company. She wouldn't deny the twinges of attraction she had for him, either. But at the same time, guilt niggled her, as though she'd somehow been unfaithful to Buck.

Restless, Molly closed the manual, rose, and went outside. The air was hot and dry, and she stepped into the shade of the sprawling maple tree by the door. Her thoughts drifted to Steve and what he told her today. How tragic that his wife had gone missing. Had he been deeply in love with her? Was he in love with her still, even though they were now divorced? Surely, he'd cared for the woman. Why else had he married her? He said their relationship was "different." What did that mean?

Also disturbing was Karli's obvious attachment to Steve. That wouldn't do. He was here only temporarily. The more attached Karli became, the harder saying good-bye would be for her.

Molly had no intention of becoming romantically involved with Steve, no matter how attractive he was. All she wanted was to be here on the ranch where she and Buck had lived and to raise her daughter in the shadow of his memory.

The phone rang. Thankful for an interruption that would force her back to work, she hurried into the office and picked up the receiver. "Rolling R Bakery. Molly speaking."

"This is Jeb at Gerson's Grocery. Over in Farley?"

"Oh, yes, I've been to your store. What can I do for you?"

"I want to order some of them cookies on a stick. My granddaughter got one somewhere, and she and her friends want some more. Thought I'd try selling 'em in the store."

Molly sank into her desk chair. She picked up a pen and poised it over a notepad. "Great! We have gingerbread, chocolate chip, and date-pecan."

"Send me a couple dozen assorted."

"You got it."

After she hung up, Molly accessed the order form on the computer, as Steve had shown her earlier, and easily filled it in.

With a surge of pride, she sat back and surveyed her work. She'd have this new program mastered in no time. Steve said to call him if she had any problems, but, chances were, she'd never need his help.

That was good.

The less contact she had with him, the better.

Chapter Five

"So, how'd it go with Steve today?" Sara asked when she returned from her Denver appointment. She set her briefcase on the worktable and approached Molly's desk.

Molly looked up from the computer. "The program's installed, and he gave me instructions." She told Sara about the call from Gerson's and showed her the computer order form she'd filled out.

"Looks good," Sara said after she perused the order. She stepped back and tucked an errant lock of her blond hair behind one ear. "Did Steve stay for lunch?"

"Yes, and he said to thank you for the invitation."

"So, ah, how'd you two get along?" Sara cast Molly a sidelong glance.

"Fine." Molly closed the screen with the order form, making sure the file went into the proper file folder. She glanced up to see a look on Sara's face that she had no trouble interpreting. "If you're trying to matchmake, Sara, please don't."

Sara's brow wrinkled. "Oh, Molly...I know I do try to matchmake, sometimes. But I want to see you happy again. Jackson thinks a lot of Steve. So do I, even though I haven't known him long."

Molly rose from her chair and strode to the window. Out on the road, a ranch hand on a horse the color of butterscotch rode by. "Do you know that Steve's wife disappeared?"

"Yes, Jackson told me. Steve must have told you, then?"

Molly hugged her arms. "Yes, after lunch. He divorced her, but I get the feeling he's not over her. And I told him about Buck's accident. So, Steve's not looking for a relationship. And neither am I."

Sara walked to Molly's side and laid a hand on her shoulder. "Okay, honey, I hear you. I want you to be happy, that's all."

"I am happy, Sara. Well, as happy as I can be, considering the circumstances." She turned and offered Sara a smile. "Now, if you have some time, why don't I show you this new program?"

****

When he arrived in Red Rock, Steve went to his hotel room where he sat at the table and checked his email and phone messages. He made a few notes then phoned his office in New York and spoke to his assistant, Beverly.

"Everything's perking along," she said in her cheery voice. "Oh, did Jerry tell you his big news?"

"He did. Pretty great, huh?"

"It is. You're next, you know."

Steve propped his elbows on the table and hugged the phone to his ear. "That's what Jerry said. Are you two ganging up on me?"

Beverly laughed. "Maybe. My niece is coming to visit next month. She's about your age. Can I tell her I have someone for her to meet?"

Steve sobered and his shoulders tensed. "We'll see when the time comes," he hedged.

After working for a couple hours, Steve shut down his computer. He'd done enough for one day. In the time remaining before dinner, he'd check around town to see if anyone had seen Angie. Yesterday, he hit a few of the establishments, showing her picture and explaining that she'd been seen in the vicinity as recently as last year. He described the distinctive butterfly and star tattoo on her left wrist. No one had any recollection of such a woman.

Once outside, he turned his steps toward the side of town he hadn't covered the day before. He visited a hardware store, a pharmacy, and a women's western clothing store, thinking especially the latter might be a place Angie would patronize. All he got for his efforts were head shakes and "Sorry, haven't seen her."

When dinnertime came, he gave up his search and headed for The Roundup, a restaurant Jackson recommended. The place was popular, with a line of people waiting for tables.

The hostess stepped forward to greet him. "There's a counter for singles."

"Sure." He nodded and followed the direction she indicated.

Single. The word lodged in his brain as he slipped onto a stool at the counter. Yep, single was what he was. And yet the word sounded alien, somehow.

A waitress came by and handed him a plastic-covered menu. He ordered a steak, and when it arrived with a baked potato and tossed green salad, and the first bite melted in his mouth, he silently applauded the chef. Jackson was right—The Roundup was a good restaurant.

As he dug into his salad, his thoughts turned to this

afternoon and Molly Henson. Was his imagination overactive or had something happened between them today? He didn't see how anything could. She was as tied to the memory of her deceased husband as he was to his worries about Angie.

Still, he could swear they'd connected on a personal level. When he sat beside her in Sara's office, attraction stirred inside him. The feeling reappeared after lunch when they were together on the porch.

He smiled to himself. He and Karli had sure hit it off, no doubt about that. But then, the little girl liked everyone. He shouldn't put too much importance on her apparent interest.

Neither would he pursue any attraction between him and Molly. Starting something wouldn't be fair to either of them, when he'd be leaving soon and returning to his life in New York.

Or, what if he found Angie? She might be in trouble and need his help. Even though divorced, he wanted to honor the promise he'd made her folks to look out for her.

Finished with his meal, Steve left a tip, paid his check, and stepped outside into the early evening. A refreshing breeze had tempered the day's heat, and the walk back to the hotel promised to be pleasant.

He had traveled almost a block when a young woman looking in a variety store window caught his eye. She wore blue slacks and a blue print T-shirt. She stood with one hand resting on her hip, setting her body slightly off balance. His pulse quickened. Angie used to stand like that sometimes, too.

The woman was about Angie's height, five-foot-five, and slender of build. When she turned and her profile came into view, another chord of familiarity jolted him. Her nose had the same curve as Angie's, as did her rounded chin.

Whether or not she was his lost ex-wife depended on one bit of identification—the butterfly and star tattoo on her left wrist. If he could just catch a glimpse...

The woman turned from the window and began walking.

He hurried to catch up, dodging a man walking a dog and a group of cowboys lounging in front of a drugstore.

Although she didn't turn around, she sped her pace.

Her movements indicated she knew she was being pursued. Caution niggled Steve. He didn't want the woman to think he was a stalker. And yet he had to know if she was Angie.

Finally, he caught up. "Oh, miss?"

"Huh?" She stopped and turned, thrusting out her left arm in his direction.

His gaze traveled to her wrist. No tattoo. Then he looked at her face. She was so unlike Angie that he didn't know how, even for a moment, he could have mistaken her for his former wife. Disappointment lumped in his stomach.

The woman propped her hands on her hips. "Were you talking to me?"

Hearing the woman's haughty tone sent heat creeping up the back of his neck. "Sorry." He made an apologetic wave. "I thought you were someone else."

She raised her eyebrows, but then gave a curt nod and turned away.

As he headed back to his hotel, Steve gave himself a mental kick in the butt. He should've known better than to follow the woman, much less speak to her. This wasn't the first time he'd been mistaken. False "Angie-sightings" occurred more frequently than he liked to admit. He always got up his hopes, and he was always disappointed. Would he ever learn?

Still, the need to find his ex-wife and discover why she'd disappeared hounded him.

****

"Mommy, wake up."

Karli's voice drifted into Molly's consciousness. She stirred and opened her eyes.

"The movie's over." Sitting beside her on the sofa, Karli tugged on Molly's arm.

Molly rubbed her eyes. She straightened and focused on the TV screen, where the program's credits were rolling. They'd been watching an animated movie featuring talking cars, and somewhere along the way, she fell asleep. She picked up the remote and ejected the DVD. "Sorry I fell asleep, honey. Did you watch it all?"

"Uh huh. So did Mr. Muggins." Karli patted the doll's head as he lay cradled in her arm.

Guilt nudged Molly. Mr. Muggins was better company than she was. She put the DVD in its plastic case then picked up the empty popcorn bowl. "Time for bed, darlin'. Go brush your teeth and pick out the story you want me to read."

As she expected, the promise of a story prompted Karli to action. She hopped down from the sofa and headed for the bathroom. By the time Molly cleaned up the kitchen and went to Karli's room, the child was in her pjs and searching her bookshelf for a story. She finally chose one they'd read so many times the pages were dog-eared.

Karli climbed into bed next to Mr. Muggins, already tucked in under the covers. She looked up at Molly. "Can Steve read me a bedtime story sometime?"

"No, honey." Molly plumped up the pillow and settled beside Karli. "He won't ever be here at your bedtime."

"Some other time, then?"

Molly opened the book's cover and turned to the first page. "I doubt it. He's busy. Besides, he's going home soon."

"Where's home?"

"Back in a big city called New York."

Karli slapped the bedspread with her palm. "I don't want him to go."

Molly chewed her lip, struggling with how to handle the unusual situation. Karli liked other males she'd come in contact with—her Uncle Harlan, and Jackson, and Dr. Mike—but she'd never grown as attached to any as she had to Steve Roper.

Laying down the book, she smoothed Karli's bangs. "He can't stay here, honey. He's only visiting. People go places to visit, and then they go home."

"Like our home was Chicago?"

"Yes, it was, but we moved, and now we live here at the Rolling R. This is home." She made a wave that included the room.

"Maybe Steve could move here."

Karli's brow wrinkled, as though she were struggling to understand the ways of adults.

Molly sighed. "No, Karli, that's not in his plans. Let's read our story now, okay?" Without waiting for Karli's consent, she picked up the book. "Once upon a time..."

After Karli fell asleep, Molly returned to the living room. A sitcom played on the silenced TV. She picked up the television guide and glanced at the evening's programs. Even though the satellite dish provided many choices, nothing interested her. She put down the guide and switched off the set.

Walking to the fireplace, she picked up the first in a line of framed photos she'd arranged on the mantel soon after moving in. The photo showed her and Buck on their wedding day, standing in front of the country church. She wore a short-skirted dress of traditional white and held a bouquet of daisies.

Buck wore a dark blue suit. Their wedding was the only time she'd seen him so dressed up. She called him "spectacular," and he said she was "the prettiest gal he'd ever seen." Not exactly original, but said with heartfelt love.

For a moment, she held the photo to her heart, and then replaced it on the mantel and picked up the next one. In this picture, she and Buck sat on the sofa with a newborn Karli cradled in Molly's arms. Half a dozen more photos, all of her and Buck and Karli, were in the group. Her family. She held and studied each one, savoring the memories until tears crowded her eyes.

The house suddenly closed in. She left the photos and went outside onto the porch. A warm evening breeze fluttered the leaves of the aspen trees, and bright stars filled the clear sky. She walked to the edge of the porch and, holding on to the wooden post by the steps, looked up. She and Buck used to stargaze a lot, especially before they were married. He proposed under the stars. They'd known each other only two weeks.

She said yes without a moment's hesitation. Deep in her soul, she'd known she wanted to spend her life with him.

Molly moved down the steps and along the path toward the road, intending to take a short walk in the moonlight before going to bed. The sweet smell of hay tickled her nose. A horse whinnied, an owl hooted—familiar and comforting sounds.

Usually. Tonight, she wasn't so sure.

Maybe the Rolling R wasn't to be their home, after all. Maybe she and Karli should have stayed in Chicago with Paige and Harlan. She was lonely here. Sara and Jackson weren't to blame. They'd done their best to make her feel welcome. No, her loneliness was her own longing, the emptiness in her heart since Buck's death. When he died, he took a part of her with him.

Molly gazed up at the stars again. *Oh, Buck, are you up there somewhere, looking down on Karli and me? Why did you leave us? Why did you have to take that last ride?*

****

"You can't live on a ranch without learning how to ride a horse." Jackson propped his hands on his hips and leveled Molly a stern look. "Horseback riding goes with the territory."

Molly sat back in her desk chair and folded her arms. "I still think Karli's too young." *And I'm afraid she'll fall off and hurt herself.*

Jackson had stopped by Molly's office to suggest they all go for a horseback ride on Sunday afternoon. Molly was glad Karli was at Teresa's and that she and Jackson could discuss the matter by themselves.

Jackson took a couple steps closer. "Ryan's two

years younger than Karli, and he already has his own pony."

Molly wrinkled her brow and turned to gaze out the window. She focused on the distant mountains, what she could see of them between the trees sheltering the office. She hated to say no, but her insides quivered at the thought of her little girl on horseback. She turned back to Jackson. "I don't know..."

"Come on, Molly." Jackson pushed back his Stetson and rubbed his forehead. "Karli will keep nagging until you let her try. She might not like riding as much as she thinks she will, and one ride might be all she'll ever take."

Jackson was right, about the nagging, anyway. Karli had talked of little else for the past couple of days. She wouldn't let the matter go, and she wouldn't take no for an answer. She was stubborn. *Like I am.* The trait came in handy sometimes, but also could be oh-so-annoying.

Molly uncrossed her arms and sat tall. "Okay, but no pony. She can ride in the saddle with me." *Then I can keep a good grip on her and make sure she doesn't fall off.*

Jackson's face broke into a grin. "No problem. That's the same way Ryan started."

Molly waited until Sunday morning after breakfast to tell Karli the news.

"Yay!" Karli yelled, and jumped up and down with glee.

As they prepared for the outing, Sara and Ryan arrived. Molly opened the screen door and motioned them inside.

Sara carried a cloth shopping bag, which she

handed to Molly. "Here's something for the big occasion."

Molly opened the bag, releasing the pleasant aroma of new leather. She reached inside and pulled out a pair of child's cowboy boots. They were red, and decorated with scrolls and curlicues. Molly smiled and held out the boots to Karli. "Look what Aunt Sara brought you."

"Wow." As she reached for the boots, Karli's eyes grew big.

Sara sat on the sofa and lifted Ryan onto her knee. "There's a hat, too."

"Hat, hat," Ryan echoed, waving his hands.

Molly plunged her arm into the bag again and retrieved a cowboy hat with a jaunty red feather. She placed the hat on Karli's head, tucking back her curls. A perfect fit.

Molly and Karli joined Sara and Ryan on the sofa. Karli slipped off her athletic shoes and pushed her feet into the boots. They fit perfectly, too. Molly wished Buck could be here to see their daughter in her Western outfit. He'd be so proud.

Molly's heart filled with affection for her friend, and her throat tightened. "You are so thoughtful, Sara. Thank you."

"Thank you, Auntie Sara," Karli echoed, settling her hat more firmly on her head.

"You're welcome, honey." Sara pointed to the bag sitting on the floor. "There's one more thing, and it's for you, Molly."

"For me?" Molly reached into the bag yet again and pulled out another cowboy hat. Of tan leather, it had a green and gold ribbon around the crown. She stared at the hat as waves of nostalgia rolled over her.

"The hat's yours." Sara's smile lit up her face. "You left it here."

Molly ran a forefinger along the hat's ribbon. The brown leather was cool and supple under her touch. "Yeah," she whispered. "Buck gave it to me. Before we were married." Her eyes burned with tears.

"Oh, Molly." Sara's eyes clouded, and she pressed her fingers to her lips. "I didn't know...I didn't mean..."

"It's okay." Molly ducked her head to swipe a fist at her wet cheeks. Then she straightened her spine and took a deep breath. "Of course, I want the hat, and I'll wear it today. Having it again will make me feel close to him." She smoothed back her hair and put on the hat. Leaning close, she gave Sara a hug. "Thank you. You are the most thoughtful person I know."

Sara brushed a tear from her eye. "You're welcome. We so much want you to be happy here."

"I know." Molly drew away and turned to Karli. She'd left the sofa and was strutting around in her new boots. Good, she hadn't noticed her mother's and her auntie's tears. "Okay, darlin', let's go get 'em!"

****

Gripping Karli's hand, Molly stepped inside the stable. She took a moment to let her eyes adjust from the bright sunlight to the dimmer interior.

Sara and Ryan, who entered behind them, stopped at one of the stalls to say hello to the horse inside. The animal nickered and shifted, rustling the hay underneath its hooves.

Halfway down the aisle, Jackson saddled a horse. Two other horses, already saddled, stood nearby. At Molly's approach, he looked up.

"Recognize Barney?" Jackson patted the horse's

rump.

Molly tilted her head and studied Barney, a cinnamon color with a white streak along his nose. "Yeah, I do. Hey, Barney." She touched the animal's nose, remembering him as a gentle animal. Jackson made a good choice for her and Karli's first ride.

Karli tugged Molly's arm. "Can I pet him, too?"

"Sure, honey." Molly lifted Karli so she could run her hand along the horse's snout.

"He's soft." Karli gave the horse a final pat before withdrawing her hand.

Karli's apparent lack of fear relieved Molly's tension. For all of her daughter's enthusiasm, Molly had half expected her to change her mind, once the ride became a reality.

As Molly lowered Karli to the floor, she spotted movement at the end of the aisle from the corner of her eye. She turned just as a man carrying a saddle and reins emerged from the tack room. At first, she thought he was one of Jackson's ranch hands, but then she realized the man was Steve Roper. Molly's heart rocketed against her ribcage. She hadn't expected him to be a part of their outing.

Today, he'd shed his city persona and was all decked out in jeans, a plaid, western-style shirt, and cowboy boots. A new-looking Stetson sat on his head at a jaunty angle.

"Set down the gear over there, Steve." Jackson nodded toward the door of a nearby stall, while adjusting the cinch strap under Barney's belly.

Steve did as Jackson requested. As he straightened, his gaze caught Molly's and a grin broke over his face. "Hey, looks like the rest of the group is finally here."

"Steve! Steve!" Karli broke away from Molly and ran to him, her boots clumping on the stable floor.

"Steve," Ryan echoed, clapping his hands.

Karli grasped Steve's hand and looked upward. "Are you coming, too?"

"I sure am. And don't you look like a real cowgirl today in your hat and boots." With his free hand, Steve straightened Karli's hat, which had tilted to one side.

Karli beamed and stuck out one leg. "Auntie Sara gave them to me."

"You said at lunch the other day that it's been a long time since you learned to ride," Molly said, aware her tone held doubt.

He caught her gaze again and nodded. "I know. But I figure I remember enough for what we're doing today."

"I wanna see the other horses." Karli tugged Steve's hand. "Can you show me?"

"I can do that. Okay with you?" He directed his question to Molly.

Molly lifted a shoulder. "Sure." What else could she say?

Steve led Karli to a nearby stall. "Let's check out this one..."

As soon as the two were out of earshot, Molly propped her hands on her hips and with a narrowed gaze turned to Jackson. "Is this a set-up?"

Jackson led Barney to join the two other horses, and then came back to Molly. "For you and Steve? Nope. He's a guest here in town. I always offer guests a ride around the ranch. But if you're not okay with him coming, you and Karli can ride some other time. I'm not telling Steve he can't come today."

Molly let her arms fall to her sides and wrinkled her brow in apology. "Of course, you can't, Jackson. I'm sorry. I didn't mean to sound rude."

He stepped close and laid a hand on her shoulder. "I know you didn't," he said, his tone gentler than before. "Try to relax and enjoy the ride. It's a beautiful day, and I'll bet once you're in the saddle again, you'll have a good time."

"Okay, I'll take your advice."

"Good. One more horse to saddle and we're ready to go." He headed for one of the stalls.

Molly folded her arms and pursed her lips. Could she enjoy herself, with Steve along? Just the sight of him a few minutes ago had sent her heartbeat into overdrive.

She cast him a covert glance. He and Karli had joined Sara and Ryan as they peeked into the various stalls and exclaimed over the horses. Molly heaved a sigh. As Jackson said, Steve was a guest, and she'd better get used to having him around.

At least, for a while.

Finally, all the horses were saddled and waiting outside the stable ready to go. Cautioning Karli to stand aside, Molly grabbed the saddle horn and mounted Barney. After she was settled, Jackson adjusted the stirrups. Then he picked up Karli and set her in the saddle in front of Molly.

Karli shook her head. "I want my own horse."

Molly had expected her disappointment. She put her arms around Karli. "This is your first ride, and you're going with me. Look, Ryan's riding with his mom." She pointed ahead to where Sara and Ryan sat on their horse, Sara with her arms tightly around Ryan.

Apparently the comparison worked, for Karli obediently settled back against Molly.

At a slow walk, they started off, leaving the stable behind and heading down the asphalt road leading to the ranch's interior. The clip-clop of horses' hooves struck a familiar, nostalgic note in Molly's brain. The sight of fields and meadows and cows grazing brought back memories, too. This was the first opportunity she'd had to venture beyond her and Karli's house.

Despite so much familiarity, sitting in the saddle again felt strange. Her legs soon ached from being stretched around Barney's girth, and, looking down, the ground seemed awfully far away. Her stomach clenched, and she tightened her grip around Karli.

Steve swung his horse into step beside them. "Hey, Karli, how do you like riding so far?"

"I like it." Karli lifted one hand from the reins and waved.

Steve's gaze cut to Molly. "How 'bout you?"

"So far, so good." Reluctant to share all her memories, Molly was intentionally vague. "You got a new outfit." She let her gaze rove over him.

He touched the brim of his cowboy hat. "Yep. When I heard about today's outing, I hit the western store. What do you think?"

Pressing her fingers to her lips, she stifled a giggle. "That you look like a dude."

One eyebrow peaked. "Should I take that as a compliment?"

"That's up to you," she said with a shrug. She didn't want to tell him that, dude or not, he was way too handsome and appealing for his own good.

The group followed the winding road through the

ranch until they came to the oval track where Jackson's horse trainer was working with one of the ranch's quarter horses. Horse and rider raced around the ring—the man leaning forward over the horse's neck, the animal's hooves pounding the dirt, raising clouds of dust.

Jackson led their group to the track's slatted wooden fence. When the trainer spotted them, he slowed and trotted the horse in their direction.

"This is Dirk Lamont." Jackson nodded at the newcomer.

Dirk smiled and tipped his hat.

Dirk's long, angular face looked familiar. While Molly was trying to place him, he gave her a wide smile of recognition.

"Hey, I remember you. Buck's wife, right?"

Molly's insides jolted. She hadn't been called "Buck's wife" for two years. "Right."

"Buck and I worked together on the Grant spread—where you two first met."

A lump rose in Molly's throat. "Ah, I knew I'd seen you somewhere."

"Buck was a great guy."

Her eyes burning, Molly lowered her gaze and fiddled with the reins. "Yes, he was."

"So how's Belle doing today?" Jackson leaned forward and rested his hands on the saddle horn. "She looked pretty good on the last lap."

Molly silently thanked Jackson for changing the subject. Taking advantage of the shift in Dirk's attention, she said in Karli's ear, "Isn't Belle a pretty horse?"

Karli bobbed her head. "She is, Mommy. Someday

I want a horse just like her."

Jackson and Dirk exchanged a few more remarks about Belle's training then Dirk said, "If you can hang around awhile, Jackson, I'll show you what she can do."

Jackson nodded. "Think I will." He turned to the others. "You folks go on ahead, and maybe I'll catch up. Otherwise, I'll see you back at the house."

Dirk tipped his hat to Molly and Steve. "Nice to meetcha, Steve. Molly, you take care now." With a tug on the reins, he wheeled Belle around and rode off.

Jackson dismounted and tied his horse's reins to the fence. Leaning his elbows on the top rail, his gaze followed Belle and Dirk.

Sara and Ryan kept the lead as the remainder of their group left the track and wound farther into the ranch's interior.

But the track was no more than out of sight when Sara reined her horse to a halt and waited for Molly, Karli, and Steve to catch up.

"My little guy is ready for his nap." Sara looked down at Ryan, whose chin was tucked into his chest. She turned back to Steve and Molly, wrinkles lining her forehead. "Sorry, but I'd better head back to the house."

And leave her and Karli to keep on riding just with Steve? Not something Molly wanted to do. "We'll go back, too."

"No." Karli shook her head. "I want to ride some more."

Molly rolled her eyes. She should have known her daughter would protest. She glanced at Steve.

He met Molly's gaze and shrugged. "I'm game."

"That's settled." Sara ran a hand over her forehead,

smoothing away the wrinkles. "You can ride on to the river. It's not far." She tugged on the reins and turned her horse around.

Now that only two horses rode forward, a sinking feeling hit Molly's stomach. This was not the enjoyable outing she'd envisioned.

That Steve had come along was bad enough, but to be abandoned by both Jackson and Sara left Molly feeling irritated. Entertaining their guest was not her responsibility.

Sara suddenly stopped and turned her horse around. For a moment, Molly thought perhaps Ryan had awoken and Sara intended to remain with them, after all. But then Sara said, "Don't forget, Steve, you're staying for dinner. And you and Karli are coming, too, Molly. Rose and Mike will be there."

Molly nodded and waved as Sara rode off. Sunday dinner with the Phillips was a frequent occurrence when she and Buck had lived there. She always looked forward to the occasions.

But tonight Steve would be there, too. On the night she and Karli arrived, he sat in Buck's place and claimed Karli's attention. A lump formed in Molly's throat. How would she get through another dinner with Steve present?

"So, what do you think?"

Steve's voice broke into Molly's thoughts. "About what?" she asked, her tone abrupt.

"About riding to the river?"

"Yes! Yes! The river!" Karli bounced up and down in the saddle.

Barney pranced and whinnied.

"Hold on there, darlin'." Molly clutched the reins

with one hand and Karli with the other.

"Can we, can we, Mommy?"

"Well, all right," Molly conceded. "But only as far as the river."

Chapter Six

As they rode on, Steve's shoulders tensed. Being alone with Molly kept him on edge. Of course, Karli was there, too, but Molly was the one he worried about. He'd tried making conversation, but her replies were short. Mostly, she stared straight ahead with her jaw set and her brow furrowed. He wasn't sure if Sara's and Jackson's absences or their visiting the river had caused her mood.

With a roll of his shoulders to ease the tension, he vowed to enjoy the ride as best he could. The winding road led them by a meadow ringed with tall cottonwood trees, where cattle peacefully grazed, and on to wide, open spaces dotted with clumps of tangleweed and scrub brush. The air was dry and hot, with little breeze, and more than once, he pulled out his handkerchief to wipe his brow.

After a while, the silence weighed on him. "Nice spread Jackson has here." He cast Molly a glance to see if she would respond.

"It is." Molly nodded but didn't meet his gaze.

"I'm guessing around seven hundred acres."

"Seven hundred and fifty-six."

He chuckled. "Hey, I wasn't too far off."

Molly clamped her jaw shut.

Okay, another conversational dead end. Steve pushed up his hat and scratched his head. There must be something they could talk about. "Say, how're you doing with the software program?"

Molly guided Karli's hands on the reins to lead Barney around a fallen branch. "No problem, so far. I've used the Order Form a number of times, and the accounting seems easy enough."

He nodded, encouraged by more than just a simple "yes" or "no." "Good. I always like to hear a client is satisfied."

"Have you met with your other clients yet?"

"A couple of them, yes. But I have more to see." Was she really interested, or just being polite? Or maybe boredom had driven her to talk.

"Do you know when you're going back to New York?"

"Trying to get rid of me already, huh?" He'd meant the remark as a joke, of course.

She pressed her lips together and said in a humorless tone, "No, I was only making conversation."

So boredom was the motive. "When I leave depends on when I see all the potential clients on my list." *And when I've made sure Angie isn't around here somewhere.*

"Oh."

"I wouldn't mind staying longer, though. I like the country here." Now, what possessed him to say that?

She turned, and when their gazes collided, the air sizzled. As confusion ricocheted around his brain, he tightened his grip on the reins.

Molly broke eye contact and lowered her gaze. "Maybe you can come back again sometime for a visit."

"Maybe I can."

No telling where the conversation would have gone

from there, because just then, Karli piped up with, "How much farther, Mommy?"

Molly favored Karli with a broad smile. "You're always impatient to get where you're going, aren't you, honey? Well, if I remember rightly, the river's around the next bend. If you listen real hard, I bet you can hear it."

Molly reined Barney to a halt. Steve pulled Rollie alongside, and they all listened. At first, the only sound was the tinkling of the wind in the nearby aspen trees. Then, in the distance, came the faint whoosh of flowing water.

Steve leaned forward in the saddle. "I can hear it. How 'bout you, Karli?"

Karli tilted her head. "I can. We're getting close." She dropped the reins long enough to clap her hands.

Molly led them down a path angling off the main road. The terrain sloped downward, and the trees thickened, blotting out the sun. The rush of the river filled the air.

When they reached the river, they reined their horses to a halt and sat watching the water foam and bubble over protruding rocks and fallen tree branches.

"What river is this?" Steve raised his voice to be heard over the roar.

"The Rolling River," Molly said. "That's where Jackson got the name for his ranch."

Steve pointed to the far bank lined with dense foliage and trees. "It's wider than I thought it would be."

"I bet I could swim in it," Karli said.

"So you know how to swim, Karli?" Steve tore his gaze from the mesmerizing water to focus on Karli.

"That's a good skill to have."

"She had lessons at a pool near our home in Chicago," Molly said. "But don't get any ideas about swimming here, Karli." She wagged a warning finger. "The river is not the same as a swimming pool."

"I know." Karli craned her neck toward the water. "It's a looong river. I can't see the end."

"It doesn't really have an end," Steve said, his gaze following the river to where it disappeared around an outcropping of rocks. "The water flows on and on until it reaches the ocean."

"Wow!" Karli looked over her shoulder, and her eyes grew big.

They watched the river in silence for a couple more minutes, their horses occasionally shifting and pawing the ground. Finally, Steve reached around and poked a sore back muscle. "I don't know about you two, but I could use a break from the saddle."

Molly nodded. "Okay. That would give the horses a rest, too."

"I'll get off first and help Karli down." Steve swung his leg over the horse's rump.

"Tie Rollie to one of those trees over there." Molly pointed to a clump of aspen trees growing along a ridge well above the river's bank.

Steve led Rollie to the trees and tied the reins around a slender trunk. Approaching Barney, he opened his arms for Karli. When she curled her arms around his neck, he lifted her off the horse and carefully lowered her, keeping a tight hold until her feet were securely on the ground.

He let his arms slip away, and a sudden lump filled his throat. He'd always wanted children, and being around Karli, even for only a few days, made him realize how much he missed having a family.

Molly dismounted. She secured her horse near Rollie and took Karli's hand. As they strolled around the clearing, he noticed that Molly kept a safe distance from the riverbank. Probably a good idea.

Karli began picking up odd-shaped stones and soon had both her and Molly's jeans pockets bulging.

"That's enough now," Molly finally said, tucking yet another stone into a pocket. "Next time we come we'll bring something to put your collections in."

"Why don't we sit for a bit?" Steve pointed to a flat spot at the base of an oak tree with a trunk thick enough to lean against. "There's a good place."

Molly frowned. "I don't know...We should be getting back..."

Steve consulted his wristwatch. "Still lots of time before dinner. Come on. Getting here took awhile. Let's enjoy it."

"Well...okay."

When they were seated under the tree, Molly emptied her pockets of the stones, laying them on the ground. "Can you arrange them with the little ones first, then the big ones?" she challenged Karli.

"'Course I can." Karli emptied her pockets. She picked up a small stone and a slightly larger one and laid them side-by-side.

Molly took off her hat and set it on the ground. She brushed strands of hair from her forehead and leaned back against the tree trunk.

Steve rested against the trunk, too, intending to relax—if that were possible with Molly sitting close. With very little effort, he could put his arm around her shoulders and...

And what?

The nearby bushes rustled. Steve twisted his head around in time to see a gray squirrel dart from the underbrush. "Look, Karli, there's a squirrel." He pointed to the animal as it scurried past.

Another squirrel scooted into view. Tails high, the two stood motionless for a couple seconds, regarding each other with inquisitive eyes. The first one wheeled around and with a swish of its tail scampered over the rough ground. The other squirrel stretched its legs in an effort to catch up.

"They're funny," Karli said with a giggle. She jumped up and took a step after the animals.

Molly caught her arm. "Don't go after them, honey. You'll scare them away."

Karli tossed Steve a questioning glance.

He nodded. "Your mom's right. Best to just watch them."

They followed the antics of the squirrels as they ran up the gnarled trunk of another oak tree. The animals skittered along the branches, their tails waving like furry flags, then jumped to another tree and disappeared into a clump of leaves.

"Oh, they're gone." Karli sighed and pushed out her lower lip.

"They don't stay in one place very long." *Kind of like you*, Steve wanted to add, but figured that, even though he wasn't, Molly might think he was criticizing her daughter.

Karli returned to arranging her stones, and Molly leaned her head against the tree trunk. Except for the roar of the river, silence reigned.

Steve cast Molly a glance. Sunlight filtering through the overhead leaves shot copper highlights through her hair and gave a glow to her cheeks. His chest tightened. "Penny," he said, needing to break the silence.

She turned, her brow furrowed. "What?"

He lifted a shoulder. "Penny. You know, a penny for your thoughts."

"Oh. Well, I was thinking how peaceful it is here. On the ranch." She made a sweeping gesture.

Her wistful expression struck a chord inside Steve. "I agree. Being here makes me think about my house in Westchester. It's not on a ranch, but I have enough acreage for a small orchard, and a stream runs through the property."

Her eyebrows rose. She folded her legs to her chest and clasped her hands around her knees. "What's the house like?"

For a moment, he closed his eyes and pictured the house. "Two stories. Wood with fieldstone trim. A peaked roof, mullioned windows, stone patios..."

"Sounds nice." She glanced down and picked a piece of tree bark from her shirt. "Buck and I were saving money for our own place," she added in a low tone.

Sensing the subject was painful, yet encouraged because she'd brought it up, he asked, "What kind of house did you want?"

She tilted her head. "One with a porch across the front, like Jackson's, with a swing hanging from the ceiling. Two stories, maybe three, with a big playroom for Karli. You'd like that, wouldn't you, darlin'?" She turned her head in Karli's direction.

Steve leaned forward, expecting to see Karli playing with her stones.

Karli was gone. All that remained were a row of stones and a pile of those yet to be placed.

Molly gasped and jumped up. "Karli!"

Alarm fueled his moves. Steve scrambled to his feet, his gaze sweeping the area. The child was nowhere in sight. "She can't have gone far."

Molly twisted her fingers together. "You don't know her. Karli!"

Steve cupped his hands around his mouth and shouted, "Karli! Karli! Where are you?"

"I don't see her anywhere." All the color had drained from Molly's face, leaving her complexion a stark white.

"She wouldn't go down to the river, would she?" Steve gestured toward the riverbank. "You told her to stay away."

"Yeah, but she doesn't mind well. Oh, this is terrible!"

"We'll hunt for her. You take that direction." He pointed toward the woods. "And I'll go look by the river."

"Okay. Whoever finds her first, hollers really loudly." She picked up her hat and put it on, giving the brim a firm tug.

"You bet. And don't worry, Molly. We'll find her!"

****

Molly ran across the clearing, shouting Karli's name over and over.

No answer. Fear clutched her insides like a vise. She stopped and pressed a hand to her abdomen. *Calm, keep calm. She can't be far away.*

She headed toward a path leading into the woods. Under other circumstances a refreshing escape from the hot sun, the forest today oozed eerie shadows and hidden dangers, from fallen trees to boulders blocking the path.

A noise in the underbrush captured her attention. Karli? No, two squirrels scrambling up a tree trunk. Probably the same two they'd seen before.

Molly made her way through the woods with no sign of Karli. Maybe she'd fallen and hurt herself. Maybe she'd...been kidnapped.

No, that was ridiculous. Her imagination was really running away with her now. Yet, her heart knocked against her ribcage, and sweat poured off her forehead. Where was her daughter? Where was Karli?

A horrifying thought popped into her mind—Karli had disobeyed and gone to the river, after all. Molly spun around to retrace her steps.

And almost bumped into Karli.

"Mommy?"

Relief weakened her stance, and Molly dropped to her knees, throwing her arms around her daughter. "Oh, Karli, you're safe. You're okay. Aren't you?" She tipped up Karli's chin and studied her face. Dirt streaked her cheeks and her forehead. Molly clasped Karli's hands. They too were gritty with dirt.

"I fell down."

"Did you hurt yourself?"

Karli shook her head. "Nuh uh."

"Where've you been? Why did you run away?"

"I went to find the squirrels."

Molly pressed her lips together. "I figured as much.

But why didn't you tell me you were going off?"

Karli shrugged and lowered her eyelids. "I don't know."

A sigh escaped Molly's lips. "You scared me, Karli. And Steve, too. You need to tell me when you want to leave my side. You know that. Now, promise me you'll tell me next time." They'd been over and over this, but Molly had to keep trying.

"I'm sorry, Mommy. I promise."

"Good." Molly rose and clasped Karli's hand. "Come on. We need to find Steve. He's looking for you, too."

They hurried back to the clearing, Molly shouting Steve's name along the way. He didn't answer, but when the river came into view, she spotted him standing atop a boulder at the water's edge, under the low-hanging branches of a willow tree. Hands on his hips, he studied the water rushing by.

"Steve!" She cupped a hand beside her mouth. "I found her."

Steve looked around. With a grin and a wave, he started toward them. He'd taken only a couple steps when his left foot hit a dip in the rock. He lurched forward then teetered backward toward the water. He swayed back and forth, arms flailing.

"Steve, be careful!" Molly pressed a hand to her chest.

He lifted his arm to grasp a willow branch, but a sudden gust of wind blew the branch out of his reach. He teetered backward again then disappeared over the side of the rock. A loud splash resounded through the air.

Molly's gut clenched. The river ran fast. She hoped

he could swim, and that he hadn't hit anything on the way down. She turned to Karli. "I've got to help Steve. You stay right here and don't move. Not one step. You hear?"

"But I want to help, too."

"No, it's too dangerous." Molly put an edge into her voice and pointed straight down at the ground. "You can help by staying here."

Karli tucked her chin into her chest. "Yes, Mommy."

Molly ran past the boulder to the river's edge. Steve was bobbing around in the water. Relief swept over her. At least, the current hadn't carried him downstream. Still, even though only a few yards from the bank, he was too far away to grasp her outstretched arm.

"Can you swim? Can you make it to shore?" she shouted over the water's roar.

"C-can't swim now...I hit my arm." His face contorted with pain.

Molly searched the area for something to use to haul him ashore. Her gaze landed on a fallen willow branch. Although it was thin and fragile-looking, she prayed the wood was sturdy enough to do the job.

Steve paddled with one arm toward the shore, but he wasn't making much headway against the strong current.

"Here!" Gripping one end of the branch in both hands, she flung it toward him, as though she were casting a fishing line. She held her breath then blew it out in exasperation when the branch fell short. She inched closer to the water, dipping her boots into the river and stepping gingerly. The bank was slick and muddy, and she could easily lose her footing.

"Hurry, Mommy! Help Steve!" Karli called.

Molly glanced over her shoulder. "I will, honey. Don't worry. Just stay where you are." She turned back to Steve in time to see him grab onto the branch. "Hold on!" Molly shouted as she tugged on her end. She walked backward, but with each step, her boots sank into the mud. Easing out one foot then another, she finally found a dry patch of ground that held her weight. With steady pressure, she tugged hand-over-hand on the branch, pulling him closer and closer to shore.

"My feet hit bottom!" he called.

"Good, but be careful. The bottom's muddy. Try to float until you get to shore."

At last, she pulled him onto the riverbank.

He lay there spewing water as he panted and gasped for breath. He held his right arm tight against his chest, cupping the elbow with his other hand.

Molly bit her lip and gazed downward, emotions tromping through her like a herd of elephants. Even though he was safe, he was obviously injured. Oh, this was awful...all her fault...they never should have come...

She knelt beside him. "We gotta get you back to the house. Your arm..."

He looked up with a weak smile. "Yeah. But...give me...a minute...Karli?"

"I found her in the woods. She's okay."

"Mommy, can I move now?" Karli's plaintive voice drifted across the clearing.

"Stay there a couple more minutes, honey." Arm extended to keep Karli in place, Molly's gaze flashed between her daughter and Steve.

"I can get up now, if you give me a hand." Steve reached out with his left hand.

Molly grasped his arm and pulled him to his feet, helping him away from the muddy bank and onto firmer ground. Clothes plastered to his body, and water dripping from his hair, he was one sodden mess. "We need to get you back to the house and into some dry clothes," she said, keeping a tight hold on him in case he should fall. "But your arm. Is it broken?"

He slowly turned his wrist from side to side, scrunching up his face. "Ow. Hurts like hell, but, no, I don't think it's broken. Otherwise, I couldn't move it." He looked around. "Hey, Karli, there you are!"

Keeping his injured arm tight against his chest, he broke away from Molly and stumbled over to Karli. "Your mom and I were worried about you."

Lower lip trembling, she looked up from under her hat. "Mommy's mad 'cause I ran away. Are you mad, too?"

"No, I'm not mad. I'm glad you're okay, but it's important to do what your mom says. She wants you to be safe. So do I."

"I'm sorry." Karli opened her arms for a hug.

Steve slipped his uninjured arm around Karli's shoulders long enough for a light hug then drew back. "More hugs later, honey, or you'll get all wet."

Touched by Steve and Karli's reunion but concerned about Steve's injury, Molly joined them. "Can you get on your horse, Steve? Maybe Karli and I should go back and send someone for you."

Steve stuck out his chin. "I'll make it back. I've still got one good arm that'll get me onto the horse."

"You'll need to see a doctor, to be sure nothing's broken."

He grinned. "Mike and Rose are coming today. I bet he won't mind turning their visit into a house call."

Chapter Seven

Molly held herself rigid in her chair while Mike examined Steve's forearm and wrist. The two men were seated on the leather sofa in the Phillips' living room. Jackson and Sara sat on the room's second sofa, while Rose occupied Jackson's favorite recliner. A pillow tucked into the small of her back pushed her rounded tummy into prominence. Karli and Ryan were in the kitchen under Anna Gabraldi's watchful eye. Sounds of their voices occasionally drifted into the room.

Mike released Steve's arm and sat back. "Looks like a sprained wrist."

Molly exhaled and let her shoulders sag. Worry about Steve's injury had kept her stomach churning all during the ride home from the river.

"Good to hear." Steve gazed down at his arm with a look of relief. "I hoped that would be the verdict."

Mike shook his head and held up a warning hand. "Not so fast, buddy. That's what I *think* it is. You need to have your arm x-rayed to be sure. For now, an elastic wrap will hold it firm."

"Where's the nearest place to do that?"

Mike reached into the black doctor's bag sitting at his feet and removed a plastic-wrapped bandage. "Valley General, in Red Rock."

Steve's eyebrows shot up. "The hospital?"

With a nod, Mike peeled off the bandage's casing.

"Okay, if you say so. I'll stop by on my way to the hotel. After dinner."

Mike furrowed his brows as he wrapped the bandage around Steve's arm. "You'd better go now. And not by yourself."

"I've still got one good arm." Steve waved his left arm. "I can drive myself."

"Not a good idea." Mike set his jaw. "You get into any trouble, you'll want both hands on the wheel. And, since we don't know the extent of your injury for sure, using your arm could make it worse. No, going alone is not worth the risk."

Jackson stood and approached the two men. "Listen to the doc, Steve. One of us can take you in."

"I will," Molly heard herself say, and then turned to Sara. "Would you mind watching Karli?"

"Of course not." Sara nodded. "She'll be fine with us."

Steve turned and frowned at Molly. "You don't have to drive me."

"Like Mike says, somebody has to." Molly rose from her chair. "And, since your accident was my fault, that driver should be me."

Steve shook his head. "How could it be your fault? I was the clumsy one."

Molly hugged her arms and paced in a circle. "I wasn't watching Karli like I should've. I know she wanders. Her behavior was nothing new."

"But I didn't have to climb up on that rock."

Why was the man being so stubborn? "You were helping me to find her."

Steve's chest expanded with a deep breath. "Yeah, I was. And she's okay. That's the important thing.

Don't put yourself on a guilt trip."

Jackson raised both hands. "Time out, you two. Steve's injury is *nobody's* fault."

"It was an accident." Rose rubbed slow circles on her stomach. "And, Steve, you'd better take my husband's advice."

"Nobody knows that better than my wife." A twinkle lit Mike's eyes as he flashed Rose a smile.

Molly wagged a finger at Steve. "See? You're outnumbered. I'm taking you to the hospital."

"Okay," he said with a slight shrug. "I give in."

"And don't worry about missing dinner," Sara said. "We'll keep everything warm for you."

****

Steve had told Molly not to put herself on a guilt trip, but all during the drive to Red Rock, underneath the surface of their small talk, that was exactly what she did. She wished she'd never agreed to extend their horseback ride to the river in the first place. Sure, Karli's wandering was a problem, but keeping her safe was Molly's responsibility, and today she'd failed. Today had shown her she couldn't let down her guard, even for a minute.

The trip into town, one Molly had made hundreds of times with practiced ease, today seemed extra long and laborious. Finally, they reached Valley General. As Molly turned the car into the driveway leading to the Emergency Room, and the five-story hospital loomed into view above the trees, Steve and his injury were all but forgotten as memories flooded her mind like a river overrunning its banks.

She hadn't been to the hospital since the day Buck was brought in after his rodeo accident. When she volunteered to drive Steve today, she hadn't thought that being here again might affect her. Her throat tightened and her hands shook as she pulled into a parking place. If only she could jump from the car and run far, far away.

Sensing Steve's gaze, she gritted her teeth and straightened her spine. She could do this.

A few moments later, as she and Steve stepped through the ER's glass doors and into the admittance area, her thoughts jumped back again to that horrible day two years ago. The waiting. The agony. The spark of hope so cruelly snuffed out when the verdict was announced—*dead on arrival.*

She hadn't even had a chance to say good-bye. Tears flooded Molly's eyes, and her steps faltered.

"Hey, are you okay?"

Steve's voice carved a path into her thoughts. "Yeah, I'm fine." She swiped away the tears and offered him a wobbly grin. "Do you need my help filling out the forms?" She nodded at the semi-circular desk where a receptionist worked at a computer.

"Thanks, but I'm sure I can manage to write with my left hand. I'll holler if I need you."

"I'll wait over there." With relief, Molly turned her steps to the row of green-upholstered chairs against one wall.

Steve had barely completed the admittance forms when a nurse appeared and guided him through the doors leading to the examination rooms. Molly was glad for the prompt treatment. Otherwise, he might have sat beside her and inquired more about her emotional state.

The ER was quiet today, and she was the only

person occupying the green chairs. She stared out the window, her thoughts tumbling through her mind. That this hospital was also where Karli was born occurred to her. Maybe dwelling on that happy occasion instead of the sad time when Buck was here would help.

Shifting her focus worked for a few minutes, but no way could she think of her daughter's birth without picturing Buck, too, and then the reminder that he wasn't here now to watch his daughter grow up plunged her into sadness again.

After half an hour, everything—battling her thoughts, worrying about Steve, the waiting—grated on her nerves. She pushed to the edge of her seat, ready to ask the receptionist to check on his status.

Just then, he came through the door.

Rather than the cast she expected, his arm was in a sling and wrapped in an elastic bandage.

"Yep, it's a sprain," he confirmed when he reached her side. "Should heal in a couple of weeks."

Thoroughly in the present now, Molly pressed a hand to her chest. "I'm glad it's not broken. A sprain's bad enough."

"Me, too. But even a sprain throws off my schedule. The doc here was as firm as Mike about not using my arm while it heals. Definitely no driving, he said." Steve tunneled his free hand through his hair. "I'll have to figure out some other way to get to the meetings I've set up with prospective clients in Denver."

Molly wrinkled her brow. "I'm sorry, Steve."

He shrugged. "The situation could be worse."

"Yeah," she said, again remembering that day two years ago. Her throat tightened. "Could be worse."

****

Steve followed Molly out of the hospital and across the parking lot to his rental car. She was right; his injury could be worse. But this was no picnic, either. He had work to do in Red Rock and Denver, people to meet, and, he hoped, accounts to land. The trip was an important part of his and Jerry's plan to expand their services all across the country. A delay such as this opened up opportunities for their competitors.

Steve set his jaw. Too late now. He'd have to make the best of a bad situation.

"I'll let Jackson and Sara know we're on our way," Steve said as they climbed into the car. He reached with his right hand to pluck his cell from his belt. Or, rather, the belt that, along with jeans, shirt, and shoes, he'd borrowed from Jackson. Then he remembered he couldn't use his right hand, and instead reached across with his left. He was glad he hadn't taken the phone on the horseback ride. If so, he either would have lost it altogether, or the instrument would be useless.

"Want me to connect the call for you?" Molly held her car keys while she waited for his answer.

"No, thanks. I'd better learn to use my left hand as much as I can." After fumbling a bit, he managed to release the phone from his belt. Laying it on his knee, he punched in the speed dial for Jackson's ranch then lifted the phone.

Jackson's familiar voice echoed in his ear. "Hey, buddy, we've been waiting to hear. How'd it go?"

Steve summarized his hospital visit while Molly started the engine and wheeled the car from the parking lot.

"Glad to hear it wasn't a break. We'll see you

soon. Wait, Sara wants to talk to you."

Jackson sounded relieved. Steve heard the phone being transferred from hand to hand, and Karli's and Ryan's voices in the background, and then Sara came on the line.

"Steve? We want you to come stay at the Rolling R while your wrist heals."

Steve gripped the phone. "What? Stay at the Rolling R?" He glanced at Molly, just as her eyebrows shot up. "Why, thanks, but I can manage at the hotel."

"No, we want you to come here. Are you still in town?"

Sara's firm tone discouraged argument. Steve looked out the window as Molly swung the car from the hospital's driveway onto the street. "We're just leaving the hospital."

"Good. Stop by your hotel and get your things, and we'll see you shortly. Dinner's waiting."

She disconnected before he could offer any more protests. Steve hooked the phone onto his belt. "Guess you got the gist of that."

"Yeah, well, staying with them is probably a good idea."

She sounded upset. Why? He doubted their paths would often cross.

No, something else bothered her. When they first walked into the ER, she had a stricken look, as though she wanted to turn around and run back out the door. Maybe she'd had a bad experience there, or maybe she just didn't like hospitals. Preoccupied with his own problem, he'd set aside her puzzling behavior.

Should he ask what troubled her? Better not. He didn't know her well enough to probe her personal feelings.

He peered out the window again. They were traveling along an unfamiliar residential street. "So, I guess we head for my hotel. Not sure I know how to get there from here."

"I know the way."

When they reached the Bingham Hotel, she parked in the guest parking lot and cut the car's engine.

He grasped the door handle with his left hand. "Instead of waiting here, why don't you wait in the coffee shop?"

Slipping her keys into her purse, she shook her head. "I'll go up to your room with you. You'll need a hand with your packing."

Steve didn't argue. He probably could pack whatever he needed by himself, but the job would go quicker if she helped. Still, the thought of her visiting his hotel room unsettled him.

Don't be a dope. There's nothing personal between you and Molly.

****

"Come on in, Molly." Steve unlocked the door to his third floor hotel room and stepped aside for her to enter.

Molly stood on the threshold, clutching the strap of her shoulder purse. For the second time that evening, she found herself in a place she didn't want to be, although for very different reasons. First, the ER had thrown her for an emotional loop. Although she'd insisted on helping Steve pack, now the moment was here, she wasn't sure she could. Being in his room was too personal, too...intimate.

She'd come this far, though, and she really had no

choice but to continue. Squaring her shoulders, she stepped inside the room.

The neatness of the place impressed her. Not a shirt or a pair of pants was draped anywhere. No nightstand clutter, and on the round table by the window, pads of paper and books were stacked alongside a laptop computer. His black briefcase rested on the floor nearby.

Molly hid a sad smile. If this were Buck's room, shirts and pants would be piled on the nearest available surface. To him, a hanger was a foreign object. And books and papers would be scattered, not stacked with the edges all aligned.

She pushed away the memories. What was the point in comparing the two men? No point, really. But Buck was so much in her thoughts that the comparison came automatically. She turned to Steve. "What can I do first?"

"Might as well start with the closet. If you could get my bag out and open it—" He pointed to a black suitcase on the floor of the alcove.

"Sure. I'll take the clothes off the hangers while you do—whatever." Crossing the room, Molly set her purse on the round table.

"Sounds like a plan."

Molly took out Steve's suitcase, lifted it onto the bed, and unzipped the opening. The corner of her eye caught Steve at the dresser pulling out what appeared to be underwear. Boxers or briefs? she wondered as she went to the closet and slipped a shirt from its hanger. She mentally slapped herself for the irrelevant thought, but not before images of him in both kinds flashed through her mind. He'd look good in either. Feeling her cheeks flush, she sighed and folded the shirt. Yep, coming here had definitely been a bad idea. Packing put thoughts in her head that she had no business having.

Twenty minutes later, Molly tucked the last pair of slacks into Steve's suitcase and zipped it shut. She joined him at the round table where he was attempting one-handed to shove his laptop into its canvas carrying case. The case flipped and flopped around the tabletop as though it had a life of its own.

"I'll help you with that." She grasped the computer and slid it into the case.

"So easy when you do it," he said.

"Good thing I came, huh?"

"Don't know what I'd have done without you."

She raised her head and met his gaze. His brown eyes were serious, intent. The air in the room stilled, and her breath faltered. She forced a swallow and broke eye contact, letting her gaze sweep over the table.

A gold-framed photo of a young woman, which she hadn't noticed earlier, peeked from between two stacks of books. The picture captured Molly's attention and made her forget about what had been happening between her and Steve.

The woman had a heart-shaped face and shoulder-length hair the color of a midnight sky. Her full lips were smiling, but sadness dimmed her blue eyes.

Although she wasn't sure when or where, Molly had the feeling she'd seen the woman somewhere. Before she could comb her memories for the answer, Steve's voice cut into her thoughts.

"That's Angie."

"I figured. She's very pretty."

"Yes, she is—was when that photo was taken,

anyway."

The wistful note in his voice touched Molly's heart. He still loved Angie, just as she still loved Buck. There was a difference, though. Steve might still find Angie, and, even though they were divorced, they might restore their relationship. In contrast, Molly would never see Buck again. Not in this lifetime, anyway. A wild bull had taken care of that.

Molly allowed herself a moment more of sadness, and then lifted the black briefcase onto the table and tucked the computer inside.

Steve added the books and papers, a handful at a time. Lastly, he slipped the photo into a side pocket.

She gazed around the room. "Anything else to pack up?"

"Nope. We're good to go."

Half an hour later, Molly sat beside Steve at the Phillips' kitchen table, eating the turkey casserole and green beans Sara had kept warm. Sara, Jackson, Rose, and Mike clustered around them, sipping coffee and munching from a plate of Sara's raspberry shortbread. Ryan had been put to bed, but Karli insisted on waiting up for Molly and Steve to return. Molly expected Karli to sit beside her at the table, but instead she sat by Steve. She hadn't left his side since he walked in the door.

While they ate, Steve fumbling now and then with his left-handed delivery, but on the whole doing pretty well, he recounted their visit to the Emergency Room. "You were right calling it a sprain." He nodded at Mike, who sat with his arm along the back of Rose's chair.

Mike helped himself to another piece of

shortbread. "Still good you went in."

Steve's forehead wrinkled. "Yeah, I know, but being laid up is gonna be hard. Ruins my schedule, my plans..."

Setting down her coffee cup, Rose leaned forward. "I can sympathize. I didn't like being confined after I broke my leg in the train wreck, either. But the ranch is a great place to recuperate."

Mike gave Rose's shoulder a squeeze. "Your staying here sure worked to my advantage. Gave me a chance to convince you to start seeing me again."

"You preyed on my weakened condition." Rose playfully dug an elbow into her husband's side.

"Yeah, I guess I did." Mike chuckled. "But it worked, didn't it? And here we are, married and expecting." He leaned close and patted his wife's stomach.

"Yes, and I couldn't be happier." Rose gave her husband a quick peck on the cheek.

As she witnessed the exchange between Mike and Rose, envy nudged Molly. She didn't begrudge them their happiness—she just missed her own. Once, she had been a wife and newly pregnant and ecstatic, too...

She glanced at Steve and met his direct gaze. Her body stilled. What? Surely he didn't think she had any designs on him while he was laid up, like Mike had had on Rose.

No. Never. Not in a million years. She broke eye contact, focusing on her plate and scooping the last bite of casserole onto her fork.

****

"I sure hate to impose on you like this," Steve said later that evening as he followed Sara up the stairs to the ranch house's second floor.

"You're not. Our guestroom has been empty for too long. Besides, I wanted you to stay here from the beginning, remember?" She tossed him a grin over her shoulder. "Looks like I got my way, after all."

When Sara led Steve into his room, he stopped and blinked. Almost as big as the one at his hotel, the room included a sitting area with two over-stuffed chairs, a straight chair, and a square table that would serve nicely as a desk. Nearby stood a TV and sound system console. Through an open door near the bed, he glimpsed a washbasin and a bathtub. His suitcase and briefcase, which Jackson had carried up earlier, sat near a large walk-in closet.

He turned to Sara. "This is great."

She grinned and bobbed her head. "Glad you like it. Will you be able to get any of your work done?"

"Some." Steve absently touched his sling. "I can poke at the computer with my left hand. My appointments are the problem. I've already set up several, like the company in Denver I'm scheduled to visit on Wednesday. I'm afraid if I don't show up, the competition will move in ahead of me." Determined not to let that happen, he sifted through the possibilities. "I suppose I could hire a driver."

Sara walked to the closet, opened the door, and took a couple of pillows from the top shelf. "Molly can drive you to your appointment," she said, adding the pillows to those already on the bed.

Steve tensed and shook his head. "Oh, no. I don't want to take her away from her job in the bakery."

"We'll work around that." Sara smoothed a wrinkle from the bedspread.

Considering the tension between him and Molly whenever they shared the same space, he wasn't sure he wanted Molly to drive him anywhere. He'd already had a taste tonight of what that would be like. "Why don't I hire someone?"

Sara straightened and made a dismissive wave. "Leave Molly's schedule to me, and don't worry." She nodded toward his suitcase. "Shall I help you unpack?"

"No, thanks. I'm kinda beat, and that bed looks awfully good right now. Unzipping the bag would be helpful, though."

"Sure." Sara laid his suitcase flat on the floor and grasped the zipper. "What do you think of her?"

She may have meant to sound casual, but he wasn't fooled. Sara wanted to set him up with Molly. People were always trying to set him up. Over the past five years, many women had been trotted out and introduced. Although some lasted beyond the first date, none endured.

He couldn't be angry with Sara, though. For one thing, he was too tired. For another, he liked Sara and knew she meant well. Still, he couldn't help saying, "I'm assuming you mean Molly."

Finished unzipping the suitcase, she stood and grinned. "Uh huh. Molly."

Steve struggled to choose his words carefully. "Well, she's, ah, very smart. She caught on to the new program fast. She's a little overbearing with Karli..."

"I agree with you there. But what do you think of her? You know what I mean."

Steve raised his hand in protest. "Sara, please don't try to fix up me and Molly. I'm not looking for anyone right now. I didn't do so well with my marriage."

Sara pursed her lips and shook her head. "What happened to you was tragic, Steve. But you're free now."

Free? Legally, yes. But not free from the responsibility he'd undertaken when he married Angie, or from the relentless wondering of what he'd done to drive her away.

"How long are you willing to wait before finding your happiness?"

Sara's tone was gentle, but firm enough to require an answer. "I don't know," he said, with a solemn shake of his head. "I just don't know."

****

"What's the matter, honey? Don't you like the story?" Molly laid the book on the bed and brushed a lock of hair from Karli's forehead. She had little enthusiasm for reading a story tonight herself, but she hated to skip a ritual both she and Karli enjoyed. Besides, after spending so much of the day preoccupied with Steve and his injury, she wanted some quality time with her daughter.

Karli shifted under the covers and looked up at Molly. Her blue eyes were solemn in the lamplight's soft glow. "I like the story, Mommy, but I can't con— concen—"

"Concentrate? You mean you're having trouble listening to the story?"

"Yeah, that's it. I feel bad that Steve hurt his arm. Was it my fault, Mommy?" Tears glistened in Karli's eyes.

Molly's heart constricted, and she gathered her daughter into her arms. Her nose brushed Karli's hair, soft as a chick's down and smelling of clean shampoo.

"What happened to Steve was an accident. An accident is no one's fault. Steve and I were worried when we couldn't find you."

Karli ran her fingers along Molly's arm. "I know you told me not to run away. But sometimes I forget."

A lot of times you forget. "Can you think of anything that would make you feel better tonight?"

"Mmmm, I guess if you stayed here with me."

"Of course, I will. I'll stay with you as long as you need me." *Days. Years. Until you grow up and leave me.* Molly turned out the light. As she snuggled down next to Karli, something jabbed her arm. "What's that?" She raised up and pulled back the covers.

Karli giggled. "It's Mr. Muggins." She lifted the doll into view.

"Mr. Muggins." Molly laughed and straightened the doll's askew hat. "I should have known."

Later, after Karli had fallen asleep, Molly eased off the bed. Leaving the door ajar, she crept out and down the hallway to the living room. The room lay in darkness with only the moon's silvery light drifting through the windows.

Loneliness filled her. She hugged her arms, her thoughts crowding her mind, pushing at the seams. Her gaze strayed to the photos lining the fireplace mantel. Zeroing in on one, she crossed the room and picked it up.

The picture showed Buck standing in front of the ranch's barn. She remembered that day, like so many others indelibly stamped into her memories. He'd given her a new camera, and for the first week or so, she carried it everywhere.

On this particular day, she followed him to the

barn, and when he emerged, she snapped his picture. The result was a rather wide-eyed look, but the pose had turned out to be one of her favorites, and she framed it. Gripping the frame now, she gazed into Buck's handsome face, her emotions churning like the Rolling River.

"Oh, Buck, I love you so much! I'll never stop loving you, and no one will ever take your place." She pressed the photo to her chest and let the tears fall.

She thought of Steve and how he also clung to the photo of his ex-wife, Angie. No doubt, he loved her as much as Molly loved Buck. Now, all they had left were their pictures and other mementoes. Poor substitutes, yet that was the way it was. And, probably, the way it always would be.

Chapter Eight

"I have an appointment in Newton this morning," Sara told Molly the following day.

Molly looked up from the computer where she was filling out a Forksville gift shop order for several dozen gingerbread men cookies. "Okay. I think I can manage while you're gone. If I run into any problems, I always have my manual." She patted the three-ring binder lying next to the computer.

"And I'm only a phone call away." Sara held up her cell phone then tucked it into her shoulder bag. "But there's something else I'd like you to do."

The tentative note in Sara's voice put Molly on alert. "What's that?"

Sara walked to the desk and perched on a straight chair. "Someone needs to make lunch for Steve. Today is Anna's day off, and I'll be gone..."

Was Sara matchmaking again? Molly pressed her lips together. "And that leaves me."

"'Fraid so. But preparation will be easy. Anna made potato salad yesterday, and there's sliced turkey for sandwiches. And cherry pie for dessert. Maybe Karli could come, too."

Molly shook her head. "Much as Karli likes Steve, I doubt she'd turn down lunch at Teresa's. Today is Joaquin's birthday, and his mother is bringing cupcakes."

"Well, then..." Sara raised her eyebrows.

Molly shrugged. "I'll make lunch."

Sara patted Molly's shoulder. "Thanks, Molly. I really appreciate your pitching in. And, honestly, I'm not throwing the two of you together on purpose." She covered a grin with her fingers. "At least, not this time."

"I know, Sara. I'll be fine."

"Good. Now, I'd better be on my way. I hope Lupe has the samples ready." She stood and headed for the door leading to the kitchen.

As soon as Sara was out of sight, Molly sagged against the back of her chair. She really didn't want to fix Steve's lunch. Not that she didn't want to help out. But being around him was...unsettling.

What choice did she have, though? Sara was her boss, and making Steve's lunch was her assignment for today. She'd have to make the best of it.

At eleven thirty, Molly closed down her computer, stuck her head in the kitchen to let Doreen and Lupe know she was leaving, and then trudged under the hot sun to the main house. Once inside, she looked for Steve, to let him know she was there. She wondered if Sara had told him she was coming.

She walked through the kitchen into the living room, but he wasn't there. He wasn't on the front porch, either. She returned to the house and called his name several times. No answer. He was probably still up in his room. Sleeping? No, she didn't think so. He wasn't a slacker. He'd be up and working, doing what he could with his limitations. Limitations that were her fault. Guilt tugged at her conscience.

In the kitchen, she took out bread, the sliced

turkey, and the potato salad, hoping he'd put in an appearance before she finished her preparations. Ten minutes later, he hadn't. She forged on and set the food on the kitchen table, but still no Steve.

Finally, she stood at the bottom of the stairs and called his name several times. No answer.

Molly blew out an exasperated breath. She'd have to go up to his room and knock on the door. She wouldn't enter his room, though. Today she had no reason to. She'd stand in the doorway and announce lunch was served.

Setting her shoulders, she marched up the stairs. At the top, she hesitated. Of the several guest rooms, which one was his? A glance down the hall revealed all the doors were ajar except one. Taking a chance that was his room, she stepped forward and tapped her knuckles on the door.

"Yes?" came his deep voice from inside.

"It's Molly."

"Molly? Hang on."

Surprise etched his tone.

Seconds later, he flung open the door. A white T-shirt stretched across his broad shoulders, and jeans fit snugly over lean hips and long legs. He wore no shoes, but only a pair of brown socks.

At the sight, Molly's pulse quickened.

"Hey, Molly, what brings you here?"

The welcoming grin on his face eased her tension. "I'm your cook for lunch. I guess you didn't get the word. Or hear me calling your name when I came in."

"No, I didn't. I've been on the phone a lot." He ran a hand through his tousled hair. "How'd you get roped into fixing my lunch?"

She explained about today being Anna's day off and that Sara had gone to an appointment. "Can you come downstairs, or should I bring your lunch up here?"

"Of course, I'll come down. Let me shut off my computer, and I'll be right with you. Come on in." He held the door open wider.

Over his shoulder, she glimpsed his bed, neatly made and piled with decorative pillows. Did he wear pajamas? Or sleep naked? Taking a step backward, she raised her hands. "Ah, no, I'm okay...unless you need help with something."

"Don't think so." He turned away and headed for the table near the window where his laptop was set up.

Did Angie's picture grace this table as it had the one in his hotel room? Probably.

He spent a few minutes at the computer, punching the keys with the fingers of his left hand then disappeared into the walk-in closet. He emerged carrying a pair of scuffed, brown leather boots.

"Good thing I brought these." He sat on a straight chair and slipped his feet into the boots. "The ones I wore yesterday are still drying out. And shoelaces are out of the question."

"I could help you with shoelaces, if there's another pair you'd rather wear."

"No, thanks. Boots will do for now."

She led the way downstairs and into the kitchen, where she waved him to a seat at the table.

Once seated, he surveyed the array of food she'd laid out. "Hey, this looks great. You went to a lot of trouble."

Molly slid into a chair across from him. "Not much

for me to do, really. Anna made the potato salad, and the turkey's left over from last night's casserole. The pie was already made, too. All I had to do was make the sandwiches."

They talked for a while about where Sara had gone for her appointment and about a new quarter horse Jackson had acquired, and then Steve asked, "So how's Karli doing?"

Molly wrinkled her forehead. "Okay—I hope. She was worried last night because she thinks your injury is her fault. I remembered what Jackson said and told her when something's an accident, no one's at fault. I didn't want her to feel guilty." *Like I do.*

Steve helped himself to another half sandwich from the plate in the middle of the table. "I don't want her to carry any guilt, either. And that goes for you, too." From under furrowed brows, he leveled her a stern look. "But you do feel guilty, don't you? I can tell."

Molly pressed her lips together and looked down at her plate. "If I do, that's my problem, isn't it?"

"If you want it to be. But I'm glad Karli's not following in her mother's footsteps. Not this time."

"We had a talk about her need to obey me, but I don't know if it'll do any good. She has a mind of her own." Molly picked up her fork and took a bite of Anna's creamy potato salad.

Steve sipped his coffee. "And when she gets excited about something—like the squirrels yesterday—she forgets she's not supposed to run off."

"Yeah. She seems to have no fear."

"Do you think that's because she's so young, or…"

Molly put down her fork. "I don't know." She hesitated, biting her lip. The urge rose to share her worries with Steve. But should she?

Before she could decide, he leaned forward, his gaze alert. "Go on, Molly. There's something else on your mind."

"Okay, I'm afraid she'll be a daredevil, like her father." Her voice cracked with the anger never far from the surface. "Buck risked his life every time he rode the broncs, and, finally, the bulls, in the rodeo." She waved a hand. "Yeah, I know, you could say we risk our lives getting out of bed every morning, but I'm talking about *unnecessary* risks."

"I understand." His brow wrinkled, and Steve nodded. "And you've every right to worry. But right now, you don't know whether she'll be a chronic risk-taker, or if her rash behavior is because she's a child and doesn't think things through the way she will when she's older."

His calm, even tone soothed Molly. She sat back and let her shoulders relax. "Maybe. I guess I'll have to wait until she's older to find out. But if recklessness is part of her nature, I want to curb it now."

"Without spoiling her spirit." Steve touched his napkin to his lips. "She has such a wonderful sense of joy in life. Lots of little kids do. I envy that. We lose our spirit, some of us, when we grow up."

"I suppose so." She took a deep breath and exhaled. "I didn't mean to dump all that on you. Raising Karli is my problem."

"Talking helps, sometimes."

He was right. Sharing *had* eased the single parenting load she'd been carrying, if only momentarily. She'd never before told anyone those deep-down fears about her daughter. Even though he had no children, Steve appeared to understand.

She cast him a covert glance while he was busy scooping more potato salad onto his plate. *I bet he'd make a good father.*

Straightening, she set her jaw. Maybe. But not for Karli. As soon as his arm healed, he'd return to his life in New York. They'd never see him again.

"Penny."

Steve's voice jolted her back to the present. "What?"

"For your thoughts. You're deep into something."

She shrugged. "Nothing in particular." Eager for a new topic, she noticed his empty plate. "Are you ready for pie?"

Steve patted his stomach. "Sure, but make it a small piece."

Molly cut a slice of pie, slid it onto a plate, and handed it to him. "Did you manage to get some work done this morning?"

"Yeah. It's slow, but I can peck the computer keys with my left hand. Same with my cell phone. How about you? How's the program?" He took a bite of the pie and his lips curved. "Mmm, this is good."

"I'll have to try some." Molly cut herself a piece and put it on a plate. "To answer your question, I did have trouble printing an order."

"I'll come out after we're through here and see what's going on."

Molly gripped her fork tighter than necessary. "You don't need to. I can figure it out."

"No trouble. Besides, I need a break." He pointed his fork upward. "I've been in my room all morning. Although it's a very nice room, I need to stretch my legs and get some fresh air."

Thinking more protests would be a waste of time, she said, "All right, then."

Molly finished her pie, wishing she'd kept quiet about her problems with Karli. Sharing personal information shifted a relationship to an intimate level. As if that weren't bad enough, she'd be spending even more time with him this afternoon.

With a twist of her shoulders, she shook off her fears. Maybe having him help her with the computer was a good idea. They'd be dealing with business, not personal, issues, which would help to put their relationship back where it belonged.

****

"You're selecting the wrong printer icon to do the job." Steve pointed to the computer screen, and then punched the keys to correct the error. The printer on the side table hummed.

Sitting next to him, Molly slowly shook her head in disbelief. "The fix was that simple? Boy, I feel stupid."

Steve rested his injured arm on the desk. "Don't be hard on yourself. Learning a new program takes time."

"Maybe so, but I'm not a computer illiterate. When I worked for the real estate firm in Chicago, most of my time was spent on the computer."

"You've got a lot on your mind right now. Moving back to the ranch, worrying about Karli—"

"True, I do." Molly blew out a breath. "But I also need to concentrate on this job. Sara depends on me to run the office."

The printer chugged to a stop.

Molly stretched to the side and scooped up the papers. As she leaned back in her seat, her shoulder brushed his, connecting with hard muscle underneath his thin T-shirt. Her pulse skittered. Clutching the papers, she tapped them into alignment on the desk. "Thanks so much, Steve." *Please leave now. If I have to work with you here, I'll make more mistakes.*

Steve leaned back and stretched his long legs under the desk. "No problem."

Molly put down the papers and picked up a pen. "I'll be okay now, so I won't keep you."

"You're not. Think I'll hang around for a while." His smile was slow and lazy.

She nodded at the stack of papers next to the computer. "Well...I do have work to do."

"I didn't mean in here. I'll go outside, get some of that fresh air I was talking about." He gestured toward the screen door.

Okay, outside was better than here in her office. She shrugged. "Feel free."

While she returned to work, he stepped out and sat on the wrought iron bench next to the building, under the shade of the towering maple tree. He'd put some distance between them, but not enough. No matter how hard she tried to ignore his presence, she couldn't. Once, he cast a glance over his shoulder and caught her looking his way. She ducked her head behind the computer, but not before she glimpsed the smile on his lips.

Next time she looked up, the bench was empty. Had he gone back to the house? No, his deep voice, mingled with Lupe's and Doreen's lighter tones, drifted in from the kitchen. Molly briefly closed her eyes and rubbed her forehead. The man was simply too distracting.

An hour or so later, while Molly was retrieving a box of envelopes from the supply cupboard, Sara came in.

"I'm back." Sara peeked around the cupboard door to greet Molly.

"How was the appointment?" Molly took out a stack of envelopes then replaced the box on the shelf.

Gripping her briefcase with one hand, Sara made a thumbs-up gesture with the other. "Very well. You'll have a couple more orders to fill out. How'd lunch go?"

Molly shrugged. "Okay, I guess. Steve's around someplace. At least, he was awhile ago." She returned to her desk and sat in her swivel chair.

Sara nodded. "I saw him in the kitchen. We're going to hang out for a while. If you need me, we won't be far away."

"All right." *If you're with Steve, far away is fine. The farther away, the better.*

Later, Molly finished putting stamps on a stack of envelopes and set them aside. First thing tomorrow, she'd trot them out to the mailbox at the main road for the mailman to pick up. Letting out a sigh, she glanced at the wall clock. Four-thirty. Time to quit. She shut down and covered the computer, and then stuck her head out the door.

Steve and Sara sat on the metal bench.

"I'm ready to leave and get Karli now."

Steve looked at his wristwatch. "Is it that late already? I've taken up too much of your time, Sara."

"Not at all." Sara shook her head. "You've given me some good business tips. But, yes, Molly, by all means, go get Karli."

Steve stood and turned toward Molly. "I'll walk

along with you."

****

He could have asked if I wanted his company. Molly grumbled to herself as she and Steve headed down the road to Teresa's. She set her jaw and kept her gaze on the fields they were passing. With only a slight breeze today, the grasses stood tall and unwavering under the late afternoon sun.

"I assume you didn't have any more trouble this afternoon?"

His question pierced her thoughts. "No, not with the *program*." She glanced his way, but his pleasant smile indicated he either had not noticed or chose to ignore her sarcasm.

"Good, good. You might be interested in some of the things Sara and I were discussing..."

He talked on, but, still irritated by his presence, Molly had trouble concentrating.

The walk to Teresa's seemed twice as long as usual, but at last, they turned down the road leading to the Halstons' house.

"Karli's probably outside." Molly led the way to the chain link fence enclosing the back yard. Sure enough, Karli sat on one of the swings, pumping herself into the air. "Karli." Molly waved her arms.

"Mommy! Steve!" Karli jumped off the swing and ran across the lawn to the fence.

Steve stooped to Karli's eye level. "Hey, Karli. How're you doing?"

Karli grinned and curled her fingers around the fence wires. "I'm fine. Are you gonna eat dinner with us?"

"Karli," Molly began, but clamped her jaw shut.

What could she say?

Steve raised his eyebrows. "I haven't been invited."

"Mr. Muggins invites you." Karli pulled the doll from her jeans pocket and waved him at Steve.

Steve laughed and shot Molly a glance.

Molly shrugged. "Tonight's menu is mac and cheese. I'm sure you wouldn't—"

"My favorite." Steve stood and shoved his hand into his pants pockets.

"Mine, too," Karli echoed, jumping up and down.

"Well, sure, then you're invited."

At the house, while Karli went in her bedroom to put away her backpack, Molly rushed to straighten the living room.

"I wasn't expecting company," she said, plumping up the sofa cushions and picking up yesterday's newspaper from the coffee table.

"So don't worry about it." Steve stood in the middle of the room, feet spread, cradling his injured arm. "This is a cozy place."

"I haven't had a chance to fix it up much yet."

"Looks good the way it is." He snapped his fingers. "I'd better let Sara know I won't be there for dinner." He pulled his cell phone from its belt holder.

She was about to ask if she could help him, but he managed to cup the phone in his palm and speed dial with his thumb. While he and Sara spoke, Molly rescued last night's empty ice cream dishes from an end table and carried them into the kitchen.

When she returned, he stood at the fireplace mantel looking at the photos. Molly stopped and sucked in a breath. Would the pictures of Buck disturb him as much as Angie's photo had bothered her?

He turned, but before he could say anything, Karli skipped in.

"Can we play a game?" Karli asked, stopping in front of Steve.

Steve ruffled Karli's hair. "That would be fun, but maybe your mom needs help fixing dinner." He gave a short laugh and pointed to his injured arm. "Not that I'd be much help."

Molly shook her head. "I'll be fine. You two go on and play. How about the Chinese Checkers Auntie Sara gave you?"

"Yes, yes." Karli clapped her hands and ran to the storage closet for the game.

In the kitchen, Molly opened the refrigerator's freezer compartment. Yes, the steaks she'd bought last weekend were still there. Should she change her menu and thaw them in the microwave? No, she'd planned to have macaroni and cheese, and she'd stick to that decision. She shut the freezer and walked to the cupboard to retrieve the package of pasta.

The meal was easy to prepare. She added a tossed salad and peas to round out the menu. Soon, they were seated at the kitchen table. Judging by the two generous helpings Steve ate, he hadn't been lying about macaroni and cheese being a favorite.

When they finished eating, Steve and Karli continued their game, while Molly took care of the dishes. As she cleaned up, she listened to the sounds of their talk and laughter floating in from the living room. Steve's presence always created an emotional tug-of-war. She was glad to see Karli having a good time. Anything that made her child happy also made her happy.

But Steve was in their lives only temporarily. Molly pressed a hand to her stomach. If Karli became attached to him, she'd be devastated when he left. Letting this relationship go on wasn't fair to her child.

But what to do about it?

Molly finished her chores, dried her hands on a terrycloth towel, and joined them in the living room.

The two sat on the floor, the Chinese Checkers board between them, and the marbles scattered about the carpet.

Karli looked up at Molly and clapped her hands. "I won, Mommy. I won."

"You sure did." Steve wagged a finger at Karli. "This kid is good."

Molly sank into a nearby chair. "She likes to win. Just like her dad. He liked to win, too." She glanced at Steve and Karli, to see if they'd heard her, but they were busy sorting the marbles. Just as well. Leaning forward, she said, "Time to put away the game, Karli. It's your bedtime."

"I want to play one more." Karli captured a marble that had rolled away from the others. "Steve does, too. Don'tcha?"

Karli gave him one of her coaxing smiles. Ready for an argument, Molly set her jaw.

"I do," Steve said, with an answering smile, "but not tonight. I'll take a raincheck." He scooped up the pile of red marbles and let them roll off his hand into the net bag that Karli held.

Karli's brow knit. "Raincheck, what's that?"

"That means we'll play again another time."

"Does it have to be when it's raining?"

Steve tossed back his head and laughed. "No, it's a figure of speech."

When Karli continued to look puzzled, Molly said, "It's something grownups say."

Karli grinned and added a couple black marbles to the bag as Steve held it out. "I can be grown up."

"You certainly can." Steve jiggled the bag to settle the marbles. "So we'll both take a raincheck."

"Okay, but can you read me a story tonight?"

"Oh, I don't think so—" Molly scooted to the edge of her chair.

"You mean a bedtime story?" Steve nodded. "That'd be cool. When I'm home, I read to my niece and nephew."

"So can you read one to me, Steve?" Karli scooted closer to him.

Steve placed the game board and bag of marbles into their cardboard box. "I gotta say again, it's up to your mom."

Molly wanted to say "no." She needed to put some space between both her and Karli and Steve. But, from the expectant look on Karli's face, she would be terribly disappointed if Molly refused her request. "Okay, but it has to be a short one. I'm sure Steve has other things to do this evening."

Steve stood and held out his hand to Karli. "Maybe so. But nothing I'd *rather* do."

Chapter Nine

After Karli was tucked into bed, Molly pulled up a chair for Steve to sit in while he read the story Karli had chosen. She stood to one side, uncertain whether to pull up another chair for herself and listen, too, or to retreat into the living room. She finally grabbed a chair and joined them, but resentment kept her back rigid. She, not Steve, should be the one reading to Karli. Yet, when Karli giggled at his deep-voiced imitation of the wolf character, Molly had to admit he was a good storyteller. She relaxed and leaned back against the chair.

At last, Steve finished the story.

They all said "goodnight," and Molly turned out the bedside light, leaving the teddy bear nightlight glowing from an outlet near the floor. She led him into the living room. "That was nice, Steve. Thanks."

"My pleasure."

Molly waited for him to say he had to leave, but instead he asked, "So, what do you usually do after Karli's in bed?"

She shrugged. "Read, watch TV." *Be lonely.* "You, ah, probably have work to do."

He shook his head. "I've done enough for today. Suppose I'd better get back to the main house. I hate to intrude on Sara and Jackson's evening, though. I could watch the TV in my room..." He cast her a sideways glance. "Unless you want some company while watching your programs."

Molly pretended to study her fingernails. She preferred to be alone, but she didn't want to be rude. "You're welcome to stay," she said, gesturing to the sofa.

A smile spread across his lips. "Thanks. I will."

She went to the kitchen and poured them cups of coffee. They sat on the sofa and consulted the TV schedule, settling on a popular sitcom. With Steve so near, Molly's senses were on high alert, and concentrating on the program proved difficult. Once, when they both leaned forward to pick up their cups from the coffee table, their elbows bumped. She jerked back, but her finger was already hooked around the cup's handle, and some of the liquid sloshed onto the table.

Steve moved his cup from the spreading puddle. "I'll get something to wipe that up."

Before she could protest, he sprang to his feet. He disappeared into the kitchen and came back with a handful of paper towels.

"You want a refill?" he asked, as he swiped the towels over the spill. "I can manage one-handed."

"I have enough left, thanks." Molly rubbed her forehead. He wasn't supposed to be cleaning up her mess. How had she gotten into this awkward situation?

Later, after they'd watched yet another program, he looked at his wristwatch. "Hey, how'd it get so late? I'd better take off."

Molly gave an inward sigh of relief.

They both stood. The front door was only a few steps away, but, remembering her manners concerning guests, Molly led him there. "Thanks again for fixing my computer glitch," she said as she opened the door.

"You're welcome. Thanks for fixing my lunch. And for dinner." He took a step over the threshold, but stopped and turned. "And for driving me to my appointment in Denver."

Molly widened her eyes. Had she heard correctly? "What are you talking about?"

His brow wrinkled. "Sara didn't tell you?"

"No, she didn't."

"She said you'd drive me into Denver on Wednesday."

"Oh, really?" Molly folded her arms. How was she supposed to do her work *and* be a chauffeur?

"I told Sara not to take you away from your job, but she insisted she could spare you." His hand rubbed over his chin. "If you'd rather not, I'll hire someone."

She unfolded her arms and pushed out her hands in protest. "No, no, I'll drive you. After all, your accident was my fault—"

With a shake of his head, he held up his forefinger. "Don't go there, Molly. My accident wasn't your fault. Or Karli's. I keep telling you that."

"But—"

"No 'but's.' I'll be fine. My work will be fine. Okay?"

"Okay."

Steve's brown eyes gleamed.

He was much too close. She wanted to step back, but before she could, he slid his finger under her chin and tipped up her head.

"Molly?"

When she looked up and met his heated gaze, corresponding warmth spun through her. Her heart thudded, her breath faltered.

He stepped closer, while she stood rooted to the spot. The air sizzled. His lips parted and his warm breath slid over her cheek.

Run, Molly!

Too late. His lips closed over hers, softly, yet firmly. She leaned into him and felt his heart beating underneath his shirt, felt the heat of his body, breathed in his masculine scent.

He rested his hand on her shoulder, while their lips engaged in a familiar dance, yet as new and exciting as though she'd never experienced it before.

Sliding his hand down her back, he drew her closer. His lips pressed against hers, his tongue roving, seeking access to her mouth.

"Mommy."

Molly jolted to her senses. Karli. Something was wrong. Karli needed her. She pushed away from Steve. "It's Karli. I—I have to go to her."

Steve dropped his arm from around her waist. "I'll come, too."

"No," she called over her shoulder, already halfway across the living room.

In the bedroom, Molly hurried through the nightlight's glow to the bed. "Are you all right? I heard you call."

Karli looked up, her eyes shadowed in the soft light, her chin quivering. "I woke up and was scared."

Molly leaned over and gathered Karli into a hug. She was sleep-warm and smelled faintly of her strawberry-flavored toothpaste. "It's okay, darlin'. Maybe you were having a bad dream."

"I don't know. Is Steve here?"

"He's just leaving." *He should have been out the door a long time ago.*

"Can I see him?"

"No, honey. He has to go back to the main house, and you need to go back to sleep." She held Karli a moment longer then eased her down to the pillow. "I'll be back in a minute and lie down with you for a while. Mr. Muggins will keep you company until then, okay?" She patted the doll lying on the pillow next to Karli.

"'Kay."

She tucked the covers around Karli's chin then returned to the living room.

Steve had closed the door and was leaning against it. Worry lines puckered his brow. "Is she all right?"

Not wanting to risk being near him again, Molly stopped in the middle of the room. "She's fine. Probably a bad dream."

"I'm glad she's okay...but what about you?" He straightened. "I'm sorry about—"

Molly glanced over her shoulder toward Karli's room, unable to shake her concern for her daughter. "Don't apologize, Steve. Let's move on, okay?"

"Sure, if that's what you want."

I don't know what I want, except I need you to leave now. "It's getting late."

"I'll be on my way." He reached for the doorknob then stopped. "We're still on for Wednesday?"

The reminder of her additional job assignment brought new tension to Molly's already frayed nerves. "Of course. Why would we not be? Sara's orders." Her tone was sharp, but she was past caring.

"Right, Sara's orders. Goodnight, then."

"Goodnight."

Molly scarcely took time to make sure the door had closed securely behind Steve before she hurried back to Karli's room. She was fast asleep, but Molly lay down beside her anyway. This was where she belonged, at her daughter's side, taking care of her, watching over her. Not falling into Steve's arms. Or into the arms of any man. She and Karli would do fine on their own.

****

Steve headed down the asphalt road to Sara and Jackson's house. Preoccupied with thoughts of Molly, he barely noticed the blue-black, star-studded sky arcing above, or the warm breeze stirring the leaves of the aspen trees.

All evening—okay, all *day*—he'd fought his attraction. He managed to keep his feelings under control until those last moments at her door, when he turned and there she was, only inches away. So close he could count the freckles sprinkled across her nose. So close he could smell her sweet perfume. So close that, with a slight dip of his head, he could press his lips against hers.

The temptation was too great. He wasn't disappointed. Her lips were soft and warm and pliant, and her body molded into his as though made for that purpose. Yep, the kiss had more than fulfilled his fantasies.

Steve huffed a breath and shoved his hand into his pocket. Becoming involved with Molly was a bad idea. There was no future for them. As soon as his arm healed, he'd be off to New York, far away from the Rolling R. Far away from the little white house where Molly and Karli lived.

Still, didn't he have *feelings* for Molly? Okay, but

he was drawn to her because they had something in common. They'd both lost their spouses. He felt sorry for her. He'd been sorry for Angie, too. That was one reason he'd proposed. And look where that had led.

The barn and the main house came into view. In anticipation of seeing Jackson and Sara, he straightened his shoulders and cleared his thoughts. As he entered the house's back door, sounds of the TV drifted in from the living room. He stepped to the doorway and peeked inside.

Jackson and Sara were snuggled together on the leather sofa. Sara had her head on Jackson's shoulder, and he had his arm around her. Both were asleep, looking contented and peaceful.

They were one of the happiest couples he knew. They deserved their happiness, too, both having been through a series of trials and heartaches before finally getting together.

Still, seeing them wrapped in each other's arms brought a bitter taste to Steve's mouth. He couldn't help envying Jackson his stable home, his loving wife, and his precious son. Everything he'd hoped to have for himself when he married Angie. But their marriage had been wrong from the beginning.

He turned away and headed for the stairs. In his room, the air smelled a bit stuffy, so he crossed the floor and opened the window. A stream of cool, night air drifted in. He gazed at the glittering stars and then at the road curling behind the house, the one he'd just traveled. Molly's house was too far away to see, but he thought he glimpsed a light from one of the windows shining through the thick foliage. Then a breeze shifted the trees and the light disappeared.

Chapter Ten

Steve sat next to Molly in the front seat of his rental car as they headed down the highway to Denver. She hadn't said more than two sentences since they'd left the ranch. Her silence, plus the set of her shoulders and the grim line of her mouth, left no doubt how she felt about her new duty as his chauffeur.

He gazed at the barren landscape, so different from the greenery he was used to seeing in New York, and then glanced at the speedometer. The needle hovered at almost ten miles over the posted limit. "Um, aren't you going a little fast?"

She frowned and pointed to the dashboard clock. "You said your appointment's at ten. It's nine now."

"Okay, but the last time I made the trip, the drive took only an hour. We've been on the road for nearly thirty minutes. We'll be okay."

"Whatever." She shrugged. "But don't blame me if you're late."

"I won't."

She pulled her foot off the gas and waited until the car slowed to the speed limit before applying pressure again.

He briefly closed his eyes then gazed out the window. He didn't need this stress. For his future appointments, he'd hire someone else. Molly could stay on the ranch, working in the bakery, where she belonged.

As they neared the city, traffic thickened, which raised a new worry about reaching his appointment on time. "The traffic will be bad when we get downtown."

"I can handle it. I'm from Chicago, remember? And we've got the GPS to help us find the Hanes Building." She pointed to the device affixed to the dashboard.

"Right. Okay, let's review the procedure. You'll deliver Sara's samples while I'm at my appointment." He nodded toward the back seat, where boxes of cookies and muffins from Sara's bakery rested on the floor.

"That's the plan. Jorgens' store is on the other side of town, but I'll have, what, an hour before I need to pick you up again?"

He checked his wristwatch. "Make it an hour and a half. That should give us both plenty of time. The corner where I want you to drop me off is coming up." He lifted his briefcase from the floor and slung the strap over his shoulder.

"I see it."

The traffic light changed to yellow. Molly barreled on through.

Steve squeezed his eyes shut, his body tensed. When he opened his eyes again, they were in the inside lane.

Molly switched on the right-turn blinker.

No one in the solid wall of cars was polite enough to let them slide over to the curb lane. Pulling up to the front of the Hanes Building wasn't going to happen. "You can drop me at the next corner." Steve pointed ahead.

"No, I'll go around the block."

Which wasn't an easy task, given the next street was one way going in the opposite direction. More traffic lights, more cars unwilling to yield their territory.

Two trips around the block later, they pulled up to the curb by the Hanes Building.

"Thanks much." Steve leaned over to open the door with his left hand. As he got out, his briefcase swung, pulling sideways, but he managed to keep his balance and land on his feet. "See you later," he called and breathed a sigh of relief as he shut the door.

He planned to wait until she merged back into traffic, but she frowned and waved him on. Reluctantly, he turned his back on her and his rental car and headed through the passing pedestrians to the glass double doors leading into the Hanes Building.

Inside, refreshingly quiet after the noise of the city, he crossed the marble-floored entry to the elevators, where he joined a group waiting for the next car going up.

He hopped on the elevator, exited at the sixteenth floor, and soon reached the door to Harwell, Inc. Taking a deep breath, he opened the door and stepped inside. The receptionist had red hair, which reminded him of Molly, not that she'd entirely left his thoughts in the few minutes they'd been separated, anyway.

The receptionist handed him over to an assistant, who ushered him into Harwell's thickly carpeted office.

Perry Harwell sat in a high-backed, black leather chair behind a mahogany desk. In his sixties, he had a thick thatch of white hair and a matching mustache. A younger man wearing black-framed eyeglasses perched on a straight chair nearby. Both men stood as Steve entered.

Harwell rounded the desk, his hand outstretched. "Steve Roper, good to meet you." His gaze landed on Steve's bandaged arm. "Whoa, had an accident, did you?"

Steve nodded. "I met up with a slippery rock on my friend's ranch and took a dive into the river. The accident slowed me down a bit, but I'm still able to work." He offered his left hand to Harwell and the two managed an awkward handshake.

"Good, good. This is Kevin Yang." Harwell waved at his associate. "He's our tech guy, and I wanted him to take a look at your program, too."

"Pleased to meet you, Steve," Kevin said as they shook hands.

Steve made a quick assessment of Yang. Early thirties, an easy smile. But behind the glasses were a pair of shrewd eyes. He'd be the one who needed convincing.

They crossed to a grouping of chairs around a rectangular table, where Steve set up his laptop. For the next half hour, he demonstrated the software he and Jerry had developed and honed to perfection. As he'd expected, Kevin Yang tested him at every turn. What happened if the accountant in charge made an erroneous entry? Wouldn't that throw off the entire program? Steve patiently demonstrated his foolproof check-and-balance system.

At last, both men ran out of questions. Harwell sat back and folded his hands across his stomach. After exchanging a glance with Yang, he turned to Steve. "Your program appears to be exactly what we want."

Yang nodded. "But we still have a couple more programs to check out."

"Of course." Steve shut down his laptop. Yang's caution neither disappointed nor surprised him. Comparison-shopping was to be expected. A program such as his included many facets, from training to transfer of data.

"Give us a couple of weeks," Harwell said. "You going to be around that long?"

"Oh, I think so." Steve pointed to his bandaged arm.

Harwell nodded. "Good, good. We'll be in touch. But, say, as long as you're in the area, come to our company party this Friday night. We're celebrating twenty-five years in the business."

Steve slipped his laptop into his briefcase. "Oh? Where is it?"

"At The Commodore Hotel. Five-course dinner, dancing, the works."

"Sounds good." Steve zipped up the case. Socializing with potential clients couldn't hurt and might help his cause. Due to his injury, he had a lot of time to spare.

Then he remembered he couldn't drive.

Before he could mention that, Harwell said, "Bring a guest, if you like."

Molly's image popped into his mind. He mentally shook his head. Who was he kidding? She wouldn't go with him. And, did he want her to, anyway?

Still, he heard himself say, "I might know someone I could ask. Is the dress formal?"

Harwell smoothed his mustache. "No need to rent a tux, but we do put on the dog a bit. Right, Kev?"

"Right." Yang's dark eyes gleamed behind his glasses.

Harwell rose, went to his desk, and picked up his phone. "Deb, give Mr. Roper one of our anniversary invitations on his way out, will you?"

Ten minutes later, the invitation stuck in his jacket pocket, Steve exited the building and scanned the nearby vehicles. He expected to see Molly waiting, but his rental car was not among those lined up at the curb dispatching and taking on passengers. Nor was the car anywhere in sight up or down the street.

A glance at his watch revealed he was a few minutes later than the agreed-upon time. He hoped Molly wasn't stuck circling the block again. The traffic was even thicker than when they'd arrived. He glued his gaze to the street, so that he'd be ready to spring to the curb the moment she arrived.

A sudden chill broke over him. What if something serious had delayed her? What if she'd had an accident? She said she was confident driving in city traffic, but was that true, or only bravado?

****

Molly peered out the windshield at the upcoming street sign. Mesa Avenue. She passed that street on the way to Jorgens' an hour earlier, but had she been at this corner or another one? Just then, the traffic light flipped to yellow, and the car in front of her stopped short. She slammed on the brakes and barely missed ramming the other car's rear end.

Relax. She puffed her cheeks and blew out a breath. *Just relax.*

Yeah, right. Relaxing while behind the wheel in this densely populated town was impossible. Besides, she had to keep moving, even if in the wrong direction.

With the help of the car's GPS, she'd found the grocery store to deliver Sara's samples. Mr. Gauge, the manager, wanted to discuss the bakery's products, and Molly obliged with confidence. She gave an inward cheer when he promised to place a large order next month. With high spirits, she started on her return trip to pick up Steve.

Despite instructions from the GPS, she'd been swept up in the tide of moving traffic, trapped into turning corners she shouldn't be turning. She should call Steve and tell him she'd be late. Trouble was, they hadn't exchanged cell phone numbers before parting.

She could call Sara or Jackson for Steve's number, but she didn't want to bother either of them. Besides, she'd gotten herself into this mess, and she'd get herself out. If Steve were standing on the street corner waiting, he could wait a little longer.

The light changed to green. Molly stepped on the gas—just as a car that had run a red light sped directly into her path.

****

After half an hour of pacing the sidewalk, Steve's nerves were ready to snap like twigs. Why didn't Molly give him a call? They had exchanged cell phone numbers, hadn't they?

He pulled out his phone and checked his contact numbers. No Molly listed. His jaw tightened. So, there was no way for them to get in touch.

Had something happened? An accident? He shouldn't have let her drive him. He should have hired a professional driver and let Molly stay on her job at the ranch.

A siren's wail split the air. Cars edged to the curb, allowing a red-and-white aide car to speed by. Steve's gut tightened. Oh, man, he hoped they weren't on their way to an accident involving Molly.

What if they were? What if she were injured and had to go to the hospital? Hours might elapse before he found out.

The siren stopped. Craning his neck, he glimpsed the top of the aide car, lights flashing, a few blocks away. He clenched and unclenched his fists. Should he continue to wait here for Molly, or should he run to where the accident was and see if she were involved?

He tapped his foot a few seconds, and then, securing the strap of his bag on his shoulder, started off in the direction of the accident.

He'd gone almost two blocks when a car's horn sounded behind him. He whirled to see a gray car similar to his rental. A redhead was behind the wheel. Molly. His knees wobbled with relief. She was okay. She hadn't been an accident victim, after all.

Blinker flickering, she pulled to the curb.

He sprinted over, flung open the door, and jumped into the car. "Thank God, you're—"

"Why were you walking down the street? I thought you were going to wait where I dropped you off?"

"I was, but—"

"Lucky I saw you. I was headed around the block but had to slow down because of an accident." She accelerated into traffic, and then, as a car cut in front of them, hit the brakes.

He kept quiet while she maneuvered them back into the traffic's flow. Her jaw was set, her brow a deep V. And all the time he'd been so worried about her. His feelings confused him. Of course, he would have been concerned, no matter who was to pick him up. But the thought of something happening to *Molly* had hit him deep in his gut...

"You didn't answer my question. Where were you headed?" Her fingers tapped the steering wheel. "Did I misunderstand where we were supposed to meet?"

"No, you didn't." He bit off the words, forcing himself to remain calm, when he easily could have fired off a few sharp remarks of his own.

"So?"

"I was headed for the accident," he said between his teeth.

She quirked an eyebrow.

"I was afraid you might have been involved. I was worried."

"Oh."

Oh? Was that all she had to say?

They passed the accident, on the other side of the street, in which an SUV had rear-ended an older model sedan. The medics loaded a victim into their van, while two cops waved their arms to keep traffic moving.

A few minutes later, he and Molly reached the freeway entrance and headed up the ramp. The open road lay ahead. He sat back, prepared to relax, at last, when his stomach gave a hunger growl. He could probably last until they reached the ranch, even though that would be another hour. Given Molly's sour mood, he didn't want to suggest stopping.

Molly broke the silence. "Were you waiting long?"

"About a half hour."

"Oh."

Another "oh," but at least they were talking again.

He was about to say something more.

But she blurted, "I got lost trying to find my way back to pick you up. Not lost, really, but I couldn't always turn where I was supposed to."

"Ah, that explains a lot. You must have been frustrated."

"You bet I was." She slapped the steering wheel. "And then a car running a red light nearly hit me."

Steve's tension spiked at the thought of her actually being in an accident, as he'd at first feared. "That must have been scary."

She pressed a hand to her stomach. "I'm still shaky inside. Then, with the next turn I took, I saw the Hanes Building."

"And I wasn't there on the sidewalk waiting, like we'd planned."

"I didn't know what to do. I didn't know which office you'd gone to."

Molly's tone had softened. Steve shifted in his seat, resting his injured arm on one knee. "You know, this whole thing could have been avoided if we'd exchanged cell phone numbers."

"I know." She heaved out a sigh. "And I'm sorry I yelled. Especially when you were worried about me. I wouldn't have thought that was the reason you took off."

"Well, that was the reason."

She glanced his way and their gazes collided. Heat flowed between them, tightening his chest. Her flushed cheeks indicated she felt the heat, too.

When she turned back to focus on her driving, he stared at her profile, mulling over a decision he needed to make. He cleared his throat. "How about getting something to eat? Don't think I want to wait until we reach Red Rock."

With a grin, Molly nodded. "I'm hungry, too, so let's stop. I know a place a few miles up the road."

Food wasn't all that was on his mind, though. He had something he needed to ask her, before he lost his courage.

Chapter Eleven

An hour later, at the Pines Café, Molly put down her fork and sat back. She looked at her empty plate, not long ago filled with a hamburger and a generous serving of fries. "I can't believe I ate the whole thing," she said, patting her stomach.

Steve, who'd polished off a similar meal, touched his napkin to his lips. "Me, neither. But, boy, that was good. You picked a great place. I've never seen so many variations of the good ol' hamburger on a menu before."

"Yep, that's their specialty. Fits right in with the décor." She gestured at the laminated tables and yellow vinyl upholstered chairs, straight out of the 'fifties.

They sipped their coffee awhile then Steve put down his mug and leaned forward. "Molly, I want to ask you something."

Molly sat straight. "Good heavens, you sound serious."

One corner of his mouth tipped up in a half-smile. "I've been sitting here trying to figure out how to broach the subject. But here goes. As I was leaving Harwell's, Perry Harwell invited me to their company's twenty-fifth anniversary party this Friday, at The Commodore Hotel." He reached in his jacket pocket, pulled out an envelope, and laid it beside her plate. "Take a look."

Molly opened the envelope and removed a cream-toned card embossed around the edges with fancy curlicues. She read the message, and then looked up. "Sure, I know The Commodore. And you need a driver, right?"

"More than that. Mr. Harwell said to bring someone, so...I thought of you."

Molly's skin tingled. "You're asking me on a date?"

He laughed. "Not very smoothly, it appears. I'm out of practice. But, yes, I'd like to escort you to the party."

Molly ran her fingers over the card's embossed edges while she formed her answer. Despite today's frustration, she still wanted to be his driver while his arm healed. No matter how hard everyone tried to convince her otherwise, she *was* responsible for his injury.

But being both his driver and his date? Uh uh. She'd decided when she met him to keep their association purely business. "I don't have anything to wear to a fancy party, Steve. I'm more at home at a grange function."

"Attire is not formal. And these days, everybody pretty much dresses however they like."

"Yeah, well, I still wouldn't wear anything in my closet to The Commodore."

Steve pushed his plate aside and leaned back. "Shall I take that as a 'no'?"

"I'm afraid so." She slid the invitation into the envelope and handed it to him. "But I'll drive you there and back."

He slipped the envelope into his pocket, and then

gripped his injured arm. "Oh, yeah? And just where will you hang out while I'm at the party?"

"I'll find something to do." She waved the air. "Maybe I'll go to a movie."

"I'm not good with that." He frowned. "We'd better forget the whole thing."

****

"I think you should go," Sara said, emerging from the bakery office's storage closet with a handful of empty cardboard boxes.

Molly plucked a freshly printed invoice from the printer. She thought back to yesterday's trip to Denver and the tension between her and Steve. "I don't want to go."

Disappointment lumped in her stomach. While Sara cleaned the closet, Molly had told her about Steve's invitation to attend the Harwell's anniversary party. She expected Sara to see her side of the situation, but apparently not. Now, Molly wished she'd kept quiet.

"An outing would be good for you." Sara tossed the boxes into the waste paper basket and brushed her hands together. "A chance for some fun. You've been home-bound since you arrived."

Molly retrieved another invoice from the printer. "And been perfectly happy. I came back knowing what life here would be like, Sara. A quiet life is what I want." She added the printed sheet to a stack on the desk.

"That's what you think you want." Sara waggled a finger in the air.

Molly sighed, remembering the heated glances she and Steve had exchanged upon occasion, as well as his tender worry when she was late picking him up in Denver. But no, she didn't want to become personally involved, especially with a man who was here only temporarily.

"Too late to change my mind," she told Sara. "Besides, I don't have anything to wear to that kind of party."

Sara's eyes sparkled as she took a step forward. "Oh, but I do. I have a dark green dress that would go perfectly with your hair."

Trust Sara, who had a closet full of clothes, to come up with an answer for Molly's lack. She groped for a reply. "But you're taller than I am."

Sara placed both hands on the edge of Molly's desk and leaned forward. "We can make it work. And Jackson and I will take care of Karli."

"Sara..." Now not a single excuse remained.

A knock sounded on the screen door. Sara turned, and Molly looked up. Steve stood outside on the steps peering in at them. Her cheeks blazed. How long had he been standing there? Had he overhead their conversation?

"Hey, can I come in?"

"Of course." Sara crossed to the door and opened it for him. "You don't have to ask."

Steve stepped over the threshold. He stopped and slid his gaze from Sara to Molly. "I get the feeling I'm interrupting something important."

"We're going over some invoices." Molly hastily shuffled the papers stacked on her desk, at the same time thinking how handsome he looked today in neatly pressed jeans and a crisp, light blue shirt. His rich, brown hair caught the sunlight shining through the window. Her pulse quickened.

"Actually," Sara said with a quick glance at Molly, "I was trying to talk Molly into accepting your invitation to the Harwell's party."

Molly's jaw dropped at Sara's betrayal. "Sara!"

"Are you having any luck?" Steve's lips quirked into a smile.

"I don't know." Sara tapped one foot on the floor and frowned at Molly.

To keep from looking at Steve, Molly folded an invoice then shoved it into an envelope. "If I recall correctly, Steve, you said we'd better forget it."

He shrugged, adjusting the sling around his neck. "I'd be happy to change my mind."

"See?" Sara tilted her head. "There's no reason you two shouldn't go and enjoy yourselves."

Molly gritted her teeth and stuffed another envelope. The two stared, as though waiting for her to say something. Waiting for her to say "yes." The silence thickened the air. Outside, a bird twittered. In the bakery, the mixers hummed, preparing another batch of dough for one of Sara's recipes.

While she filled envelopes, Molly considered her options. She could continue to protest, but she doubted it would do any good. She was stubborn, but so was Sara. And Steve, after all, was the Phillips' guest. Of course, Sara wanted to make sure his stay was the best it could be.

Quit kidding yourself. Sara's a matchmaker. And you don't need that.

Molly came to the end of her invoices. Still not sure what she should do, she looked up. Her gaze slid over Sara and landed on Steve. He stood with feet slightly apart, his shoulders rigid. The hope reflected in his eyes both shocked and touched her. Did her accompanying him to the party mean that much? Why?

Her throat tightened. Don't go there. Not now.

Pushing the worry aside, she allowed a smile to creep across her lips. "Okay," she said, making sure her voice held a resigned tone. "I'll go."

Steve's shoulders relaxed, and his brown eyes took on a new light. "Thanks, Molly."

"Yay!" Sara clapped her hands above her head and danced a jig.

Molly couldn't help laughing.

Steve joined in, tossing back his head and filling the small room with his rich laughter.

When Sara settled down, she said to Molly, "As soon as we close for the day, come on up to the house, and we'll try on the dress."

****

"Mommy, you look bee-u-ti-ful!"

Standing in front of her full-length mirror, Molly smiled at her daughter, whose eyes were wide and full of wonder. "Thank you, darlin'." She smoothed the cap sleeve of Sara's green dress then ran her fingers over the scoop neckline. Shortening the length was the only change Sara had needed to make.

"I wish I could go."

The wistful note in Karli's voice tugged at Molly's heart. "I do, too, baby. But the party tonight is for grownups. Auntie Sara and Uncle Jackson will take good care of you. You can help them with Ryan."

Karli tugged Molly's skirt. "Will you be home in time to tuck me in?"

A twinge of guilt nudged Molly. As far as she

could recall, this was the first time she would miss their nightly ritual. "No, honey. I'll see you in the morning. Now, run and get your backpack and your jacket, and we'll be on our way to the ranch house."

A few minutes later, as Molly and Karli walked along the road leading to Sara and Jackson's house, a car came toward them. Shading her eyes with her hand, Molly peered at the vehicle. The driver couldn't be Steve, but perhaps he'd sent Jackson to pick them up.

No, the car headed their way was shiny white. The Phillips owned no vehicle that color, and Steve's rental was gray.

Then she saw that the car was very long—a limousine. Her eyes widened, and she sucked in a gasp. What was going on? Surely, Steve didn't expect her to drive a limo into Denver.

Keeping a tight hold on Karli's hand, she stepped to the side of the road and waited. The limo, chrome all polished and shiny, windows tinted, stopped beside her and Karli.

A back window slid smoothly down, and Steve's head appeared. "I hoped we'd get to your place before you started out."

"What is this? Who's driving?" Molly peered inside the car. A man wearing a cap and a uniform sat in the driver's seat.

"His name is Carlos. He's from the limo service."

Molly couldn't help the smile that tilted her lips. "You mean I'm not driving?"

"No, you're riding back here." He patted the seat beside him. "I should've thought of this in the first place. Anyway, get in. We'll drop Karli off at the house." He leaned farther out the window and smiled at

Karli. "Everyone's waiting for you, honey."

Carlos, a cheerful-looking man in his forties, unfolded his lanky frame from behind the wheel and opened the back door. Molly and Karli climbed in. The interior was dim and cozy, and smelled of leather. Karli sat between Molly and Steve, bouncing up and down on the seat. "This is fun. There's a TV and everything."

Over Karli's head, Steve's gaze met Molly's. "So, what do you think?"

Touched by his thoughtfulness, Molly could only shake her head in wonder. "I'm speechless."

Steve laughed. "I'll have to take a long look at you, then. I've never seen you speechless before."

****

An hour later, after a smooth, leisurely ride on the freeway, the driver dropped off Molly and Steve at The Commodore. The building's silvery exterior glittered in light from the setting sun. A fountain that must have been at least twenty feet high, surrounded by a garden of cheerful orange poppies, filled a courtyard leading to the hotel's entrance.

Inside, a hotel employee directed them to the elevators. After a short wait with a group of other party guests, they were whisked to the twenty-fifth floor.

As they stood side by side in the elevator, Molly slanted a glance at Steve and couldn't help noticing how his black suit jacket emphasized his broad shoulders. As he shifted to allow room for other passengers, she caught a whiff of his cologne, the woodsy scent she'd come to associate with him. Her heart beat a little faster.

At last, they reached the twenty-fifth floor. From the elevator, they followed a short hallway to the ballroom where the party was in progress. Music from a live band, mingled with laughter and conversation, filled the air. While the others from the elevator eagerly entered the room, Molly stopped and stiffened.

"You okay?" Steve gripped her elbow and leaned close.

Although comforted by his touch, Molly still hesitated. "Not really. I'm sure I won't know a soul here. In Chicago, I went to a couple of realtors' conventions with parties this size, but at least I knew a few people."

Steve peered into the room. "Except for Harwell and his assistant, Kevin Yang, I don't know anyone here, either."

"But you have a purpose for being here."

"So do you. You're with me. Come on, let's have a good time."

They stepped into the room, which was a different world. The aromas of exotic spices from a nearby buffet table mingled with that of the guests' perfumes. Knowing Sara would want to hear all the details, Molly took special note of her surroundings.

At one end, an orchestra played music while the guests stood on the parquet floor sipping drinks and eating hors d'oeuvres. Round, cloth-covered tables set for dinner lined the dance floor. Thick candles in glass containers, and yellow and red roses decorated the tables. Yellow and red balloons bobbed along the ceiling, dangling curlicues of ribbon. Above the bandstand, a banner proclaimed, "Happy Twenty-Fifth to Harwell!"

A tall man with white hair and mustache broke away from a group and approached them. "Steve, glad you could make the party."

"Hello, Mr. Harwell. I'm glad I could, too." Steve gestured to Molly. "This is my friend, Molly Henson."

"Welcome." Mr. Harwell made a slight bow.

"Thank you." Molly smiled, but her lips felt stiff. Mr. Harwell reminded her of her boss in Chicago, a man who appeared congenial but who wasn't afraid to exercise his power and authority.

A woman approached behind Mr. Harwell.

"Here's my wife," he said, putting an arm around her waist and drawing her close. "Adele, these are Steve Roper and Molly Henson. Will you look after Molly while I introduce Steve to some associates I want him to meet?"

"Of course. Come along, dear."

Adele nodded pleasantly at Molly. She wore her white hair swept back from her suntanned face. Her blue earrings were probably real something-or-other and matched her blue sheath dress.

"I'll be okay by myself." Molly made a vague gesture toward the dance floor.

Adele raised carefully-penciled eyebrows.

At the look, Molly stilled. Realizing she'd goofed and that Adele's hospitality was part of the occasion's ritual, Molly pressed her fingers to her lips. "I appreciate your looking out for me, my being a stranger and all."

"Taking care of newcomers is what I do." Adele patted Molly's shoulder. "Let's get you something to drink."

Once Molly had a glass of white wine in hand, Adele steered her toward a group of women. "I'll introduce you to some of the other wives."

Molly opened her mouth to tell Adele she was not a wife then changed her mind and kept silent. Her status probably wouldn't matter to anyone, anyway.

The half dozen women, all dressed in the latest fashions and all about Molly's age or a little older, greeted her with polite interest. After Adele excused herself to greet another new arrival, Molly did her best to follow the women's conversation. Mostly, they were discussing their children and other social events they'd attended. Feeling she had nothing to contribute, she edged away.

She scanned the crowd for Steve, but he was nowhere in sight. Even though surrounded by a sea of people, she felt very alone. Her breath tangled in her throat.

What was she doing here? If she'd stayed at home, about now she'd be tucking her daughter into bed and sharing their nightly story. That was where she belonged, not here among strangers, attempting to discuss subjects about which she had little or no knowledge.

She set her empty wine glass on a passing waiter's tray and headed toward the Ladies' Room. Once inside, with the door closed behind her, she dropped into an overstuffed chair and pulled her cell phone from her small shoulder bag. She punched in the ranch's number.

Sara answered with a cheery hello.

Her familiar voice soothed Molly. Karli was fine. Was Molly having a good time? Molly told Sara she was. After a couple more remarks, they ended the call. Molly put away her phone and entered the adjoining room housing the toilets. Minutes later, she and another woman emerged at the same time from their respective stalls.

Glancing at the woman, Molly judged her to be in her early thirties. She had straight, black hair and wore a black dress that clung to her thin body.

The woman strode to the counter and squeezed a blob of a dispenser's soap into her palm. As she looked into the mirror, her gaze caught Molly's. "Ah hate these things," she said, in a thick, Southern accent.

Molly's brows knit as she pressed soap into her palm. "The soap dispenser? Mine works okay."

The other woman tipped back her head and laughed. "No, I mean these shindigs. Oops, I'm sure they wouldn't want their fancy party called that." With a sideways glance toward the door, she laughed again.

"This seems like a nice party." Molly held her hands under the faucet and waited for the water to automatically flow. She had no idea whom she was talking to and wouldn't want her criticism passed on to the wrong person.

"I guess it is, if you like this sort of celebration." The woman rinsed her hands and tore off a paper towel from the dispenser. "But maybe you do?"

Molly shrugged and rotated her hands under the water flow. "I haven't had much experience with parties such as this."

The woman nodded. "I thought you looked like a greenhorn. I'm LaTisha Melborn. Tish for short."

"I'm Molly Henson."

Tish took a comb from her clutch purse and combed her hair. "Your husband's a new hire-on?"

"I'm not here with my husband." Speaking the words caused a sudden ache to invade Molly's heart. "I'm a widow."

Tish wrinkled her brow. "Oh, I'm sorry."

Molly ducked her head in acknowledgment of Tish's sympathy. "I'm here with a friend. He's selling some accounting software to Mr. Harwell. Or hopes to." Oh, oh, had she said too much? She and Steve hadn't rehearsed what information to give out tonight.

Tish nodded. "My husband, Layton, is one of the VPs. He's probably heard about your friend."

Molly tore off a paper towel and dried her hands. "And maybe met Steve by now, too. I haven't seen him since we arrived."

"Right." Tish tucked away her comb. "Perry left you with Adele. And she introduced you to a bunch of other women then left you with them. And they were talking about stuff you didn't know anything about."

"How'd you know?"

Tish shrugged. "That's the drill. Same thing happened to me when I was new. I still feel like a stranger, sometimes. I'm more comfortable in a pair of boots and jeans than a dress."

Wow, this woman was a country girl? Molly's eyes widened. "Really? Me, too. I'm staying on a ranch right now. The Rolling R."

"We have a ranch, too, that I escape to whenever I can. But, hey, we'd better get back to the party."

Molly followed Tish from the restroom, surprised that she and Tish had something in common. Maybe she'd made a friend.

They were still talking about ranch life when Steve approached.

"Molly! I've been looking everywhere for you."

"You can blame me," Tish said with a wide smile. "I turned her five-minute powder room break into fifteen."

Happy she'd found Steve at last, Molly introduced the two.

Tish focused her gaze on Steve's injured arm. "Looks like you had a run-in with something."

Molly tensed. She hated being reminded of Steve's accident, but since the injury was obvious, comments were to be expected.

Steve shot Molly a glance then said, "Yep. Met up with a slippery river rock." Without giving Tish time to respond, he continued. "I met your husband. I think."

Tish laughed. "You'd remember Layton. He's a big guy, goatee, heavy laugh."

"Right. Say, I think you two are at our table."

"Great." Tish favored Molly with a bright smile. "I'll go round up Layton and see you two later."

****

Half an hour later, Molly sat beside Steve at one of the round tables. On her other side were Tish and her husband, Layton. The two other couples that completed their table were new to Molly. Despite having become acquainted with Tish, Molly still felt awkward and out of place, but with so many others to do the talking, she didn't have to say much. Steve, however, seemed quite comfortable as he conversed back and forth with their new acquaintances.

While they ate the chocolate mousse dessert, the master of ceremonies began the program. His deep voice boomed over the loudspeaker. Several people, including Mr. Harwell, spoke about the company's history and then about its future. Award presentations followed.

"This is the tough part," Tish whispered to Molly.

"But hang on. Dancing's next."

Dancing? Were they staying for that? With his arm in a sling, would Steve be able to dance? Would he even want to? The thought of being as close to him as dancing would require brought warmth to her cheeks.

When the formal program was over, the orchestra began to play, and the master of ceremonies invited everyone to the dance floor. Steve stretched his arm along the back of her chair and leaned close. Expecting him to suggest they leave, she readied herself to say good-bye to their tablemates.

Instead, his eyes twinkling, Steve said, "How 'bout a dance, Molly?"

She drew back. "What? Why, I didn't think you'd want to." She nodded at his injured arm.

"I'm betting I can guide us around to a slow tune. I'd like to try, anyway." His brows bunched together. "Or do you need to get home to Karli?"

Molly lowered her gaze and studied her hands in her lap. Here was a logical way out—if she wanted it. But, no, she must be truthful. "I called the ranch awhile ago. Sara said everything was fine."

"I'm glad to hear that. So, how about we give dancing a try?"

Still, Molly hesitated. If she said "no," she'd appear rude, wouldn't she? But saying "yes" might stir up dangerous emotions.

"Molly?"

Excitement building, Molly sucked in a breath. "Well...all right."

On the dance floor, after fumbling around a bit, they finally settled on a position with his left arm around her waist and both of her hands on his shoulders. Even with his injured arm between them, their bodies grazed each other's, chest to chest, hip to hip, and each contact sent a surge of heat through Molly.

"You're a good dancer," he said, as they glided around the floor.

"It's been a long time."

"Didn't your husband like dancing?"

The mention of Buck brought a soft smile to Molly's lips. "He liked country-western, but he didn't have much patience for slow dancing."

Steve guided her past a couple that swooped close with a fancy turn. "What do you like best?"

Her fingers smoothed a circle on his shoulder. "I like both. This is nice."

"It is," he said, bending his head so that his warm breath tickled her ear. A pleasant shiver rippled down her spine.

When the song ended, Steve kept his arm around her waist. "Shall we do it again?"

Being close was great, and not as scary as she'd imagined. Molly felt as though she'd had only one bite of a dish of ice cream. How could she walk away without eating the rest?

"All right."

Three songs later, they passed an open door leading to a terrace. A slight breeze blew cool air inside.

"Let's get some fresh air," he suggested, guiding her through the doorway.

On the terrace, they strolled past wrought iron tables and chairs filled with guests. The scent of flower arrangements on the tables drifted along the airwaves. They approached the chest-high stone wall overlooking the city. Lights from other skyscrapers glowed all around them. In the background, the mountains formed dark silhouettes under stars glittering in an inky sky. Muted sounds of late night traffic floated up from below.

Molly took a deep breath, allowing the cool evening air to fill her lungs. "What a gorgeous night."

He leaned his arm on the stone wall. "I agree. And you sound like you're having a good time."

A smile tilted her lips. "I am, Steve. Really." She spoke the truth. The rough spots she'd had at the beginning had faded away.

They enjoyed the view for a while longer then continued on around the perimeter, pausing now and then to look over the wall and survey the changing scene below. They passed other couples, some also strolling, others sitting at the tables.

When they came to the end of the terrace, Molly turned around to start back.

"Not yet." Taking her arm, he drew her into the building's shadows.

"What is it, Steve?" she asked, yet his husky tone told her what was on his mind. Her heart rate kicked up a notch.

"This." He lowered his head and captured her mouth with a kiss.

The thought crossed Molly's mind that she shouldn't be kissing him, but the warning lasted no more than seconds. All the physical closeness they'd shared in the last few minutes had primed her for this moment. Molly leaned into his hard body, welcoming his kiss. When his tongue probed, she readily accepted the gesture.

Long, delicious moments passed while Molly lost herself in Steve's kiss. Her fingers stroked his cheek and the other hand teased the hair along his nape. Both were breathing heavily when he finally drew away.

Steve gazed down while slowly shaking his head. "Molly, Molly, what's happening to us?"

She made a dismissive wave. "We're just—Oh, I don't know! We'd better go back inside."

"Uh uh. This is too good to give up just yet." He leaned close and kissed her again, his hand wrapping across her back.

Molly's surroundings faded away. As they stood there in the shadows, they could have been the only ones on the terrace, or on the planet. Finally, Molly came to her senses. Placing her palms against his chest, she eased away. "We must get back to the party. Someone might miss us."

He gave a low groan. "I suppose you're right." He straightened his tie, while she patted her hair and smoothed her dress, and then they started back along the terrace.

Hand-in-hand, they strolled along. Neither spoke, but when they happened to glance at each other at exactly the same moment, the energy that arced between them took away her breath. A warm glow wrapped around Molly. A glow of love. She was falling in love with Steve.

"Molly, I think I'm..."

Molly held her breath. Was he about to say he was falling in love with her, too?

Before he could finish speaking, a woman's laughter cut through the night. Molly automatically twisted her head in the direction of the sound.

The laughter came from a woman sitting with a male companion at one of the wrought iron tables. She had long, dark hair and wore a strapless blue gown. Moonlight shone on her slender neck and softly rounded shoulders.

Steve's jaw dropped, and his eyes widened. "No, she can't be!"

"What, Steve? What is it?" The back of Molly's neck prickled.

His grip on her hand tightened. "She's Angie."

Chapter Twelve

At first, Molly had trouble comprehending. Then realization dawned and she gasped. "You mean, your ex-wife, Angie?"

"Yes. At least, I think she's Angie." He stood still, gaping at the woman.

Molly laid a hand on Steve's arm. "Maybe you should speak to her and find out if she is Angie or not."

Steve frowned. "Don't want to do that. We'll walk by her first. Get a closer look." He dropped his arm from around Molly's waist and headed in the woman's direction.

Her heart hammering, Molly scrambled to keep up. What if the woman was his long-lost ex-wife? What then?

As they passed by the couple, the woman looked up and smiled. "Good evening."

Her companion, a fiftyish man wearing rimless eyeglasses that reflected the light, nodded pleasantly.

"Hello," Molly said, striving to keep her voice steady.

Steve nodded at the couple then headed toward the door to the ballroom.

As far as Molly could tell, neither the man nor the woman showed any sign of recognition toward Steve.

"Was she Angie?" Molly asked when she was sure the other couple couldn't hear. She held her breath and waited for Steve's reply.

"No, she wasn't."

His low, gritty voice conveyed more anger than disappointment. "You're sure?" Molly cast a surreptitious glance at the couple. Deep in conversation, they paid not the slightest attention to Molly and Steve.

"Yes. I knew when I saw her left wrist."

"Her wrist? Why?"

"Angie has a tattoo there, of a butterfly." With the fingers of his injured hand, he traced a pattern on the back of his left wrist. "The insect has red and blue wings, and there's a gold star above it."

"Tattoos can be removed."

"I know, but Angie never would do that. She went through too much pain to have the tattoo done. She said it was there to stay."

A butterfly and star tattoo. A memory flickered in Molly's mind, trying to make itself known. Then, just as quickly, the memory was gone.

****

Later, riding through town in the limo, the street lights flashing by, Molly glanced at Steve's profile. His mouth was set in a grim line. Since leaving the hotel, he hadn't said much, and neither had she. Tension built inside her until she had to break the silence. No point in making small talk, though. Best to address the subject that weighed on both their minds.

Keeping her voice whisper-soft, she said, "She haunts you, doesn't she?"

He turned his head and looked at her with sad eyes. "Yes, she does. Tonight wasn't the first time something like this has happened. I always get my hopes up, only to find I've been mistaken. A few days after I arrived in

Red Rock, I saw a woman I thought was Angie."

"What did you do? Did you speak to her?"

"Not at first." Steve rubbed a hand along his chin. "I followed her. She must've caught on, because she turned and confronted me. When I realized she wasn't Angie, I apologized. I felt like a jerk. But whenever I think I've found her, I lose my head."

Molly considered what she would do if she saw someone who looked like Buck. After the jolt of recognition, regret and sadness would follow. Still, she would know the man was not Buck, but only someone who resembled him.

Because he had no proof Angie was dead, Steve's response was different. Where Molly had had closure, Steve had been left hanging. Her heart ached for Steve, but she was at a loss how to help. And, maybe he didn't want to be helped.

They both fell silent again. Molly looked out the window. The freeway lights blurred as they sped along. Up ahead, the exit sign to Red Rock came into view. They'd soon be home.

After a while, he took her hand, running a thumb over her knuckles. "I'm sorry, Molly. I ruined our evening."

His fingers were warm, his grip strong. Glad for the physical connection, she squeezed his hand. "You didn't. Besides, tonight wasn't a date. Tonight was business. I was along to keep you company."

"But what about—"

The kisses on the terrace? Her stomach clenched. She didn't want to talk about that. "Please, Steve. Don't go there."

"If that's what you want." He released her hand.

Reaching the Rolling R seemed to take forever, but at last, they were heading down the side road to Sara and Jackson's house. Molly smiled to herself. Soon, she'd be with Karli again. She'd missed her daughter. She should've called Sara and Jackson a second time to make sure Karli was all right, but the troublesome incident on the terrace distracted her.

When the house came into view, she looked up at the second floor bedroom window where Karli was staying. A light beamed from the window. Why? Karli's bedtime was a few hours ago. By now, she should be fast asleep.

Molly gripped the edge of the seat. Instinct told her something was wrong.

"Are you okay?" Steve touched her arm.

A lump clogged Molly's throat. "I'm, ah, eager to see Karli."

His brows furrowed. "Won't she be asleep by now?"

"I hope so."

When the limo driver pulled up to the house, Molly flung open the door and leaped out. She ran along the walk, tottering in her high-heeled shoes, thinking—but not really caring—that if someone in the house were watching, they might assume she'd had too much to drink.

She raced up the steps and across the porch. The front door was unlocked. She burst inside. Lights glowed in the living room, but no one was there. "Sara! Jackson!" she called, as she ran across the room and down the hallway to the stairs.

Sara appeared at the top of the landing. In the dim light, her mouth was pulled into a tight line. "Molly.

I'm glad you're here."

"What is it?" Molly gripped the banister and took the stairs two at a time, vaguely aware of Steve behind her. "Is something wrong with Karli? Oh, I knew I shouldn't have gone tonight."

She reached the top of the stairs, but Sara blocked the way down the hall. She put her hands on Molly's shoulders. "Molly, calm down. Karli has a bit of a fever, that's all."

"That's all?" Molly's chest heaved from the rapid climb. She jerked away from Sara and ran down the hall to the room where light spilled through the open doorway. Molly flew into the room, Sara and Steve close on her heels.

Her gaze skipped over Jackson sitting on the bed and riveted to Karli. The bedside lamp shone down on her face. Her eyes were closed, her cheeks flushed.

"Molly, good you're here." Jackson jumped up and let her take his place on the bed.

Molly sat and, gasping for breath, leaned over Karli. "Mommy's...here now...darlin'."

Karli's eyelids fluttered then remained open. "Mommy...I don't feel good."

"Where does it hurt, honey?" Karli's plaintive tone squeezed Molly's heart.

"My head."

Molly placed her hand on Karli's forehead and her heart beat faster. "You're burning up."

"We took her temp." Jackson pointed to the thermometer on the nightstand. "A hundred and one."

Molly straightened and stared. "That's awful! Why didn't you call me?"

"We were about to." Sara stood beside her husband

and laid a hand on his shoulder. "This all happened in the last few minutes. She was fine earlier. Then when I came to check on her, she was awake and complaining that her head hurt."

"So you haven't given her anything to lower the temperature?"

Hearing Steve's voice, Molly turned to see him standing in the doorway. His solemn face reflected his concern, and for a moment, she wanted to run into his arms and have him hold her close. She didn't, though. She must focus on Karli now, not on Steve.

"No, we haven't." Jackson's forehead wrinkled. "Like Sara said, this happened right before you arrived."

"I haven't sent back the limo yet." Steve stepped farther into the room. "The driver can take us to the ER."

"I don't know what to do." Oh, how she wished Buck were here. He was always cool in an emergency. Molly turned back to Karli. "Do you hurt anywhere else, honey?"

Karli squirmed under the covers. "My tummy, a little."

Molly looked up at Sara. She was a mother, too. She'd know what was best. "What do you think?"

Sara fingered the collar of her blouse, her gaze steady. "I can't tell you what to do, Molly, honey. But if Ryan had a temp, I'd give him a children's medicine for fevers. I'd keep an eye on him throughout the night. If he got worse, I'd take him to the ER. If not, reevaluate in the morning. But, like Steve said, we can get her to the ER right away, if you want."

Molly nodded. "Your advice sounds good, Sara."

"I'll go get the medicine." Jackson headed for the door.

"You can stay here tonight." Sara pointed to the twin bed identical to Karli's, separated by a nightstand.

Molly's distress had eased a little now that a decision had been made. "I'll run down to my house for a few things."

"You don't need to. We have everything you'll need here—nightgown, toothbrush, towels."

The offer was generous but Molly hated the sense she wasn't the one making the decisions. "I don't want to cause any more trouble than we already have."

Sara leaned down and put her arm around Molly's shoulders. "You're not trouble, Molly—you're family."

"Thanks, Sara." Molly put her hand over Sara's.

Steve stepped forward. "I'll spell you throughout the night, so you can get some sleep."

Molly's mouth tightened. Although irrational, she wanted to blame him for the troublesome situation. "That won't be necessary," she ground out. She looked up in time to see Steve and Sara exchange a look. "Thanks, anyway," she said, in a softer tone.

"Well...okay, but I'll be down the hall if you need me." Steve gestured toward the door.

Karli raised up her head. "Steve? Where are you?"

"Right here, little one." He stepped around Molly and Sara and gazed down at Karli.

"I didn't know you were here." With a smile, she lay back on the pillow.

"Yep, I am. And I'm sorry you don't feel good. But we'll have you fixed up in no time and out riding those horses."

Molly pressed her lips together. *Why'd he have to*

go and mention horses? Why didn't he just leave?

Fluttering limp fingers, Karli said, "Will you stay with me until I get better?"

"Karli..." Molly shook her head.

"Your mommy's going to take care of you tonight," Steve said, grasping Karli's hand. "I'll see you in the morning."

"Will I be better then?"

He nodded. "You will. I guarantee it. And, when you're all well again, I'll have a surprise for you."

Molly expected Karli to ask more, but at that moment, Jackson returned with a bottle of chewable tablets and a glass of water. Steve stepped aside to let Jackson hold Karli while Molly fed her the tablet and water.

"Good girl." Molly set the water glass on the nightstand.

Sara and Jackson left, but Steve lingered. "I wish you'd let me help you keep watch tonight."

"No, Steve." Molly tightened the top and set the medicine bottle next to the water glass. "She's my daughter, my responsibility. I'll take care of her."

He gestured to the hallway. "Okay, but I'm—"

With a sigh, Molly folded her arms. "I know. You're down the hall, if I need you. Goodnight, Steve."

As soon as the door closed behind him, Molly turned back to her daughter. Karli's eyes were closed, and she appeared to be sleeping. Molly tucked the covers more securely under Karli's chin. Tears welled up behind Molly's eyes. She loved her child so much. She'd do anything for her. Anything.

The others thought she'd overreacted, and, okay, maybe they were right. But they didn't understand.

Karli was all Molly had. She'd never forgive herself if something happened to her daughter. Molly should've been here tonight. She had no business going off and leaving Karli with others, even people as conscientious and caring as Sara and Jackson.

Sara returned with a nightgown and a robe slung over one arm. "You'll find an extra toothbrush in the bathroom." She nodded to the door adjacent to the beds.

"Thanks, Sara."

After Sara left, Molly changed into the gown and robe. In the bathroom, she washed her face and brushed her teeth. Then she lay down on the extra bed. Spying a folded quilt at the bottom, she reached down and pulled the quilt over her. She closed her eyes, but sleep wouldn't come. Not that she expected to sleep. Not with Karli lying ill in the next bed.

An hour later, she got up and roused Karli enough to stick the thermometer under her tongue. She whispered a prayer then with baited breath studied the results. Karli's temperature had lowered a degree. Molly expelled a long, deep sigh. The medicine was working. That had to be a good sign.

Still, though, she didn't sleep. She lay in bed mentally beating up herself for being away when Karli took sick. The memory of Steve's kisses wiggled into her thoughts, but she quickly brushed aside the memory. The kisses meant nothing, absolutely nothing, and didn't deserve even a moment of her time.

****

The following morning, Karli's temperature was still above normal. Molly picked up the phone and called Mike's office to make an appointment. Luckily, he had some time to see Karli that morning.

"Getting Mike's evaluation is a good idea," Sara said, when Molly told her the news.

Anna Gabraldi made a breakfast for Molly to take up to Karli. "Some warm oatmeal and toast will make her feel better," she said, handing Molly the food-laden tray.

On her way upstairs, Molly encountered Steve, his hair slick from his morning shower, dressed in a short-sleeved shirt and jeans. Unexpectedly, her pulse spiked.

"How is she?" he asked. Worry lines crinkled his forehead, and his gaze was steady as he waited for her reply.

His concern touched her and meant more than she could have known. "Better, thanks. Her temp's down some."

"That's good news." He rubbed his forehead, clearing away the worry lines.

"Yes, it is. But as soon as she eats breakfast, I'm taking her to town and let Mike check her over. He's in his office this morning."

"I'll go with you," he said, and then frowned and patted his sling. "I'm not much use, but, still, I'd like to go."

Molly gripped the tray and took a step back. Although she appreciated his concern, she still didn't need—or want—his help. Karli was her responsibility, and hers alone. "You really don't have to."

He leveled a stern look. "You told me you felt responsible for what happened to me at the river, because I was looking for Karli when I fell. Well, now I feel responsible for your not being here when Karli took sick, because my business took you away. You can understand that, can't you? And, we can use my rental.

Then you won't have to borrow one of Sara's and Jackson's cars."

"That's thoughtful of you, but—" Molly had almost forgotten about not having her own vehicle.

"Humor me, okay?"

Feeling herself weakening, Molly offered one last protest. "She might be contagious."

"I'm not worried."

"All right, come along, then." Molly mustered a smile. "I know Karli will like that."

Steve returned her grin. "Good to know at least one of you wants my company."

****

Two hours later, Molly, Steve, and Karli were on the road to Red Rock and Mike's Timber Ridge Clinic. Karli was in the back seat, tucked in a car seat they'd borrowed from the Phillips. Her precious Mr. Muggins sat beside her.

Steve entertained Karli with stories while Molly concentrated on driving. He soon had them both laughing at the antics of a trained bear that didn't want to be in the circus anymore.

"Where'd you learn all those stories," Molly asked, when his narrative ended.

"From my grandfather." Steve settled back in his seat. "He was quite a storyteller. I don't know where he got the stories. I think he made them up. I always thought I'd tell them to my kids someday, but in the meantime, I've been entertaining my niece and nephew."

"You've still got lots of time to have your own children," Molly said, and then wished she hadn't brought up such a personal subject.

"I guess so." He clamped his jaw shut and turned to gaze out the window.

At the clinic, Mike examined Karli and questioned both her and Molly. "The illness appears to be just a virus," he said afterward, sitting on his stool in the examining room. "Although I shouldn't say 'just,' because that's bad enough. No fun being sick, is it, Karli?" He smiled at the little girl perched on the examining table.

"No, it's not." Shoulders drooping, Karli shook her head.

Mike turned to Molly sitting nearby. "Keep on with the medicine, lots of liquids, and bed rest. Call me at home tomorrow and let me know how she's doing."

"She's a tough one to keep down, but I'll do my best." Molly gathered up her purse and stood.

"You'll feel better sooner if you rest a lot," he told Karli as he patted her head.

Mike accompanied them to the waiting room, where Steve tossed down the magazine he'd been paging through and jumped up. "What's the verdict?"

"Hey, Steve, good to see you." Mike clapped Steve on the shoulder. "Looks like our little gal here has a virus."

Steve's chest expanded as he drew in a breath. "I'm glad we came in and can get her treatment started."

"Me, too," Molly said, keeping her arm around Karli's shoulder.

"She should be as good as new in a couple of days," Mike added, and then gestured to Steve's injured arm. "How's the arm?"

Steve rubbed his injured wrist. "Better, but sore if I

try to use it."

Mike turned to Karli. "See, Steve has to rest his arm, so it will get better."

"Yah, but I have to rest my whole body!" Karli said, which brought a laugh from everyone.

Chapter Thirteen

At the Rolling R, Molly dropped off Steve at the Jacksons' then she and Karli continued on to their house. After Molly put Karli to bed, she opened a can of chicken noodle soup for their lunch.

Karli ate half of hers then pushed away the bowl, saying she was too tired to eat any more.

Molly sat with her until she fell asleep. She was cleaning up the kitchen when Sara arrived.

"Here are samples of my newest recipe, Coconut Oat Cookies." She handed Molly a foil-covered plate. "I thought Karli might enjoy them."

"Thanks, Sara. I'm sure she will." Molly lifted a corner of the foil, allowing the sweet aroma of coconut to float out. "They smell wonderful."

Sara laughed. "I hope they taste as good as they smell. But, now, tell me what Mike said about Karli."

"Sit while I put these in the kitchen. Then I'll fill you in." Molly gestured toward the sofa.

After putting the cookies in the refrigerator, Molly returned to the living room. "She's got a virus," she said, dropping into a chair across from Sara. "I'll have to keep Karli away from Teresa's until she's well." She cast Sara a worried glance. "What am I going to do about my job?"

"You'll stay with Karli as long as you need to."

"But—"

With a shake of her head, Sara held up a hand. "Not to worry. We'll set you up with a laptop, and you can work from here. This will be a good time to revise the procedures manual to fit with the new software. Since your cell phone's already set up for call forwarding, taking orders won't be a problem."

"Okay, but won't setting up the laptop be a lot of trouble?"

"Not at all. Steve can help. Installing the laptop with his program is a good idea, anyway."

"I don't know—" Molly put her head in her hands. Everything was piling up, and she wasn't sure how she could tend a sick child and accomplish her tasks.

Sara stood and approached Molly. Leaning down, she slipped her arm around Molly's shoulders. "Don't worry. Everything will work out okay."

Molly took a moment to let Sara's gesture comfort her. Sara was probably right—about this particular situation. But the future, filled with potential disasters, loomed over Molly.

"I know this all looks overwhelming to you now," Sara said, as though she'd read Molly's mind. "Raising Karli, making a living. But take one day at a time, okay? You never know what's on the horizon."

Molly dropped her hands and forced a smile to her lips. "You're right. I promise to do better. And bring on the laptop. Work is good for me right now."

****

After dinner that evening, Steve left the main house and headed down the road to Molly's. Sara had filled him in on Molly working from home on a laptop and asked if he would install the software. Of course, he would. He was happy to do whatever he could to help.

Sara called Molly and set a time with her for this evening.

He had another, personal, reason for coming tonight. He'd decided to tell Molly the truth about his marriage to Angie. After the incident at the Harwell party, he figured he owed her the entire story.

"Hope I'm not too early," he said when Molly opened the door.

"Not at all. Come on in." She smiled then nodded toward the kitchen. "I was about to dish up our ice cream. Do you want some?"

"Ice cream sounds good."

He followed her into the kitchen, where the aroma of chicken soup lingered in the air.

While she dished up the bowls of ice cream, he considered launching into his story. But, no, better wait until Karli was settled for the night.

Molly put the three dishes of ice cream on a tray and led Steve into Karli's room. The air was warmer here than in the rest of the house, and the only light came from the bedside lamp with a plastic horse for the base.

Karli lay in bed, propped up against the pillows. Beside her, Mr. Muggins peeked his head out from the covers.

"Hi, Steve." Karli's lips broke into a smile.

"How're you doing, Karli?" He glanced at her face, noting pink cheeks.

"I'm better all the time. Aren't I, Mommy?"

"I sure hope so. Grab a seat, Steve." Molly nodded at a straight chair against the wall.

Steve retrieved the chair and sat.

Placing the tray on the nightstand, Molly sank into

a chair already positioned by the bed. She picked up two dishes, handing one to Steve and one to Karli. "Here, honey."

As Karli took the bowl, she looked up at Steve. "Can you tell me and Mr. Muggins a story?"

"We have a story to read." Molly pointed to a picture book lying on the nightstand.

Karli cast a frown in the book's direction. "That's old. I want to hear one of Steve's stories."

A muscle in Steve's neck tightened. Here was another tug-of-war between mother and daughter, with him in the middle. How could he keep them both happy?

To delay his answer, he took a bite of his ice cream, letting the chocolate swirl around his tongue. "I need a little more time to come up with one of my stories, so why don't we read your book tonight?"

Karli pouted and scooped up a spoonful. "All right, but you read it."

His hand stilled halfway to his mouth and he shot Molly a glance.

She swallowed a spoonful of her ice cream and shrugged. "Okay, if you really want to."

"'Course I do."

When they finished eating, he picked up the book and balanced it on his lap, so he could turn the pages with his left hand. "Ready?"

Karli grinned and snuggled down in bed, her arm around Mr. Muggins.

Molly rose and collected the empty ice cream dishes. "I'll take care of these while you're reading," she said, and left the room.

The story was about a pig and a bear that formed

an unlikely but strong friendship, first out of necessity, then with genuine caring. Karli was asleep well before he reached the last page, but he finished the story aloud anyway.

He replaced the book on the nightstand and tucked the covers under her chin. Warmth curled around his heart. With only a little imagination, he could envision himself as Karli's father. He gazed at her round face and blond curls for a few moments longer, reveling in the wonder of the experience. Then, with a deep sigh, he turned out the light and left the room.

The sound of water running led him to the kitchen. Molly was putting the last of the dishes into the dishwasher. She poured in some liquid soap, snapped shut the door, and pressed the Start button. The machine gave a loud whoosh then settled down to a steady rumble.

"Is she asleep?" Molly rinsed out the dishrag and hung it on a nearby rack.

Leaning a hip against the counter, he grinned. "Before I finished the story."

"She's on the mend. I can tell because she's getting demanding again."

"She has a mind of her own."

"Like her father."

While Molly's wistful smile touched Steve's heart, the mention of Buck Henson slipped him a dose of reality. Yes, Karli was Buck's child. A few minutes ago, he'd imagined her as his own. But that wasn't so. Never could be. He must remember that.

What if telling Molly the truth about his marriage would be a mistake? Their association was only temporary, wasn't it? Maybe he should keep that part of his personal life to himself. "Anything a one-armed guy can help with?" he asked, his gaze taking in the rest of the kitchen.

"No, thanks." She dried her hands on a towel hanging next to the dishrag. "We'd better get the computer set up."

Steve followed her into the living room, where the laptop sat on the table in one corner.

Molly pulled up two straight chairs. "Can you do what you need to with one hand?"

"I can. But tonight I'll talk you through the program and let you do the actual work." He nodded at the stack of books and CD cases next to the laptop. "I see Sara included all the manuals and software, so we have everything we need."

"Yes, I think we're all set."

He sat and opened the laptop. As she settled beside him, he caught a whiff of her hair, which smelled fresh and fragrant, like the wild flowers he'd passed along the road. With her so near, how was he going to keep his mind on business? He cleared his throat. "Okay, let's get started."

For the next half hour, he concentrated on coaching her as she installed the program. Then he showed her several formats for setting up the procedures manual.

Molly's forehead wrinkled. "I don't know which one will work best for Sara."

"Set up a few pages in each format. Then show them to her and see what she says." He liked they had this task to share and that he could offer advice.

A smile grew on her lips, and she nodded. "That's a good idea."

He sat back. "You want to start on it tonight?"

She glanced at her wristwatch. "No, it's too late. I'll wait until tomorrow."

"Okay, shut 'er down."

After she'd turned off and closed the laptop, an awkward silence descended. Molly fiddled with one of the manuals, while he straightened his sling.

Finally, she put down the manual and turned. "Would you like a cup of coffee? I can make some."

What he wanted was to kiss her, as he had at Harwell's party. If only he could repeat those wonderful moments. But that was wishful thinking.

"No, thanks. I'd better head back to the house. Today has been a long one for both of us."

As though relieved of a burden, she jumped up.

"You're right," she said. "And I'll be up and down all night, checking on Karli's temp."

"All the more reason for me to head out." He pushed to his feet.

"Thanks for getting me started on the program," she said on their way to the front door.

"No problem. You have any questions, be sure to holler, okay?"

"I will... See you tomorrow."

"Right, tomorrow." He cut her a glance, hoping to catch her eye, hoping something other than words might pass between them. No luck, though. She kept her gaze on the door.

Then he was on the road, with a faint moon shining down to light his way, and sagebrush and hay scenting the air. As he passed the stable, a horse neighed, and a second one nickered a soft answer.

Molly had been cool and distant tonight, as though they were strangers. He thought he was ready to confide in her, but tonight hadn't been the right time. Tonight was about her work for Sara, and about Karli.

Maybe the right time would never come, and, as he had thought earlier, he and Molly were destined to have only a brief time together. Steve trudged on, feeling more alone than ever.

****

Molly sat at her desk in the bakery's office working on the monthly bookkeeping. For four days, she'd stayed home with Karli, setting up the procedures manual on the laptop and taking orders on her cell phone.

Now Karli's temperature had been normal for two days, and with great relief, Molly had let her go back to Teresa's.

Sara came in from the kitchen. "Hey, Molly." She clapped her hands. "Seeing you sitting at your desk again is wonderful. I've missed you."

"I've missed being here." Sara's effusive greeting brought a smile to Molly's lips. "But I sure appreciate your letting me stay with Karli while she was sick."

Sara crossed to the supply closet and poked her head inside. "I'm glad she's better now," she said over her shoulder. "You did let Mike know she's okay?"

"Yes, I called his office this morning and told his nurse, Lucy."

"Good. When I talked to Rose last night, she asked about you and Karli."

"That was nice of her." Knowing that others cared about her daughter warmed her heart. Molly leaned back in her chair and propped her elbows on the armrests. "How is she doing with her pregnancy?"

"She's doing fine. Very excited, as you can

imagine." The sound of shuffling came from the closet. "Do you know what happened to those labels we had for the boxes? Doreen and Lupe need them."

"They should be on the middle shelf. Want me to help look?"

"No, I'll find them...Oh, here they are." Sara turned, holding the cardboard box of labels. "Steve was asking about Karli this morning at breakfast."

Molly's shoulders tightened. Steve hadn't been to the house since the night he'd set up her laptop. When Karli had asked why Steve hadn't come to see them, Molly told her he was giving her time to get well, and he'd be around later. But she wondered if he would. Perhaps her coldness that night would keep him away permanently.

Deep down, she hadn't wanted to distance herself, but she knew pulling back on their relationship was for the best. Even if doing so had hurt. Nothing lasting could develop between them. Why risk her feelings? Or Karli's?

"Molly, is there something wrong between you and Steve?"

Jolted back to the present, Molly looked up to see Sara standing on the other side of her desk. "Not really. Why?"

Sara shrugged. "I thought his asking about you was strange, because I figured you two were keeping in touch." She set the box on the desk and dropped into a nearby chair.

Molly picked up a pen and twirled it between her fingers. She wished Sara would leave and let her get back to work. "I haven't talked to him since the night he set up my laptop. Does he need me to drive him someplace?"

"I don't think so. He seems to have plenty of work to do from the house." Brows pulled together, she leaned forward. "I, ah, thought you two were beginning to—"

Molly interrupted with a wave. "Please don't go there, Sara. Steve will be returning to New York soon. Besides, he's way out of my league."

Sara frowned and shook her head. "I don't know why you say that. You two seem very well suited."

"Not at all. He's big city, and even though I came from a big city, now I'm country. We're in two different worlds. I can't get involved with him, don't you understand?" Molly's stomach knotted. "The more I let him into our lives, the harder letting him go when he leaves will be for Karli."

"But think about all you're missing if you don't get involved."

Molly shook her head, her grip tightening on the pen. "I'm not the one who matters here."

"I disagree. Putting Karli first sometimes is fine. But you need to think about yourself, too."

"I'll be glad when he's gone." Molly sighed and shifted in her chair. "Then I won't have to worry about whether anything is happening between us or not."

"Really?" Sara's eyebrows shot upward and her voice rose. "And what about the next guy who comes along? Are you going to push away every man who's interested in you to protect Karli? Or are you using her as an excuse because you're afraid of your own feelings? Afraid you might have to let go of Buck's memory and go on with life?"

Molly's jaw dropped and tears burned behind her

eyes. "What a hurtful thing to say."

"I'm sorry." Sara pressed her fingers to her lips. "I don't want to hurt you. But standing by and watching you and Steve go your separate ways is painful."

"You're assuming too much. Steve and I barely know each other. If he hadn't hurt his arm, he'd be gone by now. His accident was my fault."

"Did you ever think maybe the accident happened for a reason? So you two would have more time to get to know each other?"

Molly thrust out her chin. "Oh, yeah? And I suppose Buck's death was for a reason, too. I'm sorry, Sara, but none of this makes any sense. The only thing I know is, I have a daughter to raise. I have to do what's best for her."

"You're right, Molly. That's the bottom line." Sara stood and picked up the box of labels.

Hearing the resignation in Sara's voice made Molly regret her harsh words. She leaned across the desk and held out her hand. "Oh, Sara, I appreciate you. Really, I do. Where would I be without you and Jackson? But—"

With a sad smile, Sara grasped Molly's hand and squeezed her fingers. "I know. You have to live your life the way you see fit. I'll try to remember that."

Chapter Fourteen

Molly pulled the rake through the rectangular plot of earth behind her house then stopped to survey her progress. She finally had a chance to start her flower garden. She'd had one when she and Buck lived here before, and she always enjoyed planting and tending the flowers.

Soft evening light shone down on the newly turned ground. Pots of fledgling plants sat on a nearby bench, ready to be transferred to their new home. Next to the plants was the box of yard ornaments she'd used in her previous garden, which Sara had kept in a storage shed.

Molly put down the rake and hooked up the hose to the faucet on the side of the house. She turned on the water to a slow drizzle then dragged the hose to the plot. Picking up a trowel, she knelt and began to dig the first hole. The pleasant aroma of freshly turned earth floated up to her nose. This promised to be fun. In Chicago, while living with Paige and Harlan, she'd had only a few indoor geraniums to care for. She'd missed her outdoor garden.

Molly worked away, faintly conscious of the sounds of the TV floating out the open back door. Karli was in the living room watching her Mr. Muggins program. She'd wanted to help Molly, but in the end, the TV won out.

"Molly?"

Molly looked up just as Steve appeared around the corner of the house. Surprised at his sudden appearance, she jumped to her feet, trowel still in hand. "Hey, Steve. What brings you here?"

"Decided to take a walk this evening. Hot day and I needed to cool off." He tugged at the collar of his shirt.

Molly's pulse quickened, as it always did in his presence. "Today was hot. At least, out here there's shade." She nodded at the maple tree overhanging their corner of the yard.

"Yeah, the breeze feels good. How's Karli doing?"

"Doing well. She's in the house watching her favorite TV program." With a smile, Molly nodded toward the back door.

His gaze followed her direction. "Ah. Mr. Muggins, I assume?"

"None other."

All the time they were talking, Molly sensed something else was on Steve's mind. A thought flashed. Had he come to tell her he was returning to New York? Her heart flip-flopped. Yet, why should his leaving upset her? She'd known an end to his visit would come soon.

She cleared her throat. "I get the feeling you're here for a purpose."

Narrowing his gaze, he pressed his lips together. "You're right. I want to talk to you...about Angie."

Molly gripped the trowel and took a step backward. Why did he want to talk about his ex-wife? "Angie? Because of that night at the party, when you thought you saw her?"

"Not just that. I've wanted to tell you about our marriage for a while now. I intended to tell you that night, but when we found out Karli was sick, of course, I put it off." Steve looked out across the yard and rocked on his heels. "Then I decided to tell you the night I set up your laptop, but the time wasn't right then, either. Karli was still sick, and we had business to do."

"And the time is right now?" she asked, her voice barely audible.

He shrugged. "I don't know, but I don't want to wait any longer."

Molly swallowed against a sudden lump in her throat. His hesitant manner didn't feel right. "Well...okay. Mind if I keep working?" She tipped her head toward the garden.

"Not at all. In fact, I'll help you—as much as I can." He pointed to his sling.

"Sure. You can hand me the plants when I'm ready to stick them in the ground." She knelt and scooped a couple more piles of dirt from the hole she'd dug.

"Okay. What's first?"

"How about a delphinium?"

"Ah, right." His hand waved over the variety of plants. "And which one is that?"

They both laughed, which eased Molly's tension. "The one with the blue flower." She pointed her trowel toward the box of plants on the bench.

"Of course. I knew that." He stepped to the bench, picked up a delphinium, and handed it to her.

Molly set the plant on the ground beside the hole. "I'm listening."

Steve paced a few yards ahead then stopped and turned. He blew out a breath. "Okay, here goes. My dad died when I was five. My older sister and my mom raised me. Then when I was eighteen, Mom passed away. My sister was married by then and starting her family. I wanted to go to college, but there was no money. I decided I would work my way through, no matter how long my degree took."

"What kind of a job did you get?" Molly tamped down the dirt around the newly planted delphinium.

"As my situation turned out, I didn't have to get a job. My godparents, Ed and Jane Griffin, gave me the money to go to college."

She slanted a look his way. "Wow, that was nice."

Steve nodded. "I always intended to pay them back someday, and at this point in my life I could, but it's too late." His voice dropped. "They're both gone. They drowned in a boating accident in Mexico, where they were vacationing."

"Oh, how sad." Her throat tightened, remembering her sadness at losing loved ones. "Did they have children of their own?"

"Only one—Angie."

"Ah, I'm beginning to see..."

Steve put out a staying hand. "Don't start second-guessing, Molly. Hear me out."

Molly stepped forward along the row and began digging a new hole. She wasn't sure she wanted to hear more, but what could she say? "Okay, but get me another pot, please."

"Which one this time?"

"How about a dahlia? Those are the red blossoms."

Steve selected a dahlia and set it down beside Molly. Picking up the hose, he guided the water into the hole. "Angie was a wild kid. The Griffins were in their forties when she was born, and they never knew quite what to do with her. She was barely through high school when they died."

"That must have been tough." Molly pulled the dahlia from the plastic pot and placed it in the hole.

"She was lost without them. Before they went on their trip to Mexico, Ed Griffin must have had a premonition, because he said to me, 'Steve, if anything happens to us, will you look out for Angie?' And I promised him I would. Turns out, I did more than that. Before a year had passed, I asked her to marry me."

Molly scooped out a hole for the next plant. "You'd fallen in love with her." She couldn't look at him and focused on the damp earth. Of course, he had. Why else would he marry her?

He hesitated then said, "Marrying her seemed the right thing to do."

Okay, so he wasn't going to admit he loved her. "Were you happy?"

"I thought we were. I did everything I could to help her to settle down. She wanted to learn metal sculpture, so I found her a class at the community college. That's where she became interested in butterflies. She made yard ornaments of their shape and even sold a few at local fairs and festivals."

"Yard ornaments? Butterflies?" Molly stiffened. Her gaze strayed to the box of yard ornaments sitting on the bench. The one on top was a butterfly. The tip of one copper wing gleamed in the sun's lowering rays, like a bit of buried treasure.

"Yes, why?"

"Ah, nothing." Molly ducked her head and stabbed at the earth while her mind raced. The photo of Angie she'd seen in Steve's hotel room had pricked her memory. So had the butterfly and star tattoo he'd described on Angie's left wrist. And now, the added information that Angie had crafted butterfly yard ornaments and sold them at fairs and festivals. All pieces of a jigsaw puzzle she couldn't quite fit together.

Steve's voice interrupted her thoughts. "Angie's old friends wouldn't let her alone, and she began hanging out with them again. I was busy with my computer work. Jerry and I had started our company, and I worked long hours. I'd come home to find her gone. Sometimes, she stayed away far into the night, and eventually, all night long."

"Did you go looking for her?" Her gardening tasks forgotten, Molly sat back on her heels and gave her attention to Steve.

"Sure, I did. Sometimes I'd find her and drag her home, and sometimes I'd return home alone." Steve ran a hand through his hair. "And then, one day, when we'd been married exactly a year, she left and didn't come back. Like I told you before, I did everything I could to find her, from hiring private detectives to consulting a psychic."

Molly widened her eyes. "No trace of her anywhere?"

"Nothing that ever panned out. One detective thought he located her in one of those cults that travel around the country. One report placed the group not far from Red Rock."

"Red Rock?" The words jogged Molly's memory, but only for a moment. Then the impression vanished.

He leaned down in her direction. "Yes, why?"

Unable to meet his gaze, Molly again poked the earth with her trowel. "I, ah, maybe that's why you thought the woman at Harwell's party was Angie."

"Maybe. But, anyway, then the trail went cold."

"I can imagine how stressful her disappearance was."

"I blamed myself." He kicked at the dirt. "Her parents entrusted me with her care. I let them down."

"But you did divorce her?" She held her breath while she waited for his reply.

He nodded. "Jerry kept telling me I should, and so I finally gave in. I had to wait five years, though, to divorce her in absentia. I thought after that I could move on, but I haven't been able to. I keep thinking maybe she's alive someplace and needs my help." He held out his hand, palm up. "I feel responsible. I promised her parents I'd look out for her well-being, and they did so much for me..."

Molly focused on digging another hole while at the same time processing all Steve had revealed. "You said one detective traced her to this area. Have you asked around since you've been here, to see if anyone remembers her?"

"Yes. I've been showing her photo in various places, but with no luck."

Did that mean she wasn't in the area? Red Rock was a small town. Surely, if Angie were here, someone would have seen her. Molly's gaze strayed again to the box of yard ornaments. *Tell Steve to go look in the box.* "Steve, I, uh—" Heat crept up Molly's neck and onto her cheeks.

Steve leaned forward. "Yes? Are you okay? You look a little flushed."

Still surprised by what she'd heard, Molly fanned her face with her free hand. "Guess the heat's caught up with me, after all. I'd better quit for tonight."

Steve's brow wrinkled. "You didn't get much done. My fault."

"Don't worry about it." She made a dismissive gesture. "I planted three. That's a start."

"I can help you clean up, anyway." Steve stacked the empty plant containers then headed to the bench and put them in the box with the remaining plants. "Want me to put these inside? They look light enough to carry with one hand." He pointed to the box of plants and then to the one with the ornaments.

Molly's knees went weak. Had he seen the butterfly ornament? Apparently not, for his expression showed only slightly raised eyebrows, as he waited for her answer.

"No, thanks. I'll leave everything here until tomorrow and pick up where I left off." Her gaze flicked between him and the box. Molly stepped to the faucet. As she turned off the water and coiled up the hose, her hands shook. She prayed he wouldn't notice.

Performing the methodical tasks helped to stabilize Molly. When she finished, she longed to escape alone into the house, but her manners prompted her to ask, "Would you like to come in for coffee?"

His lips tilted in a half smile, but then they thinned and he shook his head. "I've taken up enough of your time tonight."

Although relieved, she held out a reassuring hand and brushed his arm. "Please don't feel that way. I'm glad you shared your story. I feel bad for you, and for Angie, too. She sounds like a troubled person."

He nodded, his expression still grim. "That's what I've always thought." He held up a finger. "But there's one more thing I need to say."

Molly's gaze darted to the box of ornaments and back again. Before she spoke, she swallowed hard. "What's that?"

"I told you I haven't been able to move on. But, now that I've met you...that might not be true anymore."

Molly's heart beat faster. "But, Steve..."

"There's something between us, Molly. You can't deny your feelings, and neither can I."

"But—" Her thoughts whirled.

Steve placed a hand on her shoulder. "Let's save that discussion for another time, okay?"

Before she had a chance to respond, he turned and walked away.

****

After Steve left, Molly headed for the box of yard ornaments. She picked up a butterfly-shaped one and ran her fingers over the sculptured metal. Up on the bench, the box had caught the last rays of sunshine, and the metal was warm to the touch.

She recalled the day she'd bought the ornament. Three years ago, she, Buck and Karli went to a rodeo in the neighboring town of Forksville. Buck was in high spirits because he'd won the saddle bronc riding division.

Afterward, with Karli in a carrier on Buck's back, they strolled along the row of tents where craftspeople sold their wares. Buck bought a teddy bear for Karli and a pretty green scarf for Molly, which he said matched her eyes.

They came upon a booth full of metal sculptures, many of them yard ornaments on long spikes. There were frogs and birds and squirrels—and butterflies.

"I want one of those," Molly said. "It'd be perfect for my garden."

Buck agreed. They looked over the selections, finally settling on one of the butterflies—the one Molly now held in her hands.

A young woman stepped forward from the back of the tent. Molly remembered thinking how pretty she was with her long, dark hair and large, dark eyes. But what she remembered most was the butterfly and star tattoo on her left wrist, visible when she reached out to take the money Buck handed her.

He said, "Nice tat," or something like that.

A smile lighted the woman's face. "I like butterflies," she said.

"Did you make these?" Molly asked.

The woman nodded.

"Are they in stores anywhere? I might like to buy more."

The woman shook her head. "Right now, only in fairs. We hope to get them in the stores soon, though."

"Do you live around here? Is there somewhere I could contact you?"

An older woman with gray hair tied back with a scarf came to stand stiffly beside the young woman. "We stay near here, sometimes," the older woman said.

Molly was about to ask for more information, but then one of Buck's rodeo pals and his wife and two children joined them. The man slapped Buck on the back and congratulated him on his win. The wife chattered to Molly about their respective children.

By the time Molly could turn back to the young woman in the booth, she was busy with another customer. That was the last Molly saw of the young woman who made the butterfly ornament. A woman she was sure was Angie. She recognized her from the photo Steve had and from the distinctive butterfly and star tattoo on her wrist.

Molly stared at the ornament, wondering what to do. Should she tell Steve? If she did, he might be able to find Angie, at last. Wasn't that what he wanted?

And then what?

Steve believed something was happening between him and Molly, something romantic. Molly had to admit she agreed with him. But if Angie came back into the picture... Steve took his responsibilities seriously. His loyalty and determination to keep his promise to his godparents were qualities she admired.

But, if he found Angie again, he might realize he loved her, after all, and that whatever he felt for Molly wasn't real.

She should tell him what she knew about Angie. That was the honest thing to do. Didn't she pride herself on her honesty? Molly gripped the butterfly until the sharp edges cut into her fingers. She needed to think about this—at least for a couple days.

In the meantime, she'd do some checking around town on her own. If Angie was still in the area, maybe Molly could discover her whereabouts.

She carried the ornament into the kitchen. From the living room came the sounds of the closing music for Karli's TV program. Molly needed to find a place to hide the ornament. She didn't want Karli to see it and to wonder why she was hiding it away, instead of putting it in the garden. Karli was an inquisitive child who didn't miss much, and she would ask.

Finally, Molly chose the broom closet next to the cupboards. She stuck the ornament in the back behind the broom and a mop and other cleaning supplies.

She turned her attention to story time and tucking Karli into bed and kissing her goodnight. As she performed their nightly ritual, she couldn't shake the heavy cloak of guilt that now lay on her shoulders.

Chapter Fifteen

After that night, Molly didn't know what to expect from Steve. Given his statement that "something was happening between them," she figured he'd want to spend more time together.

However, the following two days passed without a word from him. He didn't show up at the bakery office, and he didn't come to her house.

That night at dinner, Karli asked, "Mommy, where's Steve?"

Molly cut off a piece of her chicken drumstick and speared the meat with her fork. "He's still staying with Sara and Jackson. They're probably eating dinner, like we are."

"When will he come visit us?"

Molly chewed and swallowed. "I don't know. He's busy with his work. How about some more beans?" She nodded to the bowl of lima beans in the center of the table.

"Nuh uh." With a shake of her head, Karli held her hand over her plate. "But he came when I was sick."

"I know, but you're well now."

"But when is he gonna come and see us?" Karli stuck out her chin.

Molly put down her fork. Now might be a good time to remind Karli that Steve would soon be leaving Red Rock. "I can't answer your question. But, remember, Steve doesn't live here on the ranch, like we do. He's only visiting. He'll be leaving soon and going back to his home in New York City. Then we won't see him any more. Now, please, darlin', eat your dinner."

Karli wouldn't give up and talked about Steve all through the meal.

Each mention of his name stabbed Molly in the heart. Finally, in desperation, she said, "We might see him this Sunday."

Karli's face broke into a smile. "He's coming here?"

"No. Sara and Jackson are having a barbecue at their house, and everyone from the ranch is invited."

"Like a party?"

"Yes. But, remember I said, *maybe* Steve will be there. He might have something else to do that day."

Karli's smile lingered, and she said no more about him.

Molly worried that she shouldn't have raised Karli's hopes about seeing Steve. She had to admit she yearned to see him again, too. If he wasn't at the barbecue, after all, then both she and Karli would be disappointed.

****

On Sunday afternoon, a bright, hot, sunny day, Molly and Karli headed down the road to the Jacksons' for the barbecue. A wave of nostalgia rolled over Molly. She and Buck had always enjoyed attending the parties Jackson and Sara gave for their ranch employees. This would be the first one without him at her side.

Molly gripped Karli's hand tighter. "It's just you and me now," she whispered.

Marrying Molly

"What, Mommy?"

"I said, 'It's a nice day for a party.'"

"It is. And I want to hurry and get there." Karli skipped ahead, tugging Molly along.

The party was already underway when they arrived. Smoke rose from the backyard barbecue pit, where Jackson stood over sizzling steaks, hot dogs, and foil-wrapped corn on the cob. The tantalizing aroma of the cooking food filled the air.

On the other side of the lawn, a five-piece band made up of the ranch hands played a fast polka. Several guests stood nearby clapping their hands to the music's beat, while others strolled the grounds sipping drinks and munching hors d'oeuvres.

Molly and Karli greeted Sara and Jackson, Teresa and her husband, and some of the others. All the while, Molly covertly scanned the crowd looking for Steve. For Karli's sake, she told herself.

She didn't see him, and a twinge of sadness pinched her chest. However, she did spot Jackson's horse trainer, Dirk Lamont.

He caught her eye, flashed a wide smile, and headed across the lawn. "Hey, Molly, Karli. How're you two doin'?" He tipped his cowboy hat and gazed down at them with his bright blue eyes.

Molly returned his smile. "We're good, thanks. Busy at the bakery. Karli's back at Teresa's." She swung her daughter's hand.

"Right. Heard she was under the weather and glad she's better. Sara treatin' you okay?"

"She's the best."

Dirk shifted from one booted foot to the other and cleared his throat. "Ah, I've been thinkin' maybe you'd like to go into town sometime, take in a movie?"

Molly blinked. Dirk was asking her for a date. Yet when she thought about his request, why was she surprised? Over the past week or so, he'd stopped in the bakery office several times to chat.

Why not go out with him? She and Buck often went into Red Rock to the cozy movie house for a night out. And Dirk appeared to be a nice enough guy.

"Well, I..." Over Dirk's shoulder, Molly caught sight of Steve stepping out the back door of the house. Her heart rocketed against her ribcage.

Steve hesitated on the top step of the porch, looking over the crowd.

Their gazes collided. Even though a distance separated them, Molly felt a connection. Time froze. Voices and music faded into the background.

Then he smiled and lifted his left hand in a salute.

Feeling warm inside, she smiled and returned his wave.

"Steve!" Karli broke away from Molly and ran to him.

"Molly?"

Dirk's voice jolted Molly. She offered an apologetic smile. "Sorry, Dirk. I...what were you saying?"

His gaze flicked from her to Steve, and a tight smile crossed his lips. "Some other time, then." He tipped his hat and turned to leave.

"Yes, some other time," she said to his retreating back.

Molly spun to see Steve lean down and put his arm around Karli's shoulders. She beamed and snuggled against him, and Molly's heart turned over.

Steve disengaged himself from Karli and straightened. Locking gazes with Molly and taking Karli by the hand, he headed toward her.

"I wondered if you'd be here today," Molly said when the two reached her side.

"Can't miss one of Jackson's famous barbecues. But were you and Dirk..." He nodded in Dirk's direction.

Molly heard the question in Steve's voice. "We were only saying hello. I was about to take Karli to play with the other kids." She gestured to a corner of the yard where Teresa's teenage helper, Jasmine, coached the children in a game of dodge ball.

"I wanta stay here." Karli shook her head and swung her and Steve's clasped hands.

"We'll all go over." Steve smiled down at Karli. "You can join the game while I talk to your mom."

He cast Molly a meaningful glance over Karli's head.

Molly's nerve endings tingled. What did he want to talk about? More about Angie? Or about what might be happening between the two of them?

At the dodge ball game, Jasmine waved Karli into the group. After Molly and Steve watched the children play for a few minutes, Steve motioned to the picnic table holding the drinks. "How about a glass of cider?"

"I'd love one." She hadn't had anything to drink yet, and some refreshment would be welcome.

Steve filled a couple glasses with the cider, and they began a stroll around the yard. Molly sipped her drink, savoring the sweet taste. She cast Steve a covert glance, wondering when he would tell her what was on his mind.

Finally, he spoke. "I wanted to tell you why I haven't contacted you for the past few days."

Although she'd been anxious to know, she gave a careless shrug. "I figured you were busy."

"Yeah, I have been. But I've been worried I told you too much about myself. Why would you want to get involved with me and all my baggage?"

Molly thought of the butterfly ornament hidden away in the broom closet. *I'm more involved than you know.*

"I'm glad you told me, Steve. I don't think any less of you. In fact, I admire you for wanting to keep your promise to your godparents."

"Thanks, Molly. Your opinion means a lot." He looked down at his cider glass, swirling the remaining contents, and then met her gaze. "Should I disappear now?"

"Oh, no... I mean, unless you want to."

"I don't. I'd rather hang out with you and Karli."

"She'll love that." *And so will I.*

As they exchanged smiles, warmth spiraled through Molly. Perhaps this party would be fun, after all.

On the way back to the dodge ball game, Molly promised herself she *would* tell him about the ornament. But now wasn't the time. Now, they would enjoy the barbecue.

When Jackson announced dinner was ready, Molly, Steve, and Karli joined the buffet line. Molly dished up barbecued chicken for herself and Karli. Steve filled his plate, too, and led them to one of the picnic tables.

After they were settled and had spoken to the others seated nearby, Steve turned to Karli, who sat between him and Molly. "So, you're all better now?"

"I am." Karli sipped her chocolate milk through a straw.

"And you're back at Teresa's?"

"Yep. And you promised me a surprise when I got better."

A startled look crossed Steve's face.

He cleared his throat. "You're right, I did. I forgot."

"Don't worry about it." Molly buttered a roll and set it on Karli's plate.

Steve held up a hand. "No, I can't go back on my promise, can I?"

"No." Karli bounced up and down in her seat. "So what is the surprise?"

For a moment, his brow wrinkled then his eyes brightened, and he snapped his fingers. "How'd you like to ride a horse again?"

Molly's stomach tightened. How could he suggest horseback riding, of all things, without checking first with her? "Oh, no, we're not ready for that."

"This is a different kind of horse." Steve stabbed a slice of barbecued chicken with his fork and popped it in his mouth.

"Different, how?" Karli's brow puckered.

"When we go to Funland, you'll find out. That's part of the surprise."

Molly's tension eased. Funland was a theme park near Denver. Steve must be talking about riding a fake horse rather than a real one. Still, she wished he'd consulted her before revealing his surprise to Karli.

Steve met Molly's gaze over Karli's head. "But, like always, we have to check with your mom. What do you say, Molly?"

Karli turned to Molly. "Say 'yes,' Mommy, say 'yes.'" Molly idly smoothed her napkin on her lap. Despite the nature of the outing, and despite being together today, she still worried that spending too much time with Steve wasn't good for Karli. He was not someone permanent in their lives. Still, saying "no" would send a bad message about keeping promises.

She looked up and forced a smile. "Well, a promise is a promise, so I guess we'll have to help Steve keep his."

****

Saturday morning, Molly and Karli walked to the main house to meet Steve for their outing. When he came to the door, Molly noticed his sling was missing.

"Your arm." Molly pressed her hand to her chest.

"All well." Steve held up his arm and flexed his wrist. "I went to see Mike yesterday. He took off the sling and said I can start using my arm again. He wants me to have physical therapy, though, which I will start Monday."

"You went into town?" *Without me?*

Steve stepped out the door and onto the porch. "Yeah, I hitched a ride with Jackson. He had to meet one of his buyers. But today I'm behind the wheel." He pointed his thumb at his chest.

"You didn't like my driving," Molly said, as she and Karli followed Steve down the porch steps to his rental car.

He tossed a grin over his shoulder. "Your driving was fine. But I never realized how much you lose when you can't drive. So, Karli, we're both well now. What do you think of that?"

Karli jumped from the last step onto the path. "Do I still have to sit in the back seat?"

Steve laughed. "'Fraid so. That's where you're the safest, no matter who's driving."

They soon were on their way. As they drove along the freeway, Molly's thoughts drifted. She was glad Steve had regained his independence, but now he'd move back to the hotel. And then he'd leave Red Rock and return to New York. She glanced at him as he talked over his shoulder to Karli.

"...Maybe your mom knows the answer," he was saying.

"Do you, Mommy?"

Molly snapped to attention. "Hmm? What?"

"You've been off somewhere," Steve said. "Penny."

"I was thinking what a nice day it is." She gestured toward the window, glancing out at the clear, sunny sky, with only a few lazy clouds drifting over the mountain peaks. "What were you two talking about?"

"Horses."

Molly sighed. "Karli's favorite subject—next to you."

"Me?" Eyebrows raised, Steve thumbed his chest.

"Yes, that's all she's talked about all week—you and this trip. What about horses?"

"She wants to know why they have four legs, instead of two, like we have."

"Oh, boy, that's a good one." She turned so that she could better talk to Karli. "Maybe they have four legs so they can run fast."

"I already told her that one." Steve chuckled.

Molly threw up her hands. "Well, there you go. Is

that a good enough reason, honey?"

Karli's brow knitted. "I think it's so they have a back you can sit on."

"You would think of that reason," Molly said, and they all laughed.

****

Half an hour later, after parking the car in a lot and paying the admission, they walked through the turnstile to Funland. Molly gazed around. Several paths led in different directions. The hum of the various rides floated on the air, along with the aromas of hot dogs and popcorn.

"What do you want to do first?" Steve bent over and asked Karli.

"Ride the horses," Karli said without hesitation.

Steve laughed. "I shoulda known. But remember, I told you the horses we'll ride here are different than the horses on the ranch."

"Different?" Karli wrinkled her nose.

"You'll see." Steve ran a forefinger over the map they'd been given at the gate. "Okay, I know where we want to go." He pointed to one of the paths.

Steve led them along that path awhile, and then another, winding their way farther into the park.

They finally stopped in front of the merry-go-round, where Molly had guessed they were headed. She glanced at Karli expecting to see a frown rather than a smile, once she realized the horses were wooden instead of real.

But Karli clapped her hands and jumped up and down with apparent delight.

They joined the line and soon climbed on the platform for the next ride. Karli picked out her horse, painted a bright yellow with a red and blue bridle, and Steve helped her to mount. Molly positioned herself by Karli, while Steve chose a black horse nearby. The music began, and the merry-go-round started, slowly at first, and then faster and faster.

"Hang on, darlin'." Molly kept her hand firmly at Karli's back.

"I'm fine, Mommy."

Karli and Steve laughed at each other gliding up and down at opposite times. Finally, Molly let herself relax and join in the laughter, too.

After a couple more rides, Karli agreed she'd had enough, and they left the merry-go-round.

"We might as well hang around for a while," Steve said, and led them down another path.

"I want to ride in those little cars." Karli pointed to the bumper car track.

Worry shot through Molly, and she shook her head. "You're way too young."

"They wouldn't let you drive one, Karli," Steve agreed, "but you could ride in one with me."

Molly scrunched her brows into an "are-you-insane?" look.

"Yes. Yes." Karli jumped up and down. "Please, Mommy."

The cars lurched around the track like big bugs. Several of them included a child passenger. Everyone appeared to be having fun, laughing and shouting as they rammed each other's cars.

Molly sighed. "All right." She stood at the fence watching Steve and Karli in their little red bug, as they bumped and thumped around the track. Once when they passed by, she waved, and they waved back.

At last, they returned to her side, and she blew out a sigh of relief. But the sight of Karli's flushed face prompted Molly to place a hand on her forehead. "Are you okay, honey?"

"I had fun." Karli clapped her hands.

"She was a good bumper," Steve added.

Molly hoped that would be the end of the rides, but they'd no sooner started down the pathway again when Karli pointed a finger and said, "I want to ride that one."

Karli's choice this time was a long pole with a bullet-shaped compartment on either end that turned around and around like the hands on a clock.

Steve nodded toward the ride's boldly lettered sign. "Ah, the Rocket Space Ship."

Molly's chest tightened. She stopped and hugged her arms. "No. Absolutely not."

Steve stuck his hands in his slacks pockets. "I'll have to agree with your mom. Besides, there are rules about how big a person has to be to take some of the rides, and I'm betting you wouldn't pass the test for this one. Look, there's the sign that tells how tall you need to be." He pointed to a square sign near the ride's ticket booth.

Molly followed Steve's direction, and her tension eased. Here was a way out from an authority higher than hers. "Steve's right, honey. The sign says you need to be forty-eight inches tall."

"Aren't I that tall?" Karli stood straight.

"No. Don't you remember Dr. Mike's nurse measuring you when we visited him?"

"Nuh uh." Karli shook her head.

"Well, she did, and you're forty inches. You need

eight more to be able to ride the Rocket Space Ship."

Karli stared at the ground and poked out her lower lip.

"Wait until you're older." Steve patted Karli's shoulder.

Karli looked up, squinting against the bright sunlight. "Why don't you go on the ride, Steve? You're tall enough."

Steve laughed and rubbed his jaw. "I just might. Looks like fun." He turned to Molly. "What's wrong, Molly?"

He must have seen the stricken look she knew was on her face. She'd thought that with Karli being disqualified the danger had passed, but now a new fear loomed. "N-nothing." She glanced away and bit her lip. "It's just, I'm not good with dangerous rides—for anyone."

"This one's not dangerous—"

Blood pumping double time, Molly straightened and propped her hands on her hips. "I bet it is. I've read about horrible accidents on these kinds of rides. Why do you want to take unnecessary risks? You're just like—" Molly clamped her jaw shut. She'd almost said, "You're just like Buck," but stopped herself in time.

The comparison was true, though. Buck would've been on the Rocket Space Ship as soon as he saw it, never mind what Molly thought.

"Hey, calm down." Steve laid a hand on her arm.

She jerked away. "We should go now."

"Why? There's other fun stuff we can do. You don't want to go home yet, do you, Karli?"

"No." Karli shook her head so hard her hair stuck straight out.

"All right, come on." He grabbed Karli's hand and reached out to Molly.

For several seconds, she stared at his hand while her stomach churned. Then she held out her hand and let his fingers close over hers.

Chapter Sixteen

Later that evening, Molly tucked Karli into bed, and then returned to the living room where Steve waited. Her mood still sour over the Rocket Space Ship ride, she had wanted him to drop them off and leave. But he lingered, and she hadn't been brave enough—or rude enough—to suggest he return to the Phillips'.

Her gaze roved over the array of prizes they'd won at Funland, which he'd arranged on the sofa. They included a stuffed dog with a big red bow and a lapping tongue; a puppet monkey, now tangled in its strings; and a set of colored juggling balls. She smiled to herself. Karli would have fun sharing the toys at daycare.

She swung her gaze to Steve, who stood by the door. Tension lines bracketed his mouth, and his raised eyebrows asked, "Should I go? Or stay?"

Molly hesitated then gave a resigned sigh. "Would you like coffee? Or a drink? I have some wine."

The tension lines disappeared, and his lips broke into a soft smile. "Coffee would hit the spot."

They took their mugs of coffee out to the porch. She sat in the swing while he chose a nearby chair. Only a few feet separated them, but the distance might as well have been miles. She sipped her coffee, wondering if she should apologize for her behavior that afternoon.

Steve broke the silence. "Penny."

"You're always asking me that."

"When you're quiet and thoughtful, I'm interested in what's going on in that head of yours. That pretty head," he added with a grin.

Molly sucked in a breath. "I was thinking about this afternoon, and that I had no right to tell you not to ride that rocket thing."

"The Rocket Space Ship."

"Whatever."

"So, why did you?"

"I was thinking of Buck..."

He tipped back his head. "Ah, I thought maybe that was the case."

Molly pressed her foot on the floor, setting the swing in motion. "And how he always loved to take risks. The more danger, the better."

"The more danger, the more thrill, maybe?"

"I guess. But every time he put his life in danger, I went through hell." Her fingers tightened on the mug. "I thought that if he really, truly loved us, he wouldn't have taken up rodeo, especially. He would've wanted to make sure he was safe, make sure he lived..."

Steve leaned forward. "But would *not* riding in rodeo have made sure?"

Molly waved a hand in the air. "Oh, I know you're going to say that he could've died crossing the street, or from an illness. But why increase the risk?"

"I can't answer that, for him."

"Then how about answering for you? You said you thought there was something between us, and, well, maybe I think so, too. When you were about to go on that ride today, I thought, I can't go through this kind of torture again, worrying about the person I—worrying about someone I care for." She'd been about to say, "the person I love," but this was too soon in their relationship to speak of love. Even if love might be what she was feeling.

Steve rose and sat on the swing beside her. He slipped his arm around her shoulders and drew her close.

Warmth radiated from his body to hers. Her pulse quickened.

"I can't answer for myself, either," he said, caressing her shoulder. "At least, not right now. I'll have to think about what you've said. Did you ever tell Buck how you felt?"

"Oh, he knew, all right." She lifted a shoulder. "But he'd only make a joke or change the subject. Nothing I said made him change his behavior."

"And should he have changed his behavior?"

She twisted her head to slant him a glance. "What do you mean?"

"I'm wondering how much we should expect people to change because we want them to." With a shake of his head, he shrugged. "I don't know. Like I said, I'll have to think about what you've said. But maybe you don't want to see me anymore..." He tightened his grip on her shoulder.

"How much more can there be?" Her tone sharpened. "You're going away soon."

"True, I do have to go back to New York."

"And what about Angie? What if you somehow found her again? Would you try to make her come back to you? Maybe you'd realize you love her, after all."

"No, I don't think so."

He didn't think so. Not very reassuring.

Molly thought of the butterfly ornament tucked away in the broom closet. *Why don't you bring out the ornament and show it to him? Tell him the story of Angie. Let him find her. Then you'd know for sure what he would do.*

Molly pushed away the voice. Sick inside, she twisted her fingers together in her lap.

Steve gently separated her locked fingers. "Molly, honey, please, can't you relax?"

Although his touch was comforting, she shook her head. "Everything boils up inside. I'm sorry. You were so kind to treat Karli today, and I ruined our time together."

"You didn't ruin the outing for her, or for me. I think you ruined it for yourself, though."

"I couldn't help speaking out. That's the way I am. Anyway, I feel there's a big wall between us."

"We do have some challenges—but maybe this will help." He cupped her chin and guided her face to his.

The air suddenly stilled, and she couldn't breathe.

His lips softly touched hers, as though he weren't sure of her response. But when Molly parted her lips, he deepened the kiss. Heat spiraled through her. She melted into him, breathing his breath, tasting him, wanting to devour him.

This was what she needed. To be held, to be kissed.

When they finally broke apart, they both were breathless.

"Do you still feel there's a wall between us?" he asked, his breath warm in her ear.

"Not so much," she said in a playful tone.

He laughed and drew her close. She rested her head on his shoulder, and they sat in comfortable silence.

"Talking about today helped," she said.

"Yeah, it did. Tell me what you liked about today, why don't you?"

"The clown who painted the flower on Karli's cheek was funny. And riding that little train through the park was a good tour."

"Karli sure got a thrill when the conductor let her ring the bell, didn't she?"

They shared a few more stories then fell silent again. Molly gazed out at the landscape. Moonlight beamed from a clear, star-scattered sky, while a light breeze rustled through the aspens. Beyond were the ever-present mountains, on guard, as always. She let out a long sigh.

"Hey, was that a sigh that said, 'I wish he'd leave?'" Steve leaned forward and slanted her a look.

"No, one that says, 'I feel pretty good right now.'"

"Me, too. But I really do need to be on my way." He eased his arm from around her shoulders.

Suddenly cold, she shivered and hugged her arms. "Will you be around tomorrow?"

"For a while. Then I'm moving back to the hotel."

"Oh." The word came out so forlorn-sounding that Molly hastily added, "I mean, that's great you can be on your own again."

"Right. But I plan to spend all my spare time right here—if you agree."

"I do want to spend time with you. But how many days more will there be, do you think?"

He ran a finger down her cheek and across her lips. "I don't know. I should be hearing about the Harwell account soon."

Molly's shoulders slumped. "And then you'll go back to New York."

"True, I can't stay away too much longer. But don't worry about that right now, okay? One day at a time."

A few minutes later, watching his car disappear down the road and listening to the hum of the engine fade away, Molly wondered if she'd made the right decision to keep seeing Steve. Sure, the kisses and caresses they'd shared were wonderful, but a relationship needed more than physical attraction. A relationship needed time to develop and grow. They didn't have that time.

Plus, like a ghost, Angie haunted him. Although he was divorced, Steve might not be ready to move on from his relationship with his ex-wife. Even if he were ready, could Molly move on from her loss? Sometimes, she still cried herself to sleep, thinking of Buck and the life they'd had together.

She rose and went inside. Her gaze traveled to the photos on the mantel. She walked over and picked up the one of their wedding day. "What should I do, Buck?" Molly whispered. "I'm falling in love with Steve. Is that okay with you?" She half-expected the photo-Buck to give her an answer.

He didn't. He continued to gaze into the eyes of his bride, frozen there for eternity.

****

On Monday, Steve was working at the round table in his hotel room when Mr. Harwell phoned.

"I have good news for you," Harwell said. "We've decided to purchase your program.

"That's great." Steve fisted his hand and pumped the air.

"I'd like to have the training session as soon as possible, before you get too busy with the referrals I've made to our associates."

"Thanks, Mr. Harwell. I appreciate that."

Steve consulted his schedule, and they settled on a time for the training session. He punched off the call, thrust out his chest, and gave a loud "whoop." The trip to Colorado had been very profitable indeed. And the referrals, assuming they panned out, would give him a legitimate reason to extend his stay.

Nerves tingling with excitement, Steve stood and stretched his legs. He needed to call Jerry with the news. And Molly, too. Molly first. He picked up his phone again but it rang before he could make the call.

"Hey, man," Jerry said on the other end.

"I was about to call you." Steve told Jerry about landing the Harwell sale.

"Good news. You'll be coming home, then?"

"Not right away. There's the training class, plus Harwell gave me some referrals I want to follow up."

"Hmmm, that will also give you more time with the lady you met."

Steve chuckled at Jerry's sly tone. "Yes, I plan to spend more time with her. But, hey, you're the one who told me I should move on."

"You got me there. But I was hoping you'd find someone closer to home."

Home. A sudden ache filled Steve's chest. He missed New York, his apartment on the Upper East Side, the house he still owned in Westchester, his friends, his hangouts. Most of all, he missed going into the office every day and working. Work was his life, his reason for being.

But now there was Molly. And Karli. Where did they fit into his life? How did he fit into theirs?

"Steve, ya there?"

"Yeah, yeah, Jerry. I'll be coming home...soon."

Steve hung up and idly stared out the window at the distant mountains. Okay, the training class and the referrals gave him a legitimate reason to hang around. But after he dealt with those, he *should* go home. He had a business to run. Staying away much longer wasn't fair to Jerry and the rest of his staff.

Molly's image popped into his mind, as it always did when he thought about leaving. He was torn in two. One part wanted to stay and the other wanted to go home. Would he ever resolve this dilemma?

He'd told Molly they should take "one day at a time." He'd do well to follow his own advice. He picked up the phone to call her and tell her his news.

****

Molly sat at her desk in the bakery's office, working on invoices. Sara had gone into town, and Lupe and Doreen were at work in the kitchen. Bits of their conversation drifted into the office, along with the enticing aroma of chocolate chip cookies.

Checking the numbers on one of the invoices, Molly found she'd made a mistake. She deleted the error and filled in the correct number. Keeping her mind on her work today proved difficult. She kept thinking of Steve and wondering if he'd heard about the Harwell account yet. As soon as that was settled, there'd be no more reason for him to stay in Red Rock.

His leaving was for the best. Then she and Karli

could get on with their lives. They would be happy. And if someone came along who fit into their lifestyle, there might be three of them again. A real family.

That was what she kept telling herself. She just wished she could make herself believe it. She wished she didn't have this emptiness inside, this terrible sense of loss.

Time for her afternoon break rolled around. A walk outside in the fresh air might help to lift her spirits. She was heading for the door when the phone on her desk rang. She turned and stared at the phone, debating whether to answer or to let the call go to voice mail.

The call might be important, though, so she hurried back to the desk and snatched up the receiver. "Rolling R Bakery."

"Molly?"

At the familiar sound of Steve's voice, Molly's heart beat faster, yet she made herself say calmly, "Hello, Steve."

"I've got good news. Harwell gave us the account."

"Oh, that's wonderful." Her voice dropped a notch. "But then you'll be..."

"Leaving? No, I'll be conducting a training class, and he's given me some referrals to follow up on. So I won't be leaving right away."

"That is good news." *I guess. Oh, why couldn't she decide what she wanted?*

"Are you free tonight? If so, I'll pick you up and we'll go out to dinner, just the two of us."

Molly briefly closed her eyes and breathed a deep sigh. Time alone with Steve would be heaven. "Yes, I'm free tonight."

"Can you make arrangements for Karli?"

"I'm sure she can stay with Sara and Jackson."

"Great. See you about six, then?"

Molly hung up, her head spinning. Steve got the Harwell account—for which she was truly glad—and he wasn't returning to New York right away, after all. Business would keep him here awhile longer. They were going out tonight—on a date. Just the two of them.

When Sara returned, Molly told her the news.

"That's wonderful, Molly." Sara clapped her hands. "I've thought all along you two had made a connection. And don't worry about Karli. She can stay at our place this evening."

Molly gave Sara a hug. "You are my best friend, you know that?"

"And you are mine, too. Now, go get ready."

Chapter Seventeen

Later, at the ranch house, every nerve in her body tingling, Molly glued her gaze to the living room window, waiting for Steve to arrive.

Karli danced around her, waving Mr. Muggins and declaring, "Steve's coming. Steve's coming."

At last, Steve's car rumbled up the driveway. Not able to wait a second longer, Molly ran out the door and down the front porch steps to meet him. He pulled the car to a stop and leaped out. For a moment, she thought they were going to fall into each other's arms. She wanted to; but, suddenly shy, she stopped and instead gave him a tentative, "Hello, Steve."

"Hello, Molly."

His eyes were soft and tender as his gaze met hers.

"Can you come in a minute?" She gestured toward the house. "Karli would never forgive me if we left without your saying hello."

"Of course." He pocketed his keys and headed up the walk.

Excitement fueling her moves, she led him into the house, and for the next few minutes, she shared him with the others. Steve hugged Karli and Sara and shook hands with Jackson. Sara and Jackson congratulated him on landing the Harwell account and on the prospects for more business. All the while, Molly longed to have her own touch or hug, but told herself her time would come when they were alone.

Finally, she and Steve were on their way to Red Rock. Once there, he drove to The Cactus Flower, a restaurant tucked away in Old Town. The menu featured Mexican food, which they discovered they both liked.

While they ate, they talked about books they'd read, music they enjoyed, places they'd been. Molly was pleased to discover they both shared the same favorite mystery author and were following the career of a country western singer who'd crossed over to mainstream. Steve had traveled more than she, but they both had been to Hawaii.

After they left the restaurant, they strolled hand-in-hand along the streets bathed in a rich gold from the setting sun. They window-shopped antique stores, gift shops, clothing stores, and even popped into a bookstore, where Steve bought a book on local history and helped her to pick out a new bedtime story for Karli.

Eventually, they returned to his car and began the drive back to the Rolling R. Molly settled back in the seat, gazing out the window as they sped along the highway. Had the sky ever been so clear? The stars so bright?

When they reached the ranch and Steve had parked in front of the house, he shut off the engine and looked at her with solemn eyes.

"I don't want this evening to end," he said, and so they stayed in the car, talking, kissing, and then talking again, sharing thoughts and feelings.

They finally went inside and picked up Karli, who only mumbled a little and fluttered her eyelids as Steve carried her out to the car. They drove on to Molly and Karli's house, where together they tucked Karli into her bed. They were almost like a family, Molly thought.

And then, with a last, long and heated kiss, he was gone.

Molly undressed and put on her nightgown in a daze. What had happened? This morning, with the prospect of Steve's departure, her life looked bleak. Now, they'd been given more time together. What a miracle.

The next couple of weeks were full ones for Molly. She worked all day, as usual, but the nights were for Steve. He came to dinner at her house, or they went out to dinner, casual places where they could take Karli. They went horseback riding again, on real horses this time, much to Karli's delight. The ride proceeded smoothly and with no mishaps, even when they ventured along the path beside the river. On Sunday, they joined Jackson, Sara, and Ryan, and Mike and Rose for dinner.

Molly was happier than she'd been in a long time. More than once, she stopped to pinch herself to make sure she wasn't dreaming.

****

Steve sat at the counter in the hotel's coffee shop. He'd finished his breakfast of bacon and eggs and was on his second cup of coffee. Other customers came and went, and western music played in the background, but he barely noticed. His thoughts centered on Molly. They'd had a very good couple of weeks. And, he'd been right. Feelings did exist between them, feelings that had grown during the time they'd spent together.

For the first time in his life, he was in love, truly in

love. Molly loved him, too. They hadn't actually said the words, but he felt the emotion each time they were together.

Steve pasted a smile on his face. He was ready to move on, at last. And in a big way.

The waitress came by with the coffee carafe. She filled his cup then glanced up. "You're lookin' happy today. You win the lottery?"

"Better than that. I'm gonna get married."

"Married? Good for you. She's one lucky gal. If I weren't already taken, I'd give her some competition." She winked. "You pop the question yet?"

"Ah, not yet. But soon."

"Well, good luck." She smiled and moved off.

Steve sipped his coffee, his head spinning with plans. He was sure Molly would say "yes" to his proposal. They'd be married as soon as possible, and she and Karli would return to New York with him. True, Molly had said she loved ranch life, but he suspected she'd returned to the Rolling R mainly because she wanted to keep Buck's memory alive for Karli. Once Molly saw Steve's house in Westchester and had been introduced to his lifestyle, she'd forget all about the ranch. They'd have a wonderful life.

Steve left the restaurant with a new spring in his step. The future looked brighter than it had in a long, long time.

****

"Would you like more chicken, Steve?" Molly held out the plate of stewed chicken and dumplings she'd prepared for dinner. Instead of going out tonight, they were spending a quiet evening at home. When Steve mentioned chicken and dumplings were his favorites,

Molly dug out her cookbook and found a recipe.

Steve held up his hand. "Wish I could, Molly, but I'm stuffed."

She turned to Karli. "How 'bout you, darlin'?"

"I'm stuffed, too, Mommy." Karli patted her stomach.

Molly raised her eyebrows. "Both of you stuffed, hmmm? Guess we'll have to save the ice cream for some other time."

"No, no, Mommy." Karli shook her head.

Steve chimed in. "We always save room for dessert, don't we, Karli?"

"We do." Karli bounced up and down in her chair.

"Well...all right." Molly drew out the words, as though reluctant to give in. "Why don't we have our dessert outside on the back porch?"

"Good idea." Steve folded his napkin and laid it beside his plate. "We'll help you clear the table first. Right, Karli?"

Karli grabbed her plate by the edges. "I can carry mine."

"Good girl. You're a big helper."

After they cleared the table, Steve took Karli outside to the back porch. Molly followed a few minutes later with a tray of the ice cream. She'd chosen strawberry, which had turned out to be both Karli's and Steve's favorite.

Molly and Steve sat in wicker chairs, while Karli settled into her child-size wooden rocker. The air was warm, yet soft, the sky glowing pink over the mountains. A gentle breeze tinkled the wind chimes hanging from the porch ceiling.

Molly took a spoonful of ice cream and let it melt

in her mouth. Yum. Maybe strawberry would be her favorite, too. She glanced at Steve. He was gazing her way, his eyes dark and serious. "What?"

"I, ah, your garden looks good, doesn't it?" He made a sweeping gesture toward the rows of colorful flowers.

She suspected that wasn't what he had intended to say. He'd seemed preoccupied since his arrival, as though something special were on his mind.

Instead of probing, Molly chose to wait and see what, if anything, developed. "Yes, I'm pleased with the garden."

"The yard ornaments really add a lot," Steve continued.

"I like the frog." Karli pointed to the bullfrog sitting on a lily pad.

Steve tilted his head. "Where'd you get all these?"

"Oh, here and there."

Molly thought of the butterfly ornament hidden away in the kitchen's broom closet, and a lump rose in her throat. When was she going to tell him what she knew about Angie? She'd had several opportunities during the past few weeks to bring up the subject, but each time, fear of the consequences made her back off. Yet, each missed opportunity added another layer of guilt to her burden.

Molly scooped up another bite of ice cream, but now the creamy treat tasted sour. Her appetite gone, she let the rest melt in her dish. "Guess I better clean up the kitchen."

"Do you have to right now?" Steve frowned. "It's nice sitting out here, and I hoped we could talk."

The emphasis on "talk" prompted her to abandon

her silence and issue a challenge. "Something on your mind?"

Steve tapped his fingers on the arm of his chair. "Maybe."

Maybe? What did that mean? Then realization dawned. He planned to tell her he'd set a date for his return to New York. Not something she wanted to hear.

Finished with her ice cream, Karli licked her spoon. "Can we play a game, Steve?"

"Sure, but later, after I talk to your mom."

Molly dragged her attention away from Steve's perplexing behavior to check her wristwatch. "Your Mr. Muggins program is on in a few minutes."

"Yay." Karli jumped from her chair.

Molly stood. "We'll all go inside. We can talk in the kitchen, Steve." *At least, there I'll be doing something, rather than sitting passively and listening to your plans to leave us.*

Steve nodded and pushed to his feet. "Okay, I'll get Karli settled with the TV then join you."

In the kitchen, her nerves jumping, Molly began putting away the leftovers. Mr. Muggins' familiar theme song drifted in from the living room.

After a few minutes, Steve appeared. "Okay, here I am," he announced, rubbing his hands together. "What can I do?"

Molly looked up from wrapping the rolls in foil. "Why don't you load the dishwasher?"

"I'm on it." Steve stepped to the sink.

They worked in silence for a few minutes then Steve cleared his throat. "We've had a great couple of weeks, haven't we?"

"I've enjoyed your company," Molly hedged, and

placed the bowl of chicken in the refrigerator.

"We make a good team."

Her hand waved a circle, indicating the room. "If you mean right now, then I agree."

A slight laugh escaped his lips. "No, more than a clean-up team. And, well, there's something I want to say. I'm not sure this is the right time, but—" He bent to tuck the ice cream dishes into the dishwasher.

Oh, oh, here came his news. Molly picked up a skillet and held it under the faucet's running water. Her hand shook and some of the water splashed onto the counter.

Steve straightened and looked at her with furrowed brows. "Are you okay?"

"Yes, I'm fine." *No, I'm not fine. I don't want to hear about your leaving.*

She handed him the skillet then grabbed a paper towel, intending to wipe the counter. Her elbow hit a dish filled with flour, knocking it to the floor. The bowl shattered, and the flour sprayed the floor.

"Oh, for heaven's sake." Frowning at her clumsiness, she stared at the mess.

Steve jumped to her side. "I'll clean it up. Your broom's in there, right?" He pointed to the small closet at the end of the counter.

The broom closet. Molly's throat closed. The butterfly ornament was hidden there. What if he found it? No, she couldn't let that happen. She lurched forward, arm outstretched. "I'll get it."

But he had already reached the closet door.

Molly's heart thumped as though it would leap from her chest. She couldn't remember the last time she'd looked in the closet, and whether or not the ornament was still well hidden. She offered up a quick prayer that it was.

Steve opened the closet and ducked his head inside.

Squeezing her eyes shut, Molly held her breath while empty paper sacks and newspapers rustled, and broom and mop handles banged against the closet wall.

"Here it is," Steve said, his voice muffled. "Whoa, what's this?"

A sinking feeling hit the pit of Molly's stomach. She opened her eyes and drew a breath as Steve emerged from the closet. In one hand, he held the broom. In the other, as she had feared, was Angie's butterfly ornament.

"Here's a yard ornament you forgot to put in the garden." As he held out the butterfly, his eyes widened. "Wait a minute, this is one of Angie's."

Molly's shoulders sagged. If only she hadn't been so clumsy... If only he hadn't insisted on helping her clean up... If only she'd hidden the ornament somewhere else...

"Molly?" Steve waved the ornament like a flag. "Why is this in your broom closet? Where'd you get it? After all I've told you about Angie and her butterflies, didn't you know this was hers? What's going on?" The questions poured out like floodwater released from a dam.

Molly swallowed hard but couldn't dislodge the huge lump in her throat. Unable to meet his gaze, she looked away. "I—I was going to tell you."

"So, you did know this was hers."

His accusatory tone made her cringe. She nodded, misery creeping into every pore in her body.

He leaned the broom against the counter and, still

gripping the butterfly, folded his arms. "So, exactly when were you going to tell me?"

"S-soon. I—I was afraid to ruin the good time we were having."

"You were going to tell me when we were *not* having a good time? That doesn't make much sense."

Nausea bubbled up from Molly's stomach, as though not only the ice cream but also her entire meal had curdled. From the living room came the sounds of Karli's giggles mixed with canned laughter from the TV. If only Molly could be there, too, enjoying a simple pleasure with her daughter, instead of enduring this agony with Steve.

Steve paced the length of the kitchen and then back again to stand in front of her. "Do you know where Angie is now?"

Molly bit her lower lip and spoke around the lump in her throat. "I might."

"Start from the beginning, why don't you?"

Molly's knees were so weak she feared she would crumple to the floor. "All right. But I need to sit down." She wobbled to the table and slumped into a chair. He followed, looming over her like a dark shadow, blocking what little light filtered through the window over the sink.

Halting now and then to catch her breath, she told him about buying the ornament from Angie at the country fair, leaving it here with her other ornaments when she moved to Chicago, and discovering it again when Sara returned the collection. "At first, I didn't realize that particular one was Angie's," she said.

"So when did you?"

"The night you helped me in the garden, when you

told me about your marriage. After you left, I picked the butterfly out of the box, and as I looked at it, everything fell into place."

Steve absently fingered the butterfly's wings. "So, if we'd put the ornaments in the garden that night, I would have seen this one and recognized it, and..."

"And we wouldn't be having this conversation," she finished, her voice hoarse and gritty.

We wouldn't be here at all. You'd be long gone back to New York, maybe with Angie. We wouldn't have had the past few weeks together. Maybe that would have been for the best.

"You said you might know where she is now. Tell me."

Molly winced. That was what he really wanted to know, and also what hurt her the most. But he didn't need to know that. She struggled to keep her voice calm and matter-of-fact. "Okay. I bought the plants for my garden at Sky Nursery. It's on the road to Red Rock, before the cutoff to Turner Road."

He nodded. "I've seen the place in passing."

"I remembered seeing yard ornaments there. After the night you helped me plant the garden, I went to Sky and looked at the displayed items. Included was a butterfly that resembled Angie's. I asked Ned, the owner, if he knew who made them. He said they come from a local group that lives on an abandoned farm north of town, known as Dyson's. That was the name of the family that owned the place before."

"Is the group that lives there now a cult?"

Molly spread her hands. "I don't know any more than what I've told you."

Steve slowly shook his head. "So, all this time

she's been here in the area."

"Yes, and now you can go and find her."

"I will." Steve stuck out his chin. "Make no mistake about that. She might need my help, and I want to keep my promise to her parents. But what really disturbs me is why you didn't tell me all this before? What were you thinking, Molly?"

I was thinking that I love you. I was afraid that if you found her, you'd realize you still love her, and then where would I be? "I was wrong not to tell you."

A fierce frown creased his brow. "You've got that right. You've let me down, Molly. Big time."

"I know. I'm sorry." Barely able to meet his gaze, she stared at her hands.

Steve set his jaw. "I'm not sure 'sorry' is enough."

Molly closed her eyes against the burn of imminent tears. "Please, Steve, go and do what you have to do."

"Okay, I will. First, though, there is one mess I can clean up." He strode to the counter, laid down the ornament, and grabbed the broom.

"Let that go," she said, swiping away a tear that had managed to escape and trail down her cheek. "I'll clean it up."

"No, I will," he ground out. "I always finish what I start."

After he left, with a terse good-bye and not a word about when or if they would see each other again, Molly realized she still didn't know what he had wanted to talk to her about.

Chapter Eighteen

The next day, Steve sat in his car in the parking lot waiting for Sky Nursery to open. He'd been staring at the sprawling wooden building for the past fifteen minutes, especially at the windows, watching to see when the dim night lights would change to bright, a signal business was about to begin. So far, nothing. He shifted in his seat and checked his wristwatch. Ten o'clock. Come on, open up.

The lights inside the store finally blazed on. He jumped from the car and ran up the steps, barely glancing at the pots of geraniums and sacks of fertilizer and mulch on the porch. He reached for the knob just as a burly guy with a white buzz cut unlocked and opened the door.

The man's eyebrows shot up. "Well, you're an early bird, ain'tcha?"

"I sure am. Are you Ned?"

"That's me." Ned poked his thumb at the bib of his denim overalls and stepped aside. "Help ya with somethin'?"

Steve strode past the man and into the store. "Where are the seed packets?"

"Over in the corner." Ned pointed a gnarled forefinger down a nearby aisle flanked with fertilizer spreaders on one side and rakes and hoes on the other.

Steve headed down the aisle, catching whiffs of

fertilizer and potting soil on the way. The back of the store opened up into the out-of-doors, where large plants and bushes and fledgling trees were kept. Morning sunshine cast patterns of light and shadow over the area.

After studying the assortment, he selected a couple of packets containing sunflower seeds. He had no idea what, if anything, he would do with them, but making a purchase might help his cause when he got around to questioning Ned about yard ornaments.

Packets in hand, he moved to a display of trowels and clippers. Ned stood behind the checkout counter, filling a plastic container with brochures. He didn't seem to be paying any particular attention to Steve.

The bell on the front door tinkled as another customer entered. "Morning, Ned," a woman's voice called across the store.

"Mornin', Martha."

Ned came from behind the counter, and the two began a conversation. Their voices were too low for Steve to understand the words. That was okay; he wasn't interested in eavesdropping.

Moving to another aisle, Steve spotted what he was looking for—a square box of sand filled with yard ornaments. He hurried over. Made of shiny copper, their price tags waved in the slight breeze drifting in from the nursery's open back yard. He scanned the assortment, a frog, a windmill, a tulip, a hummingbird, and...a butterfly. His pulse quickened.

Steve grasped the rod supporting the butterfly and lifted it from the sand. He didn't have to look hard to know the ornament was Angie's. The cutout designs were hers, as were the exaggerated curls on the insect's feelers.

Hearing steps approach behind him, he turned to see Ned. "These are interesting." Steve nodded to the display. "Are they made locally?"

"Yup."

Steve looked at the tag, hoping for a company name, but it gave only the price.

"Someplace I could visit? I might like to order a quantity of one design."

Ned shoved his hands into his overalls pockets. "You kin place an order with me."

Steve turned the butterfly over in his hands. "Okay, but I'd like to talk to the artist. I have some ideas for special designs."

Ned's bushy white brows drew together, and Steve worried that perhaps he'd gone too far.

But then Ned said, "People that make 'em belong to a group living on the old Dyson spread."

"Are they a cult? I heard there might be one around here."

"Maybe. Something like that." Ned scratched his buzz cut. "Not sure I'd go out there. They're a private bunch. Don't like visitors."

"That doesn't seem a good way to run a business."

Ned shrugged. "I ain't no judge a that. You kin leave a message with me, if you want. They come in 'bout once a week, usually on Thursday."

Steve tilted his head, as though considering the suggestion. "Thanks, I'll keep that in mind. I'll buy this one today and see if it fits my purpose. Then, if I need to contact them, I'll let you know."

"Suit yerself."

After purchasing the seed packets and the butterfly

ornament, Steve left the store. A plan had been forming in his mind. He'd stake out the nursery on Thursday and hope to see someone from the group delivering more ornaments. If he got lucky, Angie would be the one who came.

Thursday was three days away. He filled the time with his business, although keeping his mind on computer programs proved difficult. Two of Harwell's referrals were interested in his product and services, and of those two, one was ready to move ahead in the near future. The officials of the other company hadn't come to a decision.

Molly's absence in his life had left a painful ache in his heart, and calling her, if for no other reason than to hear her sweet voice, tempted him. Once, he went as far as punching in her number on his cell phone. Then, reminding himself how greatly she had disappointed him, he cancelled the call.

****

On Thursday morning, Steve headed for Sky Nursery. Instead of parking in the store's lot, he parked at an adjacent strip mall that included a gas station, a feed store, and an espresso stand. The stand had wooden picnic tables shaded by umbrellas. He bought a coffee and sat at a table facing the nursery, waiting for it to open. Anticipation kept his nerves thrumming. Would Angie be the one who'd come? Or would anyone from the group show up?

Ten o'clock arrived. The windows lighted, and Ned unlocked the door. Cars and trucks began to fill the parking lot. Doors slammed and voices rang out as customers went up and down the steps to the building's front door. The nursery did a brisk business, but Steve saw no one he could identify. No Angie sightings. No one delivering metal sculptures.

At lunchtime, while still keeping an eye on the nursery, he wandered over to the grocery and bought a ham and cheese sandwich. The afternoon crept by. Despite stretching and short walks around the lot, his muscles cramped from so much sitting.

He was about to give up when a black SUV carrying a driver and a passenger drove into the nursery's lot and slid into a parking space.

The driver's door opened, and a middle-aged woman with a gray ponytail stepped out. Her denim jeans hugged ample hips, and her blue T-shirt stretched across a sizable chest. She strode to the back of the SUV, opened the hatch, and took out an oblong wooden box.

An object from the box fell to the ground. Bright copper on a long pole gleamed in the sunlight. A yard ornament.

Steve's blood surged through his veins. Payoff time. Finally.

The woman snatched up the ornament, stuffed it back in the box, and then carried the box up the steps to the nursery's front door.

Steve strained to see the SUV's passenger, but sunlight glinting off the hood obscured the person's face. He was ready to head over there for a closer look when the SUV's door opened, and the mysterious person stepped out.

A woman. Considerably younger than the driver, she appeared to be in her twenties. Like her companion, she wore jeans and a blue T-shirt.

As she rounded the nose of the car, she raised her

left hand to brush back strands of her dark hair. On her wrist was a tattoo. Even from a distance, he could make out the wings of a butterfly, the points of a star.

Steve caught his breath and stared. For a moment, he thought he was having another Angie-sighting. He'd had so many over the past five years his mind wouldn't accept that this was not one more disappointment.

He gave himself a mental shake. This was no false Angie-sighting. The woman was Angie. And, she was headed his way. Had she seen and recognized him? Now what? He stiffened his shoulders for a confrontation.

Instead of approaching him, she angled off toward the espresso stand's order window. She passed within ten feet of him and never looked his way.

Covertly, he watched her place her order. When the cup arrived, she took a couple sips, nodded at the barista, and placed some money into the woman's outstretched hand. Still without glancing Steve's way, she started back to the SUV.

Steve continued to sit there, as though glued to the wooden bench. What was wrong with him? Wasn't this the moment he'd waited five years for? Now that the time had finally arrived, he wasn't going to act? In a couple moments, she'd be back in the SUV, her companion would exit the store, and then his opportunity would be over.

He jumped up and sprinted across the parking lot. "Hello, there."

She kept walking.

"Hello."

No reaction, no response.

"Angie."

She stopped short, stood as still as a rock for a couple heartbeats, and then slowly turned. Recognition flickered in her eyes, like a beacon shining through a fog.

"Were you talking to me?" She pressed her fingers to her chest.

"Yes, you're Angie. Angie Griffin Roper."

Eyes narrowing, she lifted her chin. "No, you're mistaken."

He pointed to her left hand curled around her coffee cup, with the butterfly tattoo on her wrist in full view. The insect's wings were red and blue, and a tiny gold star hovered above the tip of one wing.

"You're Angie. I know you by your tat, if nothing else. And I'm Steve. Your husband?"

Her shoulders sagged and a sigh escaped her lips. "Okay, what do you want?"

Steve's jaw dropped. After all this time, this was not the attitude he expected to face. "What do I want?" he said when he recovered. "Well, for starters, I want to know why you left. I want to know if you're okay. I want to know—"

The nursery's screen door banged. Steve's gaze left Angie and followed the sound.

Angie wheeled around.

The woman who'd driven the van had emerged from the store and was crossing the porch. Her gaze zeroed in on Steve and Angie. "Miriam," the woman called across the parking lot.

Miriam? For a moment, Steve thought she was addressing someone other than Angie. Then she lumbered down the steps and made a straight line for the two of them.

"Please go." Angie hissed the words.

Steve leaned his head closer. "What's going on? Why can't you talk to me?"

Shoulders stiff, she shot a glance at the woman then turned back. "Tonight," she whispered. "The Dyson place on Old Canyon Road...seven o'clock."

The woman reached them. She propped her hands on her hips and glared at Steve. "What's the trouble here?"

"No trouble." Steve kept his tone firm as he met the woman's steely gaze. "I saw this lady drop some change on her way back from the espresso stand." He pointed to the nearby building. "I picked it up and chased her down to return it."

The woman's eyes narrowed as she focused on Angie. "Is that so, Miriam?"

"Why, yes, Sister Joan." Angie lowered her eyelids.

Sister Joan tilted her head and studied Steve.

Afraid anything he might say would only turn up the heat, he clamped his jaw shut.

"Come along, then." Sister Joan grabbed Angie's elbow and steered her toward the van. "Brother Michael will wonder what's keeping us."

Steve stared after them, clenching and unclenching his fists, fighting the urge to follow and wrest Angie from the other woman's clutches. Had Angie not told him to meet her later at the Dyson place, he would've done exactly that.

Before disappearing inside the SUV, while Sister Joan's back was turned, Angie glanced over her shoulder. Her gaze met Steve's only briefly before she climbed into her seat and Sister Joan slammed the door shut.

The vehicle wheeled from the parking lot, stirring up clouds of dust and spitting gravel from under the tires. At the end of the block, the vehicle swerved around the corner and was gone.

****

Back in his hotel room, Steve sat at the round table, studying the photo of Angie that he'd carried for the past five years. She was the same woman he'd seen today, and yet not the same. Photo-Angie was younger, of course, and, although her eyes were sad, innocence radiated from them, too, and softness shone in the smile on her lips.

The Angie he'd seen today had cold eyes and a tense mouth, with lips that hadn't smiled once. Yet, the butterfly and star tattoo proved she was the same person.

"I finally found you," he whispered to the woman in the photo. "You might call yourself 'Miriam,' but you are still 'Angie' to me. Why would you give up the privileged life I gave you to join a cult?" He tapped the photo with his forefinger. "You'd better give me some answers tonight, Angie."

Setting aside the photo, he rose and strode to the window. As he gazed out at the buildings and the mountain backdrop, his thoughts turned to Molly, and his chest tightened. Should he call her and tell her of these latest events? Did he owe her that? Did he owe her anything? He set his jaw. No, he didn't. Not when she'd betrayed his trust. He'd come close to proposing to her that night. What a mistake that would have been.

Yet, the longing to hear her voice continued to hold him prisoner. He paced in front of the window then pulled his cell phone from his belt and made the call to the Rolling R.

****

"One, two, three." Molly counted the bags of walnuts in the cupboard, and then noted the number on her clipboard checklist. She was in the bakery's kitchen, taking inventory of food supplies and making a shopping list for tomorrow's trip to the grocery supplier.

Across the room, Lupe poured flour into the large mixing vat, while Doreen measured out the carob chips and dried mixed fruit for Sara's latest cupcake recipe. Lupe was teaching Doreen to speak Spanish. "*La cucina*," she said with a sweeping gesture at the room.

"*La cucina?*" Doreen repeated, a puzzled frown on her round face.

"*Si*. Kitchen. *Estamos en la cucina*. We are in the kitchen."

"Ah. *Lo entiendo*. I understand."

The phone in Molly's office rang. Laying her clipboard on the counter, she ran into the office. She picked up the receiver and heard the dial tone. Whoever the person was had hung up. Usually, a caller waited to leave a voice mail message. She checked voice mail, but no message was recorded.

A tingle crept down her spine. For some strange reason, she had the feeling the caller was Steve. She'd thought about him almost constantly since that horrible night at her house when he discovered her deception.

She stared at the phone. Should she call him? If she got him on the line and he hadn't been the one, she'd feel stupid. Yet, there might be a way to determine whether or not he had made the call.

Picking up the phone, she punched in the code to learn the number of the last received call. "Anonymous," the recorded voice reported.

Molly hung up the phone. Okay, so much for that. Just as well. If he wanted to talk to her, he could keep calling.

Or, he could come and see her in person.

****

At six forty-five that evening, Steve exited the freeway onto Old Canyon Road. He hoped he'd allowed enough time to find the Dyson place. Angie had said seven o'clock, and he didn't want to be late. If he were, she might assume he wasn't coming and not wait.

Old Canyon Road was narrower than the highway but well paved. Traffic this time of night was light; he passed only a couple vehicles headed in the opposite direction. Farmland stretched on either side of the road, punctuated by stands of weeping willows, aspen, and fir. Mailboxes on posts, as well as gates and arches, marked each property.

An overhead arch announced Dyson's Double D Ranch. He drove through the arch onto a road that disappeared over a rise in the distance. What now? He didn't have a plan; he'd been intent on finding the place, period. If the Double D was anything like the Rolling R, he could wander around for hours and never find Angie.

He set his jaw. That was not going to happen. He'd waited five years for this. Even if he had to stay all night, he wouldn't leave without seeing her.

Spying a section of land thick with trees and underbrush, he headed in that direction. If she were meeting him on the sly, as he figured she would be, the trees would provide a good cover.

When he reached the woods, he pulled to the left side of the road, cut the engine, and stepped from the car. The air was dry, with no breeze, and still hot from the day's sunshine. Listening, he tilted his head. In the distance, faint sounds of voices drifted through the air. Not talking or singing, but more like chanting. The back of his neck prickled. Maybe the cult was having some kind of service. Maybe Angie would have to participate and not be able to meet him. Maybe she'd decided to not meet him, anyway.

He thought about sneaking up to the camp, but decided not to. He didn't want to get caught. Who knew what they'd do to a trespassing stranger?

Leaving the car where it sat, he paced the road, his boots crunching on the dry gravel. He stopped now and then to scan the woods. What if she didn't show? Would he make good his vow to camp out all night?

She would show up. She had to.

The chanting ceased, but the silence was just as nerve-wracking. The sinking sun sent long shadows across the road. Steve wiped sweat from his forehead. Where was she? He set his lips in a tight line and stared into the silent woods.

The underbrush nearby crackled and snapped. He stood rigid, arms hanging at his sides, feet planted solidly on the road. He focused on the spot where he heard the sounds and held his breath.

The bushes parted, and a large, black and brown dog plunged into view. The animal had a drooping jowl and pointed ears, like a cross between a Rottweiler and a Doberman.

A leash extended from the dog's collar.

At the other end of the leash stood Angie.

Dressed in the same blue T-shirt and jeans she'd worn earlier, she advanced to the edge of the woods, leaning forward as the dog strained at the leash and barked at Steve.

"Noble, quiet!" Angie tugged on the leash.

The dog issued a low growl then clamped its jaw shut.

Now that they were face-to-face at last, Steve's stomach churned. He'd no idea how this would all play out.

"Hey, Angie," he said, with a casual wave.

"My name is Miriam."

Her defiant tone grated. Yet, in as calm a voice as he could manage, he said, "Okay...Miriam. And you do know who I am?"

"Yes, of course. You're Steve."

He stared at her somber expression, trying to find some indication of the old Angie. But this woman, with her cold eyes and tense mouth, was a stranger. "Are you okay?" he asked, intent on keeping their conversation alive. "Are you in good health?"

"Yes, I'm fine."

"You don't need my help?"

She gave a slight laugh. "No, of course not."

To honor her parents' memory, he forced himself to push on. "Angie...uh, Miriam, I need to know why you left."

A frown wrinkled her forehead, and she gazed down at her hand holding Noble's leash.

She remained silent so long he thought she wasn't going to answer.

Finally, still without looking at him, she said, "I couldn't be the person you wanted me to be."

He wanted to say, "What does that mean?" but bit back the words, as well as the anger that bubbled up from his churning stomach. "Can you tell me more?"

She shrugged. "I couldn't be the wife you wanted. I don't belong in your world."

"And you do belong here?" He waved at the surroundings.

"Yes, I do."

"Is this a cult?"

Eyes narrowing, she stuck out her chin. "No, we're not a cult. We're a community. People living together with common interests and goals."

Steve shifted from one foot to the other. Dry leaves crackled under his feet.

The dog growled low and deep in its throat.

"Noble, hush." Angie held up a finger.

Steve slowly shook his head. "I don't think your parents would approve of your new lifestyle."

"I'm not living my life for them. Or for you. I'm living my life for me."

Another bubble of anger escaped and charged to the surface. His voice rose a notch. "But I promised them I'd watch out for you, take care of you after they were gone."

"That was between you and them. That has nothing to do with me." She shook her head. "No one asked me if I wanted to be taken care of."

"You agreed to marry me. I didn't force you, did I?"

Angie pressed her lips together. "No, but I didn't know what I was doing then."

His stomach tightened, and he said through gritted teeth, "Did you know what you were doing when you left without any word? Do you realize how worried I was? I did everything possible to find you."

She lowered her gaze, fingering the leash. "I was afraid to face you, afraid to tell you I wanted out of the marriage. So, I left."

Steve fisted his hands to keep from grabbing her and shaking her. How could she be so casual about what she'd done, when her leaving had torn apart his world?

"I suppose you want a divorce now." She looked up from under her lashes.

Unable to hold back, he gave a harsh laugh. "I've already divorced you. But I had to wait five years, Angie. Five years of my life."

Her brow puckered. "I'm...sorry."

A bitter taste filled his mouth. Sorry. That was all she could say? That she was sorry? Anger churned inside Steve. He wanted to yell and rant. He wanted her to suffer as much as he had. Then he reminded himself she wasn't the Angie who'd been his wife. The "community"—whatever that was—had surely brainwashed her.

Moments passed with no sound but the rustle of aspen leaves and the dog's whimpers. Then a shout pierced the woods, like a shot from a cannon. "Miriam! Miriam!"

Alarm flickered across her face. "I have to go."

"Yeah, sure," he said dully, kicking at the underbrush.

"Good-bye, Steve."

"Good-bye, Angie."

What else was there to say? He'd asked his questions, and she'd answered them. What had he expected? That she'd rush into his arms, begging him to rescue her, the way he'd rescued her before? Was that what he wanted?

The dog leading the way, she plunged into the underbrush. After a few steps, she stopped and turned. A light flickered in her eyes, and, for a moment, he thought she'd changed her mind and wanted to go with him. Shoulder muscles taut, breath suspended, he waited.

Right before disappearing into the woods, she said, "My name is Miriam."

Chapter Nineteen

Back on the freeway, Steve clenched his teeth and gripped the steering wheel until his fingers ached. His mind played again and again the scene with Angie. She claimed she couldn't live up to his expectations and be the wife he wanted. Okay, so maybe he'd had expectations. He'd also given her a good life, including a beautiful home and whatever she wanted that money could buy. He'd shared all the perks that went with his success.

Instead, she chose to live on a run-down farm with a bunch of hippies. She had her metalworking craft, but she could've had that in New York, with him. He was the one who'd sent her to school and paid for her training.

Still, she claimed she was okay and where she wanted to be. He should leave her here.

Who was he kidding? Other than kidnapping her, what choice did he have? His gut churned, frustration eating at him.

Now what should he do? Could he pick up the pieces of his broken life and move on at last? What about Molly? Was there any way he could put their relationship back together? The night he discovered Molly's deception, he'd stormed off. He acted in haste, he realized now. If he apologized and asked her forgiveness, could they work things out?

Aching to hear her voice, Steve pulled off the road and reached for his cell phone. He stared at the phone in the dying light, fingering the buttons, pausing on the one that would connect him to Molly.

But his mind wouldn't focus on what to say. His thoughts swirled and churned like the mighty Rolling River the day he'd fallen into it. Finally, he tossed down the phone and wheeled back onto the road.

****

Molly sat on the sofa in her living room, her gaze darting to the phone and then away again. As she had each night since their painful parting, she waited for a phone call from Steve. A call that never came.

When eleven o'clock rolled around, she turned out the lights and climbed in bed. She lay there with a heavy heart. Had he found Angie? Had he talked to her? Did she want to come back to him?

If so, Molly would have to accept that. She'd have to forget about Steve and concentrate on her life here at the Rolling R. Concentrate on her job. Most important of all, concentrate on raising Karli.

All the logic did nothing to ease the ache that had spread from her heart to every corner of her body.

Oh, Steve, please call. I need to hear your voice and to know you care for me the way I care for you.

****

The following morning, Steve was ready to head out for breakfast when his cell phone rang. He pulled the phone from his belt and answered the call.

"Steve speaking."

"Hey, buddy." Jackson's deep voice echoed in Steve's ear. "I know it's early, but I wanted to catch you before you started your work day."

"Good timing. I was just on my way to breakfast." Steve took a few steps back into the room.

"I won't keep you long, but how've you been? Haven't seen you around for a few days."

"I've been busy." Jackson was a good friend, but Steve didn't want to tell him about Angie. Not now, when he still had decisions to make.

"Yeah, I'm sure you have. Everything going well?"

"Real good. I've set up a couple more accounts." He glanced at the round table, where the paperwork waited, a task he planned to do after breakfast.

"Have you decided when you'll be returning to New York?"

Steve raised his gaze to the window. In the distance, an airplane cruised against the clear blue sky, and sudden homesickness gripped him. "I haven't set a date yet, but I can't stay here too much longer."

"Sara and I would like to get together with you at least one more time before you leave."

The thought of seeing Sara and Jackson again brought a smile to his lips. "That goes for me, too. Did you have something specific in mind?"

"Yeah, there's a party at the grange Friday night. Buffet dinner, music, and dancing. Why don't you join us? Come out to the house and we'll all go together."

A party at the grange? Would Molly be there? Steve's stomach tightened. "I, ah, suppose I could..."

"Hey, I'm not hearing a lot of enthusiasm. If you'd rather not, don't feel obligated."

Steve automatically raised a staying hand. "No, no, I want to see you. But—"

"You want to know if Molly will be there, too."

"I really messed that up." He ran a hand through

his hair. "Too long a story to go into right now. But, yeah, is she coming?"

"She'll be there. Maybe that will be a good thing."

"Maybe." But showing up at the Phillips' beforehand might be awkward. "Why don't I meet you at the grange hall?"

"Works for me. I'll give you directions, and we'll look for you. Party starts at seven."

A few minutes later, Steve hung up, shaking his head. Was he making a big mistake? Or was there still a chance he and Molly could get together?

On Friday night, the dashboard clock registered eight o'clock when Steve pulled into the grange hall's parking lot. His late arrival wasn't because he'd put off making the trip. He really had been busy tying up loose ends with his accounts. By the time he put away his equipment and changed his clothes, the time was already well past seven.

He still hadn't decided exactly what he would do when he saw Molly. Should he apologize? Suggest they start over? Tell her about his meeting with Angie?

Still undecided, he parked and got out of the car. Lights spilled from the hall's windows and the open door. A country-western tune, mixed with talk and laughter, drifted along air that smelled of hay and wildflowers. He wished he were more in a party mood, but the circumstances kept his stomach churning.

He climbed the steps and crossed the porch to the open door. Reluctant to enter, he stopped on the threshold. How would Molly react when she saw him? Did she even know he was coming? Maybe he should have called her and arranged to meet in another setting.

No, this was the best way for them to reconnect.

With people around, they wouldn't get into any heavy discussion. Serious talk could come later.

He scanned the crowd looking for Molly. He didn't see her, but he spotted Jackson and Sara standing with some others by the buffet table. Joining them might be a good first move.

As he stepped inside, his gaze roved the dance floor—and landed on a red-haired woman. His stomach jolted. Molly. No one had red hair quite like hers. Tonight, instead of her usual ponytail, she wore her hair loose, the way he liked it best.

To get a look at her partner, he angled his head, but the man's cowboy hat hid much of his face. Then he twirled Molly around and under his arm, and Steve glimpsed his features.

He stiffened. Her partner was Jackson's horse trainer, Dirk Lamont. Yet why should that be so surprising? Dirk had paid special attention to Molly at the Phillips' barbecue, and Steve had spotted him hanging around the bakery's office a time or two.

Dirk pulled Molly back into his arms, close to his chest. She looked up at him, and they both laughed, as though they were having a great time.

Steve's throat tightened, and he stepped back into the shadows. He watched and waited. When the song ended, instead of returning to their seats, Dirk and Molly stood on the dance floor talking. When the music started again, he took her into his arms for another dance.

Steve curled his fingernails into his palms. He wanted to march out to the dance floor and claim Molly. Dirk had no right. Dirk wasn't the man for her.

Then, as the minutes passed, Steve calmed and

thought more rationally. He'd been planning to take Molly away from the Rolling R and introduce her to his life in the city. He'd been ready to give her the house in the suburbs, the social life, and the money he enjoyed as a successful businessman.

But, just as Angie hadn't wanted that kind of life, maybe Molly didn't want it, either. He tried to mold Angie into his idea of a wife, and that hadn't worked. Wasn't he now planning to do the same thing with Molly?

When they first met, Molly told him she returned to the Rolling R because she wanted to raise Karli where she and Buck had made their home. Did Steve have the right to suggest she change her plans?

Maybe Dirk was the man for her, after all. He appeared to be a nice enough guy. Steve had nothing against him. He'd probably make Molly a good husband and Karli a good dad. If not Dirk, then someone else would eventually come along, someone with the kind of lifestyle Molly wanted.

And yet, as he watched her waltzing around the room in Dirk's arms, he wanted to rush to her side and claim her for himself. Gathering every ounce of his willpower, he turned in the opposite direction and made his way through the crowd and to the door.

As he left the building and headed for the parking lot, he half-expected to hear Jackson, or Sara, or even Molly call his name and summon him back.

The only sound was the music. The words floated out, something about "lost love." An appropriate send-off, he thought, as he climbed into his car.

****

As Dirk led Molly back to her seat, a tingle

traveled down her spine. She could swear Steve was nearby. Since she'd learned he was coming tonight, her nerves had been on edge.

When Sara first suggested Molly attend the dance, she declined. She was too upset and distressed over Steve to think of going anywhere, least of all to a dance. But Sara persisted, as only Sara could, and Molly gave in.

On the way to the grange hall, Jackson dropped his news that Steve would be at the party, too. Molly wanted to be angry with him for not telling her earlier, but kept her emotions in check. Jackson and Sara knew something had happened between her and Steve, but, thankfully, they respected her privacy and hadn't pressed her to confide in them.

"Sure you don't want to go 'round again?"

Dirk's voice cut into Molly's thoughts. She looked up and saw a sparkle in his eyes that indicated more than casual interest. She'd suspected he was pursuing her. Too bad her interest in him went no further than friendship.

She laid a hand on his arm. "I think my feet need to rest for a while. But thanks, Dirk. You're a good dancer."

"Same goes for you." He patted her hand. "I'll catch you later, then."

They reached the table where Molly sat with Sara and Jackson and two other couples. Molly slipped into her chair, and Dirk headed for his seat at another table.

The feeling Steve was nearby whispered over Molly again. She scanned the room but didn't see him. Yet, as though an invisible cord connected them, she sensed his presence. She leaned toward Sara. "I'm going to the ladies' room. Be right back."

"Okay, hon." Sara's brow wrinkled. "Are you feeling okay?"

"Yes, I'm fine. Just gotta go."

Instead of heading for the restrooms, Molly veered off toward the hall's front door. A large group blocking the way slowed her progress, but she finally stepped through the door and onto the porch. A rush of warm night air brushed her cheeks as she peered into the growing darkness. Clouds covered the moon, and only a few dim night lights hovered over the parking lot.

The sound of a car's engine rose above the band's music. She located the car as it headed out of the lot toward the main road. She couldn't be positive, but the car looked like Steve's rental.

When she returned to the hall, her earlier sense of Steve's presence had vanished. Emptiness filled Molly, as though she'd lost something very precious.

****

Monday morning, Molly sat at her desk in the bakery's office, working on the monthly accounting. Sara had gone into town, and Lupe and Doreen were busy in the kitchen. Bits of their conversation drifted into the office, along with the enticing aroma of shortbread cookies.

"Molly," a deep voice said.

She looked up to see Steve standing in the doorway. Pulse racing, she gulped a breath and pressed a hand to her chest. After wanting so badly to see him, now that he was actually in her presence, she was tongue-tied.

He took a step into the room then stopped. "Got a few minutes? I'd like to talk to you."

At his serious tone, her heart skipped a beat. "Well...sure. Sit down." She motioned to the chair across from her desk.

He sank into the chair and met her gaze. "I came to tell you I'm returning to New York tomorrow."

Her stomach lurched, and Molly wrapped her arms around her middle. "Time to go home, huh?" She struggled to keep her voice light.

He nodded. "I've been gone longer than I intended, and I need to get back."

Molly wanted to yell, "Don't go!" She wanted to jump up, run around the desk, and throw her arms around him. Kiss him with all her heart and soul. Make him stay. Make him know he couldn't leave her.

Instead, she twisted her fingers together—in her lap where he couldn't see them—and pressed the soles of her shoes hard to the floor.

Steve's gaze strayed to the window. "I'm taking the train into Denver and catching a flight there."

"Is Angie going with you?" The words almost stuck in her throat. She hated to ask, but she had to know.

"Angie?" Steve turned and gave her a wide-eyed look. "No, no, she's not."

"Did you find her?"

"I did." He ran a hand over his face. "Like you said, she's living with her group—she calls it a 'community'—on the Dyson farm. She's where she wants to be."

Molly could swear she heard pain behind his matter-of-fact statement. *He still cares for Angie. He doesn't want to go back to New York without her.*

Steve picked up a paperweight from her desktop, a

chunk of granite with silver mica that sparkled in the sunlight. "I don't know quite how to say this," he began, idly fingering the paperweight, "but we're in different spaces right now, you and I. And so I thought it best that I say good-bye and wish you every happiness in the future."

"Happiness to you, too, Steve." Molly could hardly believe how calm she sounded, when her heart was breaking into pieces. "You'll say good-bye to Karli, won't you?"

"Already did. I stopped by Teresa's before I came here."

Oh, my poor little one. "And what was her reaction?"

He replaced the paperweight and met her gaze with a faint smile. "She said she'd miss me, and I told her I'd miss her, too."

"She will miss you, Steve." *And so will I.*

"I'll be keeping in touch with Jackson and Sara, so I'll find out from them how you and Karli are doing."

Emotion clogged her throat but she forced out the words. "We'll be doing fine."

"I'm sure you will." He stood and came around the desk.

At his nearness, her insides trembled. For a moment, she thought he was going to lean down and kiss her. What would she do then?

But he didn't lean down, and he didn't kiss her. He simply laid a hand on her shoulder. "Take care, Molly."

"You, too, Steve."

Then he was gone. And her heart ached so badly she could barely breathe.

Chapter Twenty

That afternoon, when Molly picked up Karli at Teresa's, she expected her daughter to quiz her about Steve. Instead, she chattered about her day.

"We played dodge ball," Karli said, skipping ahead of Molly as they headed down the road to their house. "And no one was able to tag me out until the very end."

Molly smiled at Karli's enthusiasm. "Sounds like you are a good dodger."

"I am."

As they climbed the steps to their porch, Molly brought up the subject that weighed on her mind. "Steve told me he came by Teresa's to say good-bye." She held her breath and waited for Karli's response.

Karli grabbed the banister and hopped up to the next step. "Yeah, he did."

"And how do you feel about that?"

Karli's brow puckered.

"I mean, are you sad?"

"Sorta. But Steve said that even though he was going away, we'd always be friends. But I'll miss him."

Karli's voice held a wistful note that touched Molly's heart. Unshed tears burned her eyes and she blinked them back. "So will I, honey. So will I."

****

The following day during her afternoon break, Molly sat outside on the wrought iron bench under the maple tree. She liked to take her break there, shaded by the big tree and cooled by the light breeze sweeping in from the mountains. She liked listening to the distant sounds of horses neighing and cows mooing. She liked breathing in air tinged with all the smells of the ranch—horses, hay, grass, wildflowers.

This was country. This was home.

Today, though, her usual pleasures were missing. All she could think about was losing Steve. Last night, she cried herself to sleep, and all day, she'd barely been able to do her work.

The drone of an airplane overhead caught her attention. She shaded her eyes with her hand and looked up at the plane shining like a silver bullet against the sky's vivid blue backdrop. Maybe that plane was the one Steve had taken. She imagined him sitting back in the seat, enjoying a drink and reading one of his business journals. He'd probably forgotten about her already.

Molly brushed a tear from her eye. She would never forget him. Never.

****

Jerry met Steve when his plane landed at JFK. Instead of his usual baggy pants and shirt, Jerry wore fitted brown slacks and a crisp tan shirt that looked fresh off the store's clothing rack.

"Hey, Jer." Steve slapped him on the back. "What's with the new look? I almost didn't recognize you." Then realization dawned and he laughed. "Ah, I get it. Candace took you shopping."

Jerry grinned. "Yeah, I let her have her way on that, but I'm holding out on a few things, this being one." He pointed to the trimmed stubble on his chin.

"Good for you, though I gotta say, the new clothes are an improvement. But, what's with the big welcome?"

"My partner's return deserves special notice. I'm sure glad you're back, buddy."

"Thanks. Glad to be back."

At baggage claim, they picked up Steve's suitcase then headed outside. Steve was ready to take one of the taxis lined at the curb, but Jerry pointed farther down the walk. "We've got one waiting."

When they stopped beside a black limo, Steve's jaw dropped as he took in the shiny vehicle. "Part of your welcome?" he asked when he recovered.

"Just wanted to celebrate your return first-class. Not to worry—we can afford it. We're rolling in dough. Wait until you see our profit margin for last quarter."

Steve grinned. "Hey, maybe I should leave town more often."

The limo driver hopped from the car and helped stow Steve's luggage in the trunk, and then they were on their way. Well, sort of, Steve reflected, as they joined a long line of other vehicles crawling at a snail's pace from the terminal.

On the way into Manhattan, he told Jerry about finding Angie. "She calls the place she's staying a 'community,' but it sounded more like a cult. Can you believe that?"

Jerry pressed his lips together. "Yeah, I can believe it."

His disgusted tone prompted Steve to ask, "Why? Is there something you're not telling me?"

"Let's hear the rest of your story first."

Jerry listened without much comment, looking out

the window most of the time, his square jaw set. Steve was so wrapped up in his narrative that he barely noticed when they reached Manhattan, until Jerry said, "Let's stop for a bite."

"Good idea. I haven't eaten since breakfast."

They went to Manoli's, one of their favorite hangouts on the Upper East Side. Over cannelloni and a glass of red wine, the likes of which Steve hadn't seen since he'd been there the last time, he finished his story. He sat back and took a deep breath. Sharing had taken a toll, but he felt relief, too.

Jerry leveled Steve a serious gaze. "You want my opinion?"

"Of course."

"Stop taking all the blame for what happened and get on with your life."

"What life? I mean, what personal life?" For the past five years, his career had been his main focus.

Jerry leaned forward. "That's for you to figure out. But, for starters, get rid of everything that connected you to Angie. She's where she wants to be. You can stop being responsible for her well-being. You've paid your debt to her parents. You did the best you could."

Jerry's words lingered in Steve's mind. That weekend, he visited the house in Westchester, which, anticipating Angie's eventual return, he'd kept intact. The two-story, four-bedroom home sat on a quiet, tree-lined street amid similar homes. He walked through the rooms filled with furniture and other items he'd bought for her, remembering incidents from the past that he hadn't thought of for years. They hadn't been happy here, he realized. The entire place resonated with their unhappiness.

He left the house and walked out into the front yard. On either side lived families whose kids had been toddlers when he and Angie had lived there. Now they were riding their two-wheeled bicycles up and down the sidewalk. But inside his house, time had stood still while he waited for Angie to return.

Jerry was right. He'd been longing for something that hadn't existed in the first place. So intent on honoring his marriage vows, on living up to his promise to Ed and Jane, he hadn't realized his marriage was a total sham. His stomach churned. What a fool he'd been.

At that realization, he climbed in his car and drove to the nearest real estate office. A few hours later, after an agent had visited the house and arranged for an appraisal, Steve signed papers to put the house on the market.

"I know that was tough for you to do," Jerry said the following day when Steve told him about putting the house up for sale. "But, trust me, you'll be better off. And, what about the woman you met in Colorado? Can you put that relationship back together?"

The mention of Molly brought an ache to Steve's chest. He shook his head. "No chance of that."

He couldn't go crawling back to Molly. If only he could have found Angie and realized the truth about her and about their marriage *before* he met Molly.

But that hadn't happened. By a cruel twist of fate, Molly had come somewhere in the middle.

Chapter Twenty-One

Molly stood beside Sara at the fence enclosing the ranch's oval training track. They were watching Jackson break in one of his quarter horses. A late August sun shone brightly overhead. Molly tipped back her hat and rubbed away the perspiration dotting her forehead.

Sara had coaxed her into an afternoon walk. "You've been working hard all day," she said with a smile. "Come with me to deliver some refreshments to Jackson."

Molly had agreed. She helped Sara pack a wicker basket with soft drinks and fresh-from-the-oven raspberry scones, and they headed down the road to the training track.

"How're Rose and the new baby doing?" Molly asked Sara. Rose had given birth to a seven-pound, three-ounce baby girl a week ago. Molly visited her and the newborn at Valley General Hospital but hadn't seen them since.

The picnic basket at her feet, Sara rested her arms on the fence's top rail. "They're all doing fine. Of course, there is an adjustment when a new baby comes home."

"I remember those days." Molly smiled at the memory. "Have they settled on a name yet?"

"Finally. She'll be Melissa Ann."

"Melissa Ann Mahoney." Molly rolled the name over her tongue. "I like it."

Jackson's horse gave a loud, shrill whinny, and Molly turned her attention to the track. Jackson was leading the horse around, working him through paces before he attempted to mount him for the first time.

"Hobo looks like he has a mind of his own," Molly remarked.

Sara nodded. "Unbroken horses always do."

"He looks like a winner, though." Molly's gaze took in Hobo's broad chest and sturdy legs, characteristics of a good quarter horse.

"Jackson hopes Hobo will be a winner. He and Dirk will train him for racing—once he gets saddle broken."

Jackson continued leading Hobo around the track, while the horse pranced and tugged on the reins. Then Jackson stopped and approached Hobo, reaching for the saddle horn.

Hobo's defiant whinny cut the air. He tossed his head, his mane flying, and reared up on his hind legs, hooves pawing the air.

Jackson's face contorted as he gripped the reins in an attempt to control Hobo.

Still on his hind legs, the horse danced closer to Jackson, until his raised hooves were mere inches from Jackson's face.

Molly cringed and gripped the fence rail, unmindful of the wood splinters digging into her fingers. She was sure the horse would strike Jackson. In her mind's eye, she saw him falling to the ground, his face all bloody, and with the horse looming over him, ready to inflict more damage.

Sara gripped Molly's arm then rubbed a soothing line up and down. "It's okay, Molly. Relax."

Molly remained rigid. "How can you be sure?" she ground out between clenched teeth.

"Because I just am. I trust in Jackson's abilities."

Sara's voice was soft and reassuring, and Molly relaxed a little.

Sure enough, Jackson skillfully jumped aside, avoiding Hobo's menacing attack. Jackson tugged on the reins and gave verbal commands to the horse. His exact words were too faint for Molly to hear, but they apparently calmed the horse. Soon all four of Hobo's hooves were on the ground. A few minutes later, Jackson sat astride the horse. He looked over and gave them a big grin and a salute.

"Yay, Jackson and Hobo!" Sara clapped her hands then circled a hand in the air.

Molly cheered, too, although the lump in her throat kept her from yelling as loudly as Sara.

Later, when she and Sara were on their way back to the ranch house, Molly asked, "Don't you ever worry about Jackson getting hurt?"

Sara shifted the picnic basket from one hand to the other. "I won't lie and say I never worry. I know working with wild animals can be dangerous."

"Look what happened to Buck." Molly dipped her head and kicked a stray rock from their path.

Moving closer, Sara put her arm around Molly's shoulders, and they fell into step. "Yes, that was tragic. And I'm not comparing bull riding to horse training. Of course, there's a difference in the degree of danger involved.

"But, Molly, if Jackson and I are to have a

successful marriage, I need to let him be who he is. He loves horses and he loves to train them. Horses are his life." She laughed. "Besides me and Ryan, of course."

Sara's words echoed in Molly's mind. *I have to let him be who he is.* "Was that my mistake?" she asked. "When I tried to stop Buck from rodeo riding, was I also trying to prevent him from being true to himself?"

"I'm not passing judgment on you, Molly. You'll have to decide. But don't be too hard on yourself. When you first met Buck, you didn't know he would join the rodeo. Bull riding wasn't something you were prepared to cope with." Her hand on Molly's shoulder tightened. "But I do know Buck loved you and Karli. Don't ever doubt that."

Molly looked up, fastening her gaze on the mountains in the distance. "And I loved him. I still do."

"Of course, you do. But, have you considered there might be another man you could love now? I know you and Dirk have decided to be only friends, but what about Steve?"

They had reached the bakery. Molly shook her head as she pulled away and opened the kitchen door for Sara. "No. Steve and I are from different worlds, and he's already returned to his."

Sara stepped inside the kitchen. "He found his ex-wife, didn't he?"

"Yes, and that was part of the problem."

While they emptied the picnic basket and put away the leftover scones, Molly told Sara about hiding the butterfly ornament. "I felt awful about that. So foolish." She stopped and covered her face with her hands.

Sara put her hand on Molly's shoulder. "Do you know what happened when he finally came face-to-face with Angie?"

Molly met Sara's concerned gaze. "Just that she said she was happy where she was, and she wasn't going back to New York with him. But for all I know, she may have changed her mind."

"He didn't share much with Jackson, but I do know he returned to New York alone."

"Maybe she joined him later." At the thought of Angie and Steve being together again, Molly's chest tightened. She knew she should be happy for Steve, but the pain of her own loss was difficult to ignore.

"I don't think so."

"Well, it doesn't matter now, does it?"

Sara gave a wry smile.

"I'm beginning to sound like a broken record, but I have to say again, that's up to you."

****

"You can't do it, Molly." Teresa took a carton of milk from the refrigerator and stepped to a row of empty glasses lined up on the kitchen counter.

"I'm betting I can." Molly folded her arms and stuck out her chin.

She was using her break time to talk to Teresa about an important matter that had been weighing on her mind. She'd arrived just as Teresa was preparing the children's afternoon snack.

Teresa shook her head as she filled the first glass. "You're telling me you can drive Karli back and forth to kindergarten every day and still put in your hours at the bakery? Uh uh. I don't think so."

"Well...Sara would have to be flexible," Molly admitted.

But would Sara be flexible? She'd been firm about

Karli attending day care, rather than spending her days in Molly's office.

"My children take the bus." Teresa filled the last glass and put the milk carton in the refrigerator. "The driver is a good friend of mine. She's very caring and responsible. And the teachers meet the bus each day and see that the children get on it to come home."

"But you know Karli tends to run off." With stiff steps, Molly crossed to the window over the sink and looked out at the play yard. Karli and two other children were tossing a ball back and forth. Molly's heart swelled with love. She would die if anything happened to Karli.

"I know." Teresa placed the filled glasses on a tray and added a plate of whole-wheat crackers. "We've been working on that. I know you have, too. And I agree, there's a risk factor. When isn't there?"

Molly's shoulders tightened. "I'm not good with risks."

"I understand. But you have to let go sometime, Molly." Teresa raised her eyebrows. "Come on with me while I give the kids their snacks." She picked up the tray and headed for the back door.

You have to let go sometime. Teresa's words echoed in Molly's mind, along with Sara's words about Jackson. *I need to let him be who he is.*

Had the time come to let Karli go out into the world under someone else's watchful eye?

****

"Look, Mr. Muggins, here comes the bus." Waving Mr. Muggins in the air, Karli jumped up and down and then looked up at Molly. "Do you see it, Mommy?"

Molly shaded her eyes with her hand and gazed

down the highway to where a yellow school bus had appeared over the horizon. "Yes, the bus is almost here. But, be careful. Don't jump into the road."

Molly glanced at Teresa, who stood nearby with her two children, Lani and David. "Come on, bus." David made a fist and swung at the air. Lani, who was two years older than Karli and in the second grade, grabbed Karli's hand. "You're going to school. You'll have fun."

Teresa tucked a lock of hair back into her braid and rolled her eyes. "Don't you love their enthusiasm?"

"I guess." Molly swallowed against the lump that clogged her throat.

After Molly and Teresa's talk two weeks ago in Teresa's kitchen, Molly had done some heavy thinking.

The decision to allow Karli to ride the bus to school in town hadn't been an easy one. But after Molly attended the new parents' meeting, met the teacher and the principal and other staff, she knew Karli would be in good hands.

The bus arrived, pulled to a stop, and the door swung open. The driver, Francine, whom Molly had also met, smiled and waved the children aboard.

"'Bye, Mommy." Karli held out her arms for a hug.

Her eyes brimming with tears, Molly gathered Karli close and hugged her tightly. "'Bye, darlin'. Have fun. I'll be right here to meet you when the bus brings you home."

Karli planted a big smooch on Molly's cheek, and then ran after Lani and David to climb onto the bus.

As the door closed, Molly blinked away the tears. She kept her gaze glued to the bus until it was out of sight.

Teresa linked arms with Molly. "She'll be fine."

"I know." Molly mustered a wobbly smile. "But does it ever get any easier?"

Teresa shook her head. "No, I can't say that it does. Every letting go rips something out of you. But you'll be fine, too. Trust me."

That afternoon, Molly met Karli's bus. Happy and relieved to see her, Molly hugged her tightly. As expected, Karli was full of stories. Her excitement lasted all through dinner and story time. Finally, clutching her precious Mr. Muggins, she fell asleep.

Returning to the living room, Molly crossed to the fireplace mantel where the framed photos sat. Her gaze skimmed over them, each one setting off a flood of memories. Looking at them was like living her life with Buck all over again. She thought some more about letting go. Today, she'd taken a big step in letting Karli go. Maybe the time had come to take another step.

Molly walked down the hall to the laundry room. From a storage closet, she took out a cardboard box and a handful of old newspapers. Returning to the living room, she picked up each photo and, after gazing at it awhile, wrapped it in newspaper and put the bundle in the box. Soon tears were running down her cheeks.

"I wish your life hadn't ended the way it did," she whispered to the photo of her and Buck on their wedding day. "But I know you loved us, and we loved you. A part of me will love you always."

One photo, which showed the three of them standing in front of their house, she let remain on the mantel. Wiping away her tears, she carried the box back to the storage closet.

Then, she opened the back door and stepped out

onto the porch. Warm night air washed over her, and the smell of sagebrush scented the breeze. She sat in one of the wicker chairs and listened to the crickets chirping. Down the road at Teresa's, a dog barked.

Somehow, she felt lighter, as though a burden had been lifted from her shoulders. A burden that, until recently, she hadn't even known weighed her down.

And yet, there were still decisions to be made.

She'd come back to the ranch because this had been her home with Buck. She thought if she returned, she could have that life back again.

Now she realized this wasn't the place for her and Karli, after all. A tear slid down her cheek and she flicked it away. The reminders of their previous life here, instead of offering comfort, brought mostly pain. No matter how hard she tried, she hadn't put her old life back together again.

As much as she loved Sara, Jackson, and Ryan, and Mike and Rose, and baby Melissa, this wasn't home. The simple truth was, without Buck, she and Karli didn't belong at the Rolling R. They needed to move on and make a new life—and new memories—somewhere else.

Molly leaned her head back against the chair's cushion, her thoughts whirling now she had admitted the ranch was not the place she wanted to be. She hated to take Karli away from kindergarten, when she'd only recently begun, but Karli was resilient. She would adjust to a new school.

Where to go, though? The most obvious place, for now, was Chicago. Her old boss had said he'd always have a job waiting, and she and Karli could find an apartment near Paige and Harlan. But she didn't know if she wanted to stay there permanently.

A deep sigh escaped. Well, one step at a time. The first step was to realize she needed to move on.

Her gaze drifted out to her garden. Moonlight shone on the yard ornaments. The humming bird, the frog, the duck—and the butterfly. Angie's butterfly. She'd meant to give the ornament to Steve, but there'd been no opportunity. So, she placed it in her garden, as had been her original intent. The ornament was too pretty to hide away anymore, and she might as well enjoy it. Trouble was, every time she looked at the decoration, she was reminded of Steve. She sure had ruined that relationship. She hadn't been ready then. Now, it was too late.

"Oh, Steve," she whispered into the night air, *"I hope you're happy with your new life."*

****

"Here is today's mail, Steve." Beverly placed the stack of papers, which she'd opened and sorted, on Steve's desk.

"Thanks," he said without looking up. "I'll get to it later. Right now, I've got a problem with one of our new programs." He pointed to the computer screen.

Beverly propped her hands on her slim hips and pursed her lips. "You've been working like a hound dog on a scent since you returned from your trip. When are you going to slow down and enjoy life?"

Steve's lips twisted into a grim smile. "This is my life."

Beverly shook her head and made a "tsk tsk" sound before heading back to her office.

Afternoon arrived before Steve gave his attention to the stack of mail. On the bottom was an envelope

Beverly hadn't opened, addressed to him in handwriting and postmarked Red Rock. What could this be? He slit the envelope and took out a printed card:

You are cordially invited to attend the christening of Melissa Ann Mahoney at the Red Rock Community Church, September 30, at 1:00 p.m.

Reception to follow at the Rolling R Ranch.

Steve sat back and smiled. Well, well. During a phone call, Jackson told him of the baby's birth. Now, she was ready to be christened. Time had flown. Almost two months had passed since he'd left Colorado and returned to New York.

The invitation included a separate note:

Hi, Steve,

We know it hasn't been that long since you were here, but, if possible, we'd love for you to come to our celebration.

Hope you're doing well.

Love, Rose and Mike

His thoughts whirling, he put down the note and stared into space. Yeah, he'd like to see all his friends in Red Rock, especially Molly. Whenever he thought about her—which was more often than he wanted to admit—a longing consumed him. Man, but he wanted to see her again.

But, after leaving her to run after Angie, why would she want to see him? Why make them both uncomfortable by attending the christening?

He picked up the invitation and read it again. Maybe she wouldn't be uncomfortable. Maybe she'd already moved on and was involved with Dirk, or someone else. She was still living on the ranch, because on his last phone call with Jackson, he'd casually inquired about her and Karli.

Jackson had said they both were doing well.

Should he go to the christening or send a gift and his regrets? He brought up his schedule on the computer screen. A technology convention that he'd thought about attending was scheduled in Vegas the week prior to the christening. Traveling from there to Red Rock would work, wouldn't it?

After office hours, he was still mulling over his decision when he and Jerry went out for drinks. They sat at the bar at Dugan's. The place was packed, as usual. Raising his voice over the din, he told Jerry he might want to attend the convention.

Jerry eyed him with one eyebrow peaked. "Okay with me. But I have a feeling there's something else going on here."

Steve grinned and sipped his gin and tonic. "You're too smart for your own good, my friend. Yeah, okay, I was invited to a christening in Red Rock, for Mike and Rose's baby daughter. It's the week after the convention."

"Keep going." Jerry made a spinning motion with his hand.

"I'm debating that, because Molly will probably be there." At the thought of seeing Molly again, Steve's heart beat faster.

"So?"

"So, I don't know if my being there, too, is a good idea or not."

"You're in love with her. Still in love with her, I should say."

Steve stared at his drink. A yearning for Molly filled him. If only he could restore their lost relationship. "Yeah," he said in a low voice. "I am. Haven't been able to get her out of my mind since I've been back. But I know I hurt her. Why would she want to see me again?"

Jerry scooped up a handful of mixed nuts from a bowl on the bar and popped a few into his mouth. He chewed and swallowed. "Hey, you did what you had to do at the time. If Molly is the woman I think she is, she'll understand. I say, go for it."

Steve looked his partner in the eye. Putting his partnership on the line was a risk he had to take. "Okay, but if the trip turns out like I want it to, I might have to make some big changes in my life—and my work."

"We'll deal with whatever you decide." Jerry clapped him on the shoulder. "The only thing I need for sure is that, come December, you show up as best man at my wedding."

"You have my promise on that."

The following day, he called Beverly into his office. "I need a favor," he said when she stood on the other side of his desk.

She cast him a sideways look. "Something I'm going to like doing?"

"You like babies, don't you?"

A twinkle gleamed in her eyes, and she laughed. "I hope so. I've had three of them."

"Right. So, I need help in picking out a baby gift. For a christening..."

Chapter Twenty-Two

In the Phillips' living room, Molly hovered at the edge of an admiring group gathered around the guest of honor, Melissa Ann Mahoney. Rose held the baby in her arms. Melissa's long white christening dress, decorated with tiny silk roses, trailed over Rose's arm. A narrow white headband, also decorated with rosebuds, encircled the baby's head.

"Isn't she the sweetest thing?" a woman said, her eyes sparkling, her hands clasped against her chest.

Along with the others, Molly nodded her agreement. Melissa Ann's wispy black hair, big brown eyes, and tiny, bow-shaped mouth, gave her a special charm.

As much as Molly wanted to focus on the party, another matter kept her mind occupied and her nerves thrumming. A couple hours ago, after Pastor Logan conferred the blessing on Melissa Ann, and as Molly and Karli were leaving the church, the most amazing thing happened. Her eyes had no more than adjusted to the bright September sunlight than who should she see but Steve Roper. He stood at the end of sidewalk leading to the church, scanning the exiting crowd, as though waiting for someone.

Her heart started to pound. He was the last person she expected to see today.

His gaze landed on her and Karli. His lips broke

into a smile as he hurried to their side. "Molly!"

Before she could say anything—not that she could, anyway, with surprise rendering her speechless—Karli shouted, "Steve! Steve!"

Karli broke away from Molly and ran to meet him halfway.

"Hey, Karli." He bent and gave her a hug.

Molly wished she could run to him and so easily receive a hug, too. But she wasn't five years old. She was twenty-five and, besides, they'd parted as strangers. Fear rooted her feet to the sidewalk, and she held herself steady.

Steve stood and their gazes met. His was tentative, questioning. Hers—well, she couldn't be sure what showed on her face, but she hoped the expression wasn't the strong emotion that had filled her heart.

"I didn't see you earlier," she said, when he'd let go of Karli and approached her side.

He gave a slight shrug, never taking his gaze off her face. "I got here a little late and sat in back."

"Oh." Words failed her. Hearing the sounds of car doors slamming, she glanced at the parking lot. Sara and Jackson and Ryan were climbing in their SUV.

She turned back to Steve. "We're riding with Sara and Jackson, so we'd better go."

"I'll see you at the party. I want to talk to you."

Now, at least half an hour had passed since Molly and the others arrived at the Rolling R. The party was well under way. Drinks had been served, and Anna and her daughter, Doreen, were passing around the hors d'oeuvres.

But no Steve. Molly rubbed her forehead. Had he changed his mind and decided not to come? What did he want to talk to her about, anyway? Hadn't they said everything there was to say on that last day before he returned to New York?

The crowd around Rose and Melissa parted, and Rose approached Molly. Glad for the distraction, Molly said, "I'm so happy for you and Mike." She ran her finger along Melissa's silky cheek. The baby smiled and waved a chubby fist.

"Thanks." Rose's eyes sparkled. "I never dreamed I could be so happy myself. I have the love of my life"—she nodded to where Mike stood talking to several of the guests—"and now my daughter."

"Are you quitting your job?"

"I am. I love working for TransAmerica, but I want to be a stay-at-home-mom." Her gaze drifted to her daughter's face. "For a while. Then I'll get my degree in counseling. After that, I'll join Mike at the clinic as a social worker."

Molly clapped her hands. "That's wonderful. I remember counseling is something you've always wanted to do. There's a lot of cause for celebration today."

"Uh huh. And that includes Sara. Did you know her father is here?" Rose nodded toward the sofa.

Following her direction, Molly saw Sara sitting with an older, distinguished-looking man with gray hair and a gray mustache. "I met him yesterday. I was surprised to learn he was coming. I know they've been estranged for several years."

"Ever since Sara came to Red Rock. But she called him recently and they reconciled. This is the first time he's seen his grandson." Rose straightened the baby's dress. "I hope you find happiness, too, Molly. I hear you're leaving us, though. We'll miss you."

"I'll miss you, too. But Karli and I will come back to visit."

"You'd better. Any idea who'll replace you at the bakery?"

"Teresa's sister, Ellie, is interested." She gestured to the buffet table, where a tall, blonde woman was sharing a laugh with Dirk Lamont. "Looks like my job on the ranch isn't all Ellie's interested in," Molly added with a chuckle.

Rose lifted her eyebrows. "They make a nice-looking couple, don't they?"

Molly nodded as Dirk placed a possessive arm around the woman's waist. "They do. And Dirk's really a nice guy. I hope things work out for them."

Another guest joined them. As they chatted, the sound of a car pulling up outside caught Molly's attention. Steve? She excused herself and hurried to the window and peered out. The white car was not one she recognized as belonging to a local. She kept her gaze pinned to the driver's side. The door opened, and a man stepped out.

Steve.

Molly's heartbeat quickened.

He shifted the gift-wrapped package he carried from one hand to the other and looked up at the house. Molly ducked out of sight. She didn't want him to think she was eagerly waiting for him—even though that was exactly the case.

As Steve climbed the porch stairs and approached the front door, Molly stepped farther back into the room. She watched as he entered and shook hands with Mike and Jackson.

He was even more handsome than she remembered, tall and sturdy in a navy blue jacket, navy slacks, and black boots. Sunlight from the window accentuated the strong lines of his cheekbones and jaw. Molly felt light-headed, as though she might faint. She reached out and grasped the arm of a nearby chair for support.

Anna Gabraldi took Steve's coat and the gift. Jackson led him to the portable bar and poured him a glass of wine. As Steve sipped his drink, his gaze swept the room.

Molly knew instinctively he was looking for her. Suddenly afraid to talk to him—although she wasn't sure exactly why—she joined a group of guests. For the next half hour, she mingled with the others, managing to stay far away from Steve.

And then, after a short conversation with the Russian-born wife of Mike's clinic partner, she turned around and bumped into the solid wall of a man's chest. "Excuse me..." The words died on her lips as she looked up into a pair of all-too-familiar brown eyes. "Hello, Steve."

"Sorry, I didn't expect you to turn so suddenly. Are you okay?" He briefly touched her shoulder.

Molly steadied her trembling lips into a smile. "No harm done."

"I saw you earlier, but couldn't get over to say hello until now."

Heart pounding, she gazed at the person she'd missed so much over the past two months. "I saw you, too, but there are a lot of people here to talk to."

"How've you been? You're looking good."

"I've been fine. You're looking good, too."

"Is there somewhere we can talk privately?" Steve frowned and nodded at her left hand. "Or, are you and Dirk..."

"We're just friends," she said quickly. Maybe too quickly. She didn't want Steve to think she had any designs on him. What did she want him to think? She frowned. "Leaving the party would be rude, wouldn't it?"

"I promise not to keep you too long." He looked over Molly's shoulder and nodded. "I see we have Sara's okay."

Molly glanced around to spot Sara smiling and making shooing motions. "But Karli..."

"Is with the other children in the den. Teresa's keeping an eye on them."

She shrugged. "I can't think of any other excuses."

"Good. We'll grab our jackets and go outside."

Outside, Molly blinked in the bright sunlight beaming down on the warm autumn day. Yellow, orange, and red tinged the leaves on the maple trees, while the aspens' leaves were pure gold. A bit more snow than usual draped the mountain peaks, but the sky was as blue as any day in summer.

"I've missed this place," Steve said as they strolled the path leading to Sara's garden. His voice dropped a notch. "Most of all, I've missed you."

She wanted to say she'd missed him, too, but uncertainty kept her silent.

They reached the barn, and through the open door, a horse's neighing drifted along the air, accompanied by the soft shuffle of hooves on the barn's brick floor.

"I felt badly about the way we parted," Steve continued. "We left so much unsaid. I want to talk now and be honest with my feelings. I've been kicking myself for the way I acted that night—you know—when I found the butterfly ornament."

Molly stuffed her hands in her jacket pockets and tucked her chin into her chest. "I was wrong to keep the information from you."

"I'd like to think that had something to do with how you felt about me?"

Hearing the question in his voice, she darted him a glance. He was turned in her direction, and under slightly furrowed brows, his gaze was steady and unwavering. Although still not comfortable with the situation, his honesty reassured her.

"You're right." She took a deep, fortifying breath. "I was afraid that if you found Angie, you might realize you still cared for her, even though you'd said you didn't love her."

"And that was because—"

Molly briefly closed her eyes before replying. "Because I had feelings for you myself."

His wrinkled brow relaxed. "Ah, that's what I hoped you'd say."

If you only knew how much that admission cost me. My stomach is rumbling like a freight train, and my nerves are strung tight.

They came to the pond where the resident ducks drifted in and out of the weeping willow tree's overhanging branches. The birds' green and gray feathers were shiny and water-slick.

"Want to sit?" Steve pointed to the wooden bench facing the pond.

"I guess we could—for a while."

Steve brushed away a few fallen leaves and

gestured for Molly to sit.

Still a bit apprehensive, she sank onto the bench, conscious of the wooden slats pressing into her back. She expected him to join her. Instead, he paced toward the pond and back again, his feet crunching through piles of dried leaves.

At last, he spoke. "When I finally talked with Angie, she made me realize that during our marriage, I'd been trying to make her into the wife I wanted, the wife I thought I should have. I wasn't letting her be herself. Plus, I married her for all the wrong reasons. I wanted to rescue her. I wanted to keep my promise to her parents that I'd look out for her after they were gone. But you know about all that." He made a dismissive wave.

"Yes, and keeping one's promise is a good quality for a person to have. You must never be ashamed of that." Steve's loyalty was a trait she'd always admired.

His gaze radiated appreciation before he looked away and began pacing again. "Anyway, I knew I loved you, but I was afraid I'd make the same mistake all over again. When I went to the grange dance that night—"

"So you were there. I had a feeling you were." She recalled the uncanny sense she'd had that Steve was nearby, and the sense of loss she'd experienced when she thought she saw him driving away.

He stopped, placed his hands on his hips, and nodded. "Yes, and when I saw you with Dirk, I realized you'd be better off with him, or someone like him, and living here in Colorado, where you want to be. So I said good-bye and returned to New York." He slowly shook his head. "So many times, I wanted to call you, but didn't feel I had the right. I'd treated you badly, starting a relationship then running off to find Angie. But I never forgot you, Molly."

Steve's words warmed Molly's heart. "I never forgot you, either. I've thought about you so many times."

"That's good to know." He flashed a smile. "So, when I got the invitation to Melissa Ann's christening, I debated, knowing you would probably be here and fearing my presence might make us both uncomfortable. But the desire to see you won out, and I decided to come." He waved a hand. "Well, okay, I wanted to pay my respects to Mike and Rose and the new baby, too, but you're the biggest reason I'm here. You and Karli."

"I'm glad you came, Steve."

"And I'm glad to see you're doing well and are happy." He approached her and, leaning down, looked into her eyes. "You are happy, aren't you?"

Struggling to choose the right words to explain her change of plans, she studied her hands in her lap. Finally, she found her voice. "No, not really. In fact, Karli and I are leaving." She looked up in time to see his mouth drop open.

"What? Why?"

"I came back to find the same life Buck and I had here when he was alive, but that didn't work." The old ache nudged her. Giving up her original plan had left a lingering sadness. Still, she'd made her decision and she must move on. She straightened and leaned back against the bench.

"Oh, Sara and Jackson have been wonderful. I couldn't ask for better friends, better family. But I realized I need to make a life somewhere else." She lifted one shoulder. "So, we're leaving."

"Where are you going?"

"Back to Chicago."

His brows drew together. "You think you'll be happy there?"

"We'll see. I plan to get an office job—that seems to be my talent—and find an apartment near my sister and her husband." But even as she spoke, now that Steve had returned, she wondered if her new plan was what she really wanted.

Steve turned away to gaze in the direction of the pond. "I wish we could start over, you and I. If only I hadn't made such a mess of things."

Start over. Dare she hope that was possible? "What happened to us is not all your fault. Don't you remember that when we first met, I didn't want to get involved with you because of Buck's memory? And you needed closure to your marriage with Angie. Neither of us was ready for a new relationship."

"That's true. Then, when I found Angie, she made me realize I played a part in her leaving." Steve rubbed his chin and stared at the ground. "I orchestrated our lives, deciding where we would live, what we would do. Her leaving was my fault."

"I felt guilty about my marriage, too."

He turned, eyes widened. "You did?"

"Yes, because I objected so strongly to Buck's rodeo riding." Molly picked up a leaf Steve had missed when he brushed off the bench. She idly ran her fingers over the leaf's veined ridges. "Sometimes, I made our lives miserable with my disapproval. My reaction was due to my fear, of course, fear that he'd hurt himself— which he did." With a surge of the old anger, she tossed down the leaf.

"But your disapproval was justified."

Molly briefly closed her eyes and took a deep, calming breath. "Not exactly. Yes, what happened to Buck was a tragedy, but Sara helped me to realize I need to let people be who they are. Like with you that day at Funland, when I didn't want you to take the Rocket Space Ship ride."

"I see what you mean." He smiled and placed a hand over his heart. "But knowing you were worried about me was also kinda nice."

She clasped her hands together in her lap. "Okay, but, still, I wish I'd been more supportive of Buck."

He nodded, his expression solemn again. "We both were trying to control our mates."

"At least in some ways." She hesitated, uncertain how much more to share. But Steve's honesty about his feelings gave her courage. "I know I try to control Karli, too. Again, out of fear. But she has to learn who she is and how to be herself. I've been able to let go, a little. Did you know she's been riding the school bus into town to kindergarten?"

"Yes, she told me when I talked to her earlier. I'm proud of you, Molly."

His praise brought warmth to her cheeks. "Thanks. I'm still learning, but maybe there's hope for me yet." She laughed.

"Of course, there is. And for me, too?" He raised his eyebrows and tilted his head.

"Most definitely."

He sank down beside her and grasped her hand. "With all this deep insight, I'm ready for a new relationship." He stroked the back of her hand. "With you, Molly. What do you say? And, no, I'm not going to convince you to come to New York. I'll come to Chicago, if that's where you want to live. I'll open a branch of my business there. If Jerry doesn't agree, I'll go out on my own."

His touch tingled all the way up her arm. But his sacrifice was too much. Molly wrinkled her forehead. "Oh, no, Steve."

He held up his free hand. "I won't risk making the same mistake with you that I made with Angie. Where I live and work are not as important as being with the one I love. And the one I love is you, Molly. That I know for sure."

Molly's heart filled with a joy she thought she'd never again experience. "I love you, too." She'd never stopped loving him, not even when she was hurt and angry that he'd left her. "And I want to be where you are."

"We'll work out the details later." He put one arm around her and drew her close. "For now, why don't I go with you to Chicago?"

"That would be wonderful. I'd love for you to meet Paige and Harlan." Could this really be happening? She laid a hand on his chest and tipped up her chin to gaze into his eyes. "But, we're going on the train. Karli's choice."

He leaned back and caressed her shoulder. "No problem. I'll cancel my airline ticket and pick up one for the same train you're taking. Being together for a couple days will give us time to talk and plan. I can stay in Chicago and help you get settled. Then we'll go from there."

Although his steady voice gave her confidence, she

had to ask, "Do you really think our being together will work?"

"Our love will make it work."

Love. Yes, that was the key. And, deep in her heart, Molly knew their love for each other was strong and everlasting.

Steve brushed a lock of hair from her forehead. "Come on, let's find Karli and tell her the good news. But first—" He enfolded her in his arms, drew her close, and kissed her.

Molly wound her arms around his neck and gave herself up to a kiss that went deeper and deeper, until her very soul blended with his. This was where she belonged. She'd never doubt that again.

Steve was her future. Her forever.

Epilogue

Six months later.

"Looks like we got a message from Molly." Jackson gazed over Sara's shoulder as she sat at their computer checking email.

"Yes, let's see what she says about our invitation." Sara opened the message and read aloud:

"Hi, Sara and Jackson,

You two are wonderful, you know that? Steve and I would love to be married at the Rolling R. The ranch holds so many fond memories for both of us. Now that our hearts and minds have been healed of the past, we are ready to move on with our lives. Karli, of course, has been ready from the beginning!

We'll be leaving to honeymoon in Hawaii after the ceremony, but we thought we'd come out a week early and look at some of the ranches there that are for sale. We love our new home on Long Island, but wouldn't it be nice for us all to be neighbors for part of the year?

Looking forward to planning the details with you and, above all, to seeing you again. Give our love to Mike, Rose, and Melissa Ann.
Molly and Steve and Karli.

Sara looked up at her husband. "I'm so glad their relationship finally worked out."

He gave her a fond smile and leaned down to kiss her cheek. "Me, too. Their getting together took some time, though."

"But I never doubted that love would win out in the end. Love always does."

"Yes," he agreed. "No matter what happens in this old world, we can always count on love."

Linda Hope Lee

SARA'S COCONUT OAT COOKIES

1 egg
½ cup honey
1 teaspoon oil
½ teaspoon vanilla
½ cup rolled oats
½ cup chopped nuts
½ cup shredded coconut
¼ teaspoon salt
¾ cup whole wheat flour

Beat egg, add honey gradually, then oil and vanilla.
Add oats, nuts, coconut, and salt.
Gradually stir in flour.
Drop by teaspoons onto greased cookie sheet. Flatten.
Bake at 350 degrees for 10-12 minutes.
Makes approximately 2 dozen cookies.

A word about the author...

Linda Hope Lee writes contemporary romance, mysteries, and romantic suspense. Also an artist, she works in watercolor, colored pencil, and pen and ink. Collecting children's books and anything to do with wire-haired fox terriers occupies her spare time. She lives in the Pacific Northwest, a setting for many of her novels.

Visit her website at: http://www.lindahopelee.com
Email her at: linda@lindahopelee.com

~

Other books in The Red Rock Series by this author are:
Finding Sara
Loving Rose

Thank you for purchasing
this publication of The Wild Rose Press, Inc.
For other wonderful stories of romance,
please visit our on-line bookstore at
www.thewildrosepress.com.

For questions or more information
contact us at
info@thewildrosepress.com.

The Wild Rose Press, Inc.
www.thewildrosepress.com

To visit with authors of
The Wild Rose Press, Inc.
join our yahoo loop at
http://groups.yahoo.com/group/thewildrosepress/